MADE OF STEELE

STEELE GUARDIANS SERIES - BOOK 4

SUSAN SLEEMAN

Published by Edge of Your Seat Books, Inc.

Contact the publisher at contact@edgeofyourseatbooks.com

Copyright © 2022 by Susan Sleeman

Cover design by Kelly A. Martin of KAM Design

1

Teagan froze, her mind locked with choices, her heart racing.

She couldn't make a mistake. Just couldn't. The wrong move could cripple the family business her father and uncle had started.

Perhaps destroy it.

"Ms. Steele," the solid male voice of Patrick, one of Steele Guardians' best guards, came through the phone.

"Sorry." She paced through her office and stopped at her desk. "I need more information before I decide how to handle this. Run through the situation again. Don't leave any details out."

He let out a frustrated breath. "I was in the lobby of World of Crafts monitoring the live security feeds for the building. The main warehouse feed flickered. It was the area in the back where the owners' office and private entrance is located. So I investigated."

She stared at the glow her lamp cast across her sparkling glass desk. "You went into the warehouse?"

"Yes. Made my way to the back. That's when I saw four men standing next to a large shipping crate. Since I'm subbing for the regular guard who's at training this week, I've never met the owners, but figured that explained the ID of three of the men."

"The three Conti brothers own the company so that makes sense."

"Still, I hung back to watch. They took a bunch of boxes labeled glitter out of the crate. Then one of them lifted out padded packages from the bottom. The items he opened looked old. Way old. And this guy handled everything very carefully. I figure it's ancient artifacts or something like that. They got super excited. Spoke in a foreign language. I couldn't make out what they were saying."

"Likely Italian." She thought about the Italian-American owners as she turned to face the window overlooking their parking lot. She'd known the Contis for years. Honest. Hard-working men.

Or so she'd thought.

Could they be involved in something illegal?

She had to learn more. Delve deeper. "Artifacts, like what?"

"A couple of sculptures and something decorative that looked like it would be mounted on the outside of a building."

"How could you tell they were ancient?" she asked, pausing at the window to look over the night sky.

"I don't know. They just looked old. Figured you would know what was going on and should call you before I barged in on the owners and made them mad. But before I could make the call, one guy stayed behind to pack up the crate again and the others came my way. I hightailed it back to the security booth and relaxed so they didn't have any idea I'd seen them. You know. Just in case."

Interesting to say the least. "Did they come through the lobby?"

"No. So I checked warehouse video to see what was going on."

"Were their faces captured on it?"

"No, and that was odd too. I played it back and it wasn't the live action I witnessed. Just a boring feed of the area. No people at all. They had to have looped in an old feed to cover their actions. Only thing that makes sense and explains the flicker."

Even more interesting. Bordering on intrigue. "And you're sure you didn't recognize them?"

"Never seen them before."

She had to know who was in the warehouse before making a decision. "The owners' pictures are on their website. Check it now and see if it's the men you saw."

"Hold on."

She resumed pacing, getting more frantic with each step, her mind racing.

World of Crafts had sixty stores in the Pacific Northwest and ran a very lucrative online supply business. The brothers were eccentric at times, but she'd always found them trustworthy. Maybe she was simply overreacting, her former detective roots begging to be reactivated.

Seriously, Teagan. You are letting your imagination go wild.

Why suspect them of dealing in illegal goods?

"Yeah, it's them," Patrick said. "The fourth guy isn't on the site though."

"Go back to the warehouse. See what's going on. Make sure the brothers aren't under duress. But whatever you do, don't get caught surveilling them. I'm on my way." She kicked off her pumps.

"Should I call the police?"

"No." She slid her feet into her running shoes. "Make sure the brothers are okay. When I get there, we'll inspect these items. See if they're really what you think and not

3

some mass-produced décor pieces that World of Crafts plans to sell."

"How are you going to do that?" His breathing increased as if he was heading to the warehouse.

"I honestly don't know, but I'll figure it out on the way." She ended the call and shoved her phone into the pocket of her suit jacket. She tied her shoelaces, grabbed her backpack, and raced for the door.

The office hallway was dark and ominous feeling. Not because she feared an intruder waited in the dark to assault her, but that phone call could mean her worst fear was coming true. She'd been the chief operating officer for Steele Guardians for the past two years, and she'd already made one mistake. Big, giant, colossal mistake right after she'd taken charge that had nearly taken the company down. Each and every day since then, she feared she would fail her family again.

World of Crafts importing stolen antiquities right under Steele Guardians' noses could not only destroy their business reputation but could destroy Steele Guardians too. If they didn't have their reputation—they didn't have anything. She had to do the right thing here.

Maybe she should call 911. Or was this really something simple? If so, why were the brothers hiding their actions with a looped-in security feed?

I wouldn't mind some guidance here.

She kicked up her speed, pausing to get a key for WOC's main door from a locked cabinet at the end of the hallway before getting into her car. Her tires rolled over wet roads, mile after mile, toward the industrial area with warehouses and shipping containers near the airport. Not a vehicle in sight. Not unusual for midnight on a weekday.

She passed Christmas lights, but for once, they didn't do a thing to improve her mood. Thankfully, the usual winter rain had taken a break and continued to hold off for her drive.

She approached WOC's main headquarters, the sign at the road matching the garish red and blue neon ones at their retail stores. Shadows shrouded the single-story building with large glass block windows and the overcast night hid the moon. The only light came from a streetlight to her rear, the red and blue glow of the sign, and the twinkling white Christmas lights lining the front window. An older model red Jeep sat in the lot. Surely not one of the owners. They seemed to be swimming in money and drove flashy vehicles. Most likely Patrick's Jeep.

She started to climb out of her vehicle when her grandad's and dad's warnings came to mind.

Forget how headstrong you are. Take care. Don't rush. Approach with caution.

Former law enforcement officers, their warnings had saved her life numerous times as a deputy. They'd drilled caution into her, but since she'd left law enforcement, her leap-before-you-look personality had returned.

And tonight? Tonight she needed to take a moment. Be proactive. Protect herself.

She retrieved her Glock from her backpack and clipped the holster on her belt.

She took out her phone and located the group text for her sisters and typed—*Heading into WOC headquarters. Patrick says something is going down with antiquities. Maybe stolen. Call me if you haven't heard from me in 30 minutes.*

Roger that, came the text from Teagan's youngest sister, Ryleigh, who was a night owl too.

Seriously, Mackenzie texted. *Can't this wait for morning?*

Urgent. Teagan typed back. She could easily imagine Mackenzie in bed, the text having just woken her up, pushing her long blond hair from her face as she grimaced at the phone. Ryleigh, on the other hand, would be sitting behind her computer, tracking some cyber creep for her job as an FBI agent and wouldn't be hitting the sack for hours yet.

Teagan silenced her phone and stepped into the brisk evening. The sweet, pungent zing of coming rain filled the air, but not a drop fell on her walk to the front door. She looked inside the big lobby window to the security desk in the corner, where Patrick should be sitting behind the tall desk with multiple monitors. Or would be, if she hadn't told him to return to the warehouse to check on the brothers.

Had she sent him into danger?

Her stomach cramped as she unlocked the door. Inside, she paused to listen.

Nothing save the door whisking closed behind her.

"Patrick!" she called out, hoping he'd returned and had gone to the restroom at the far side of the space.

No response.

She locked the door and pulled her jacket back for access to her weapon. Stepping across the room, she passed the long reception desk painted a bright red to match the sign. The company's logo, a world with its name in blue letters, had been painted on the front. The graphic had seen better days, the top letters worn, maybe from visitors leaning against the desk over the years.

The unisex restroom door said *unoccupied*, but she jerked it open anyway. The overhead light flashed on. She took a quick look.

Empty.

Her heart thumped, and she let out a long breath before heading back to the other side of the space where a steel door led into the warehouse. She took a moment to consider her options.

Enter the warehouse or wait for Patrick to return? No brainer. She wasn't a waiting kind of person.

She pulled the handle and slipped into the dark room. The glowing red exit signs above the doors and a few single bulbs at ceiling height cast shadows and left the space dark and eerie. She let her vision adjust to the dim lighting.

Voices sounded ahead. Not Patrick's. Urgent. Demanding voices.

She drew her weapon and started forward, walking on her tiptoes. Silently. Cautiously. Entering the online sales storage area holding rack after rack of steel shelves with crates of supplies boasting easy-to-read labels.

She moved deeper into the space. Inching toward the loading dock.

Closer to the voices.

A hand shot out of the dark aisle behind her, cupping her mouth. Another arm, strong, like iron, jerked her body into the nearest aisle. Patrick sat on the floor, wrists and ankles bound. Gagged. His eyes wide. Worried.

She struggled to free herself. Kicking. Squirming. Jabbing with her elbows. No success. The man's rock-hard arms held her in place. Not one of the Conti brothers. The fourth man. Or maybe another person Patrick had not seen.

Her mind raced, flying over possibilities as she kept struggling.

What in the world had she and Patrick stumbled upon?

More importantly, would it cost them their lives?

Drew kept his arms around the woman he recognized as Teagan Steele. She kicked. Fought. Tried to scream. Her strength surprised him. She was slender but packed with muscle. Solidly packed.

"Shh," he whispered in her ear. "I won't hurt you. Just keeping you from making a mistake you'll regret."

She struggled even harder.

"If these men find out you're in the room they'll kill you. Same goes for your guard here. So stop moving and making noise. If not for yourself, for his sake." Drew put as much urgency into his voice as he could while still whispering.

She went slack in his arms and planted her feet on the floor. He didn't let go of her mouth or her very shapely body. A body he'd admired several times when she'd stopped by to talk with the Conti brothers about how her company's security guards were performing their duties. She was all about customer service, and Drew suspected she would comply with his demands not for herself but for the guard. Drew had restrained the guy to keep him from stumbling into something that would get him killed.

The fake feed was supposed to have prevented all of this. So what had brought the guard back here?

And now this! Seriously. This was not how Drew had expected the night to go. He could only imagine the questions going through both of their minds, the first being who the heck he was and did he plan to kill them? As much as he wanted to explain, as an undercover ICE Agent investigating antiquities theft, he couldn't say a word.

"I'm going to secure you, just as I did your guard," he said. "I have to release your mouth. If you say a word, I'll kill your guard. Do you understand?"

She gave a soft whimper.

Oh, man. The defenseless sound tore at his heart. He hated putting her through this and wanted to confess his real identity. That was one of the greatest challenges of undercover work. Keeping in character no matter the situation. No matter how beautiful and charming the women he ran into.

To see a strong woman like her defenseless like this? And at his doing? That was rough. He wanted to tell her he wasn't killing anyone but needed her compliance for her own good.

He released her mouth, keeping his hand close for a moment to see if she would cry out, ready to clamp down again.

She let out a long burst of air, but didn't speak. He retrieved a zip tie from his pocket. When the guard started getting nosey, Drew had found ties next to flowery quilt fabric in the warehouse to contain the guard and tied a strip of the floral fabric around his mouth.

He bound her wrists together, trying to be as gentle as he could. He used the same fabric to gag her and eased her down to the floor, then zip-tied her slender ankles. She wore a body-hugging skirt and matching jacket in a pale blue color, accenting her shiny black hair. He'd never seen her this close up and looked in big brown eyes that were glaring at him with an icy stare that would freeze his emotions if he didn't find her so very intriguing.

"Sorry about this," he whispered. "It's for your own good."

She murmured something. Not likely a kind sentiment.

"Both of you stay here until we're gone. Then you can call for help."

Drew took one last look into those rich chocolate eyes pleading for help he couldn't provide. He took off for the trio of men. Drew had been undercover for nearly a year and the Conti brothers had only recently come to trust him. When a noise had sounded while they were looking at their stolen antiquities, he'd been dispatched to look into it. He'd found the guard. Another noise and there was Teagan Steele. Sneaking into the space.

He slipped through the warehouse and found the

brothers gathered around an open crate. The middle brother, Aldo, held one of a pair of tablets with cuneiform inscriptions etched into the fragile clay. They were believed to have originated in an ancient Sumerian city located in present-day southern Iraq.

Vito, the youngest and chubbiest of the trio, looked up at Drew. "Everything okay, Dylan?"

Drew nodded as his undercover name was mentioned. "Just the wind. Looks like we might have a real storm brewing."

Sal, the oldest, the brother with piercing black eyes, caught Drew's attention. "If it was nothing, why'd it take you so long?"

"I checked every inch of the warehouse. Thorough, like you taught me."

Sal didn't move for a long moment. "My brothers and I'll get these items repackaged so we can get out of here before the rain hits. Make another pass around the building to be sure it was just the wind."

As the oldest, Sal called most of the shots. Not easily though. His younger brothers tried to buck his authority whenever possible. Drew still hadn't figured out which one of them had gotten the family involved in importing and selling illegal antiquities, but Aldo seemed to possess the most knowledge about them.

"On it," Drew said and gladly took off to check on Teagan and her guard. He strode through the rows of tall racks until he reached the pair. He paused for a brief moment to glance down the aisle. Teagan and her guard remained in place. Both sitting rigid and attentive. Both firing an angry glare at him. Too bad. He wanted her to look at him with one of the warm smiles he'd seen when she'd stopped by the warehouse. But he had to let her think he was a criminal who was willing to restrain a defenseless woman.

He gave her another apologetic look and moved on to the lobby door, where he poked his head out. An SUV pulled up out front. Two women got out. The blonde was another Steele Guardians executive, but he didn't recognize the one with near-black short hair. Likely another Steele sister.

He'd heard Sal say they were all former or current law enforcement, and Teagan had likely called them here before he subdued her. He had to get the Contis moving and fast. Stop these women from getting inside. The men would have to get the goods out of here or Drew's undercover assignment would abruptly end before they could find the source for the stolen antiquities.

Drew had invested too much of his life to let that happen. He'd go down swinging if he had to.

Anything short of committing grievous bodily harm and murder.

2

Teagan had failed. She'd let this guy the Contis called Dylan get the jump on her. Despite his unwelcome handling, he seemed kind. Like he really regretted tying them up. Didn't stop him though. He secured them both.

He was a criminal. Plain and simple.

She cut her gaze around the place again. Searching for any way to get free and catch the Contis and this guy in the act of receiving stolen goods. She'd clearly heard the brothers' voices, especially Sal, barking orders to his brothers, but he didn't mention anything about the product they were dealing with.

She could relate to Sal. Not that she called all the shots in the family business. Her sister, Mackenzie, and two cousins ran the company like a democracy, but as the oldest, Teagan often had the final say. Ryleigh and their oldest cousin, Londyn, were the only holdouts who still worked in law enforcement.

What she wouldn't give at the moment for any one of her sisters or cousins to arrive. She'd been at the warehouse for more than the thirty minutes she'd warned her sisters to follow up on, and her phone had vibrated against her side several times. So they should know she was in trouble.

But would they think to come to her rescue? Or would they think she couldn't answer for a legit reason? They wouldn't have a key and would have to force their way into the building.

Would they do that? Would she do that in their position? Yeah, she would, but then she was the leap before looking member of the family. The others were more conservative. Especially Mackenzie. She was controlled but clever. Prim and proper too. Ryleigh was a free spirit. Acting on a whim. Following her heart. So maybe she would be the one to bust down the door.

Nothing was a given, and Teagan couldn't sit around and wait any longer.

Maybe she would have a better chance of seeing something they might use to get free if she got to her feet. She signaled her intentions to Patrick to move back-to-back with him and rise up. He was a strong and fit guy, and she worked out nearly every day. They would be a good match for each other.

His eyes narrowed, and he shook his head.

He was probably right. She could fall and draw the brothers over here. But the guy who'd zip-tied her had charged back to the group and urged them to get moving. Telling them to take the goods with them and flee before someone arrived.

Had he seen something? Maybe Mackenzie and Ryleigh had arrived?

Maybe.

She gave Patrick a direct stare. The one she used as a boss. He nodded, and they scooted into position, back-to-back. His muscles were firm as expected, giving her confidence. She lifted her feet to flatten the soles of her shoes on the floor. She felt him doing the same thing. She waited for him to stop moving then pressed against his back. They rose, wobbling a bit as they found the right pressure and she made adjustments for her slim skirt.

On her feet, but still leaning on Patrick, she hopped to bring herself into an upright position. He followed suit. *Great!* They were standing. Now what?

She spotted a crate labeled *Exacta Knife Refills*. Could she get a package out and open it without it falling?

She had to try.

Footsteps rushed back and forth in the rear of the warehouse. She had to hurry. Even if she fell, they wouldn't likely hear it with their movements.

She hopped one step. Wobbled. Remained standing. Another. Hopped and turned. Swayed but stayed upright.

Patrick moved too. Faced her. Concern etched in his expression.

She leaned back to the shelf and reached upward. Feeling for the right crate. Her fingers clasped the package. Cardboard and plastic. The cardboard tore. The blades spilled out. She grabbed one. Slashed her finger.

She bit down on the gag to keep from crying out. She maneuvered the blade between her fingers and signaled for Patrick to turn. The blade was slippery with her blood. She clamped onto it tighter to keep hold. Her finger burned with pain. She forced her mind away from it and onto her work.

Patrick took three hops. She felt for his zip tie with her free hand. Held it with her fingers and began sawing. Tiny small movements were all she could make.

Would this actually work in time?

She heard a car door slam and an engine start. The outside door closed.

No. They were leaving.

She sawed harder, but could only go so fast and not risk injury to Patrick's wrists. The tie gave way.

Patrick's hands disappeared, and he hopped to change position. He took the blade from her and bent to release his feet. He cut her wrists free. And her feet.

They both tore off their gags. She tied hers around her bleeding finger. They drew their weapons.

"The back door," she whispered and eased around the end of the shelves to move silently down the aisle.

The soft thump of Patrick's steps behind her gave her assurance. Former military, he would have her back if needed.

She reached the end of the aisle. The open crate sat by the exit. As she suspected, no sign of the men. She rushed to the door. Flung it open.

Two women stood there. Her sisters. Guns drawn.

They wore rain jackets and water pooled at their feet.

"Teagan." Mackenzie let out a long breath and brushed her shoulder-length hair back. "Thank goodness you're okay."

"Fine, but thanks for coming to my rescue." She holstered her weapon and looked at Patrick. She didn't want him to listen in to the discussion she planned to have with her sisters. "You good to go back to the desk?"

He nodded.

"Not a word of what you saw tonight to anyone. Not even to a wife or girlfriend."

He mimicked zipping his lips and marched away.

Teagan looked at Ryleigh and explained the situation, including the wounded finger. "The FBI works stolen antiquities cases, right?"

"Sometimes, but ICE does too." Ryleigh stowed her weapon, the holster looking very odd over the Duck Tales pajama pants. "As far as I know, our office hasn't investigated it."

Didn't mean they couldn't. "Since this involves Steele Guardians, can you get your supervisor to open an investigation?"

"Into what?" Ryleigh asked. "I believe in Patrick and what he saw, but he wasn't close enough to prove they were illegally importing antiquities, right?"

"Right," Teagan admitted, albeit reluctantly.

Ryleigh continued to eye Teagan, her sister's narrow-eyed stare likely the one she used when questioning suspects. "And you didn't see them."

"No, but we were restrained by a guy working with the brothers. No need to tie us up unless there was something going on that they didn't want us to see."

"That's awful," Ryleigh said. "It really is and I'm sorry it happened, but you seem to be all right."

"Physically yes. Not so much inside." Teagan sighed. "I want him to pay."

"I'm sorry it happened, too, but we need to think clearly," Mackenzie said. "Not with our emotions. That's what Grandad and Dad have always told us."

"I know," Teagan said. "But I'm not there yet."

"Say they *are* engaged in something illegal." Ryleigh tucked her short hair behind her ear. "They could claim they thought you were up to no good, and they were only trying to protect their property. And there's nothing on the video as proof of any of it, right?"

"So? They restrained their security guard and the company COO." Teagan's voice was rising out of control so she swallowed to keep her cool. "That doesn't play."

Ryleigh frowned. "It could with a good lawyer. Either way, that's something for the local police not the FBI."

"But you won't press charges," Mackenzie said. "We need

16

the revenue from our contract with WOC, and without any proof of wrongdoing, we can't do anything."

"I won't let them get away with breaking the law." Teagan held her throbbing finger up to ease the pain. "And I'll do everything within my power to find the evidence to prove their guilt."

"You should let it go." Often the peacemaker, Mackenzie rested a hand on Teagan's arm. "Think of our contract with WOC. Not your pride."

"It's not about my pride. It's about something illegal going on under our company's nose." Teagan firmed her stance. "If the Contis are arrested, they could drag our company's name through the mud."

"It's possible, I suppose," Ryleigh said.

"Besides, I aim to find the guy who tied me up." Teagan eyed her sisters. "That *is* personal. You don't tie me up, gag me, and get away with it. No way."

Drew slipped through the shadows behind the coffee shop and leaned against the wall. Joining him any minute for an update would be Gala Harris, his supervisor and Special Agent in Charge of the Portland ICE field office. He'd been seen by the Steele Guardians' guard and their COO. Sure he maintained his cover, but Harris needed to be updated. He wasn't sure if Teagan Steele had seen the antiquities, but he thought the guard had gotten close enough to get a look, and he would report his findings to her.

Of that, Drew was sure.

Harris rounded the corner, a purpose in her step as she approached him. She wore all black and had glossy black hair cut bluntly by her chin. "Why the unplanned meeting?"

He told her about the situation. "The way I see it, Teagan

Steele has a few choices. She has no real evidence of the stolen antiquities, but she could report the problem to federal law enforcement and hope they'll look into it. Either us or the FBI who deal in stolen antiquities. My guess is she would go with the FBI as her sister is an agent. Or she could settle for reporting my restraining behavior to local law enforcement. She could also talk to the Conti brothers and investigate the situation on her own. Or even do nothing."

Harris gritted her teeth and clamped her hands on her hips. "Any of the above will likely end our investigation."

"Exactly."

She ran a hand through her hair, but it fell back into place like her agents did when she ruffled them. "Do you know anything about this Steele woman?"

"I've seen her a few times at the warehouse and did a little online recon before calling you. She was a Clackamas County detective and comes from a law enforcement family. She must know she doesn't have anything to stand on and might not file a report. I'm sure she wouldn't want to jeopardize their account with the Conti brothers either. But..." He let the word linger. "She doesn't seem like a do-nothing kind of person."

"Not that I know her, but regardless of what she might do, her law enforcement background won't likely allow her to let it go," Harris said, though she didn't often speculate. She made her decisions based on fact and fact only. No gut moves. No hasty decisions. No emotions. The word around the office was that she had ice flowing through her veins. "So what do you want to do about it?"

"Good question." One he'd been thinking about since he left the Contis with the stolen antiquities. "We've worked too hard to let Steele end this investigation."

"True. We're closer to the source for the stolen goods than we've ever been, and it would be a shame to cut our losses before we had the name." She took a long breath and locked eyes on him. "But we're already nearing the end of our second six-month undercover approval."

"Sure," he said. "Four days left, but there's no reason to believe that Undercover Review Committee won't see this through and approve another six months, right?" He'd worked long days and nights to prepare the package for the URC to discuss at one of their review meetings called a scrub meeting. They were just waiting for the official approval to proceed.

Harris swiped a hand over her face and let out a long noisy breath. "Word coming down from a member of the URC who's chairing the scrub meeting says we'll be lucky to get another reauthorization."

What? News to Drew. But he nodded when he wanted to rage.

When had she planned to tell him this?

He figured he'd demonstrated enough progress on the op in the prior term and had hoped for another six months, but now the clock was ticking on completing his assignment.

Four days. Ninety-six hours.

A good thing, maybe. With Christmas just ahead, he could resume his life, and his mother wouldn't have to be alone for another holiday.

All of that didn't matter at the moment. Teagan Steele could end things before then. Before he got results. Problem was, despite thinking about the situation non-stop, he didn't have an answer on what to do about her.

Harris looked him in the eye. "What if I met with Steele? Tell her that she stumbled on something she needs to forget about. Play on her former law enforcement experience. Hope she'll cooperate and not tell anyone."

"Sounds like a plan," he said. "One I think you need to

carry out as soon as possible. Can't afford for her to bring me up on charges when my days on this op are already numbered."

~

Two hours after leaving WOC headquarters, Teagan opened the front door of the Steele Guardians offices to let Clay Byrd inside. He entered and slowed, his gaze going over the space.

Not surprising. His expression held the same interest that most people had when they saw the converted fire station for the first time. Her family had left the brass fire pole in the back, the concrete floors unfinished, large metal stairs climbing to a second story, and the original truck doors so the space still felt very much like an operational firehouse.

She'd hated to wake Clay at this time of the morning, but she needed an expert's opinion on what Patrick had discovered. She'd heard Clay tell stories of his former days as an ICE agent, stories that had included stolen antiquities.

She closed and locked the door. "Thanks for coming, and sorry to get you up at this time of the morning."

"You said it was urgent." He planted his feet, looking alert even at three a.m.

She stood back so he could access the truck bay where her sisters sat at a large conference table. He strode with purpose across the space, his tactical boots thudding on the concrete. He wore black tactical pants and a polo shirt with the Nighthawk Security logo embroidered on his broad chest.

"You know my sisters," Teagan said, though she knew he did. Especially since his wife Toni was an FBI agent and worked with Ryleigh at the Portland field office. "Go ahead and have a seat."

He dropped into a chair across from her sisters, a shock of hair falling over his forehead, and he swiped it back.

Teagan sat next to him and explained what had happened at the WOC warehouse. "I don't know if I have a leg to stand on here, but I can't let it go. So I thought I'd get an unofficial opinion from you."

Clay frowned. "I agree that the men were acting suspiciously, and you being restrained further cements that in my mind. But you didn't actually see any items and your guard only saw them from a distance. So honestly, the only thing I think you can do is report the physical attack."

"That's what we were thinking too," Mackenzie said.

Teagan resisted firing an angry look at her sister. She had a right to her opinion, even if it wasn't what Teagan wanted to hear. But for now, she'd keep her attention on Clay. "You're sure ICE wouldn't at least look into this?"

"I can't speak for Agent Harris—she's the Special Agent in Charge of the local office—but unless she's changed, she's a facts only kind of person, and you don't have any real facts."

Teagan didn't like that answer either. "What if I went to see her anyway?"

Clay rested his hands on the table, staring at them for a long moment as if he was trying to find the right words. He looked up. "Honestly, I don't know if she would even take the meeting. Unless you had someone who could bypass intake, you'd have to talk to an agent first. They won't likely recommend she see you. At least, I wouldn't have if I were the one you came to. Not with her personality."

The wrong answers just kept coming, but she could still feel Dylan's arms restraining her, and she would keep pushing. "Could you bypass the intake? Call her for me?"

Clay took a long breath and reclined his chair back to put his hands behind his head. "Honestly, I'd rather not, but if I were in your shoes, I would want someone to help me. So yeah, I can call her in the morning."

She gave him her most thankful smile. "I'd appreciate that."

"Whatever you do, don't take any action until after I talk to Harris." Clay looked her straight in the face. "The last thing I want to have to tell Harris is that you let your emotions get to you and you did something stupid."

"I wouldn't."

Her sisters snorted, and she fired them a sharp look.

Clay snapped his chair forward. "Every law enforcement officer or former LEO would want to pay back a person who forcibly restrained them. It's in the law enforcement DNA. We may leave the field but we never leave that behind. Never."

"He's right," Ryleigh said.

Of course he was. She didn't like it, or like Ryleigh pointing it out, but Teagan knew she had to follow his suggestions.

He stood. "I'll give Harris a call first thing and get back to you after I talk to her."

She got up too. "Thanks, Clay, I owe you."

"No worries."

Teagan looked at him. "We need to keep this between us until we decide what to do."

"Of course."

"Means not telling your wife, brothers, or sister." His brothers ran an investigative firm and his sister was the trace evidence expert at a local private lab that handled work for law enforcement.

He tapped his chin. "Gonna have to tell Toni something

about why I took off in the middle of the night, and I won't lie to her."

"Okay, tell Toni but swear her to silence too." Teagan felt this getting out of hand. The fewer people to know what was going on, the better. Not only because letting a guy get the drop on her was embarrassing but because she didn't want the rest of her family to find out either.

"She won't tell anyone." He headed for the door.

When the black steel framed glass door whisked closed behind him, Teagan turned on her sisters. "And that goes for the both of you. Not a word about the incident to anyone."

Mackenzie's mouth dropped open. "You mean keep it from the rest of the family?"

"That's exactly what I mean." Teagan planted her hands on the table. "You know Dad and Uncle Gene. If they heard I was manhandled, they'd be down to WOC in a flash to confront the Contis. We can't have that happen until after I locate the guy who restrained me."

3

"She what?" Drew gaped at Harris, once again in their concealed meeting place in the alley, dark with overhead clouds blocking the early morning sun.

"You heard me." Harris scowled. "Steele went to her friend and former agent, Clay Byrd. Had him call me to see if we're interested in pursuing the lead she found. Told me all about your attack and how eager they were to locate a man named Dylan."

Drew figured Teagan would be persistent. He'd worried about it for the rest of what was left of his night, and now she'd proven him right. And far faster than he'd expected her to act. He couldn't fault her for her sense of urgency. Just that it was pointed at him. "And you told Byrd what?"

"No, of course." Harris crossed her arms over her gray suit jacket. "Said Steele had nothing to go on. Which she doesn't. But we have to figure a way to stop her from spreading this info across the whole world."

Drew's thoughts exactly, but how? "I hope you have a good idea because I've been thinking about it all night. Can't come up with a plausible plan other than arrest her and put her in solitary until the investigation is over."

"You know we can't do that," Harris said, as if she believed him to be serious. "What if we joined forces with her?"

Drew worked hard not to frown at his supervisor's idea. "What do you mean join forces?"

"We read her in on the investigation and swear her to secrecy. She had a stellar reputation as a detective for Clackamas County. I did some digging and learned they were sad to lose her, so she must've been a valued member of their team."

"But we can't work with a civilian," he said, thinking more that he couldn't work with the woman who could easily distract him.

"Then let's not. I'll get on the horn to Lieutenant Gutierrez at Clackamas County. Persuade him to deputize her for the duration of our investigation and have her join the team if necessary."

Drew knew his boss could bend even the staunchest advocate to her will. She could do most anything she put her mind to, but him working with Teagan? Not a good idea. Not at all. "I really don't need her help."

"Maybe not, but if she's deputized, we can at least read her in and swear her to secrecy. She'd be bound by code to keep quiet."

Drew got the feeling that once she knew about the op, she would keep quiet no matter her status. All they would have to do was ask her, but he didn't say anything. When Harris got an idea in her head, she wasn't looking for any more input.

She widened her stance. "I'll call Gutierrez as soon as I get back to the office. Once he's onboard, I'll get approval from upper management to bring her in to your op with limited duties."

"What about UCOS?" he asked. "How do you plan to

bypass the requirement of her attending Undercover Operatives School?"

"Don't you worry about that. I can claim exigent circumstances and get approval. You be thinking how to bring her in and how much to tell her. The less the better in my mind."

"If she's not fully read in, how exactly do you see the two of us working together? The Contis know both of us, and I doubt they would see us forming any kind of business partnership."

"Okay, you're right. Then let's not do business." She raised her shoulders. "Dating. You could form a fake relationship."

His mouth dropped open, but he snapped it closed. "Don't you think the Conti brothers would argue about me dating the COO of their security company? I've presented myself as a guy who's willing to break the law, help with their antiquities smuggling, and am looking for opportunities to launder my illegally gotten money. Doesn't seem like they would want the two to mix."

"You can figure it out. Convince them. I have confidence in you." She held his gaze. "Frame it right. Say it could help you see if the Steele family knows anything about their side hustle. Or you could simply say the heart wants what the heart wants." A surprise statement coming from the ice queen.

"You're forgetting one thing." He didn't look away from his boss's inquisitive stare. "I tied the woman up, and she was furious. I'm probably the last person she wants to work with, much less fake date."

"Then use those charms I've seen you train on women. They're potent and bound to work."

He doubted her assessment when it came to Teagan Steele, but Harris was giving him no choice. Looked like before the day was out, he would be trying to date Teagan Steele no matter what the very feisty woman wanted.

Teagan tried to relax on the park bench after her run, but she couldn't wind down or improve her mood. Not even after a three-mile run through her favorite park. She'd run fast and hard, hoping the sweat pouring from her body would wash off the touch of that man's hands. She even had a soft breeze cooling her body and a hint of sunshine glimmering through pillowy white clouds instead of rain, and yet, her dark mood continued.

Most likely because no one seemed eager to move forward with an antiquities investigation. Sure, Clay was hopefully on the phone with Agent Harris, but Teagan suspected the woman would say no. Everyone but Teagan was approaching this situation logically. Not her. Nope. She was fully fueled by emotions. She wanted this Dylan guy to pay. Oh how she wanted it. Sure her desire went against her Christian upbringing unless you went with an eye for an eye logic, which didn't apply to today's world. Vengeance was the Lord's.

Fine. She got it. She could embrace that thought, but did it calm her frazzled nerves? No.

She hopped up and pulled her phone holder from her arm to check the time and for a call from Clay. Fifteen minutes after eight.

"C'mon, ring already." The device sounded in her hand, and she jumped before taking control and answering it. "Please tell me Harris said yes."

"Sorry." Clay's deep voice rumbled through the phone. "She was a no go as I predicted."

Teagan had to fight the urge to hurl her phone to the ground. "Guess I'm on my own then."

"Hey, I'm glad to help and offer our team's resources if you need them. Smuggling stolen goods can get dangerous, and I don't want anything to happen to you."

"Thanks, Clay. I'll let you know if I need help." She ended the call and frustration flooded out of her pores.

She'd predicted this outcome. But now that it was reality? A total disappointment.

So what did she do now? She couldn't sit back and do nothing as Clay, Mackenzie, and Ryleigh all suggested. She had to act or the anger burning in her gut would set her on fire.

She marched to her car and climbed in. She plugged her phone into the vehicle and woke it up. About to send a text to Ryleigh and Mackenzie, her phone rang. The automated voice announced the incoming call was from her former lieutenant, Merle Gutierrez at Clackamas County.

"LT," she answered using the nickname the team had called him, including her.

"You available to come in for a meeting?" he asked.

"Now?" Her mind raced with questions. She'd left her detective's job nearly two years ago and not a peep from him since. What could he want?

"As soon as possible." That iron fist that he'd ruled his department with rode through his tone.

"I just finished a run, and I'll need to clean up first."

"Then double-time it. This is important." He ended the call.

Curious, she backed out of her parking space.

Could this meeting have to do with the situation with the Conti brothers and Dylan last night? Not likely. But if not, why would he insist on seeing her now?

Teagan adjusted her blouse at the collar and sat in the waiting area outside Lieutenant Gutierrez's office. He'd practically ordered her to appear this morning. No reason given. She didn't have to follow his orders any longer, but she respected him. If he called her, he needed her help on something, and she would give it. No question.

She rubbed her wrists. She could still feel the tight straps circling them from last night. She could also feel the gag at her mouth and the sharp slice into her finger. If she ever saw that Dylan guy again, she would give him a piece of her mind. Maybe more.

And she would see him. Of that he could be sure. She planned to hang out at the WOC warehouse until she did. She'd find a reason. Maybe say she was evaluating guards. Something like that. She'd figure it out. He needed to be told off and paid back for his rude treatment. He'd said her life was in danger, but the Contis weren't killers. She'd worked with them for years, and they were just big teddy bears.

The office door opened, and Lieutenant Gutierrez poked his head out. He still wore his silver hair cut in a high and tight military style, and the same deep wrinkles grooved his high forehead.

He beamed a tense smile her way. "Steele. Good. Glad you're here. Come in."

He disappeared into his office, and she stood. She smoothed her hands down her dress slacks and brushed her hair over her shoulder. She'd almost automatically pulled it back like she had when working as a sworn officer, but she was a civilian now. No need to consider how she would appear to her fellow deputies and people she stopped while on patrol. She could wear her hair however she wanted.

She entered the room and came to a sudden stop. Gutierrez wasn't alone. A woman with jet black hair and a sharp expression sat in a chair by the desk. But Teagan's gaze went to and lingered on the man causally sitting on the corner of the desk.

Dylan. The creep. The man who tied her up.

She went straight for him.

He stood. She shoved him against the wall as she would a suspect, her chest heaving with anger. His corded muscles remained firm under her fingers. She was no match for him. He could take her out if he chose to. Subdue her again like he'd done last night, even though that had been a surprise attack.

He flashed a look of amazement before a smile slowly slid across his mouth.

Fine. Smile. Make me madder.

She took a breath. Couldn't gain much air. Tried again. Failed. Went on anyway. Poked him in those pecks made of steel. "You best be here to apologize for last night. If not, I'm headed back out that door."

"Why don't you sit down." Gutierrez's calming voice came from behind. His words normally would be a suggestion, but not the way they were issued.

She didn't have to comply, but she did have to gain control of her emotions—and fast. Her breathing had become so shallow she could hyperventilate and pass out. Sitting would be good. Sitting and gaining control of her rash behavior. Acting like a professional.

She dropped into the chair next to the woman dressed in a plain gray pantsuit that screamed Fed. She'd crossed her legs, her hands pressed on her bony knee as a black pump dangled from her foot.

Gutierrez gestured at the woman. "Meet Gala Harris, Special Agent in charge of ICE's Portland field office."

Pegged her. Teagan held out her hand, hating that it was still trembling with anger. "Teagan Steele. Nice to meet you."

They shook hands, a contest of strength ensued. Teagan let go. No point in getting into a contest with this woman. If Clay's description of Harris was accurate, the older lady liked to win no matter the cost.

Teagan lifted her shoulders and looked at Dylan. "And you are?"

He remained against the wall, but those very broad shoulders relaxed. How could he be so calm when she'd slammed him against the wall? Infuriating. Maybe he had an abrasive personality and was used to people going after him.

He held out his hand. "Agent Drew Collier, working undercover with the Conti brothers."

Her mouth flapped open. She snapped it closed, her mind racing with the news. "You're an ICE agent?"

He nodded, and when she didn't reach out to shake his hand, he rested it on his trim waist. No way she would touch him again. Not with the way she was reacting to him. Not the anger, but her interest in him.

"Sorry about last night," he said casually as if they'd simply bumped into each other. "I couldn't have you walk in on the brothers and risk a year of my undercover work going up in smoke. And I had no idea what they might do to you either. I couldn't risk your life that way."

He sounded sincere on both points, but then he lied for his job, living as someone else in a world where lie upon lie kept him alive. Odds were good that he was playing a part now too.

So how did she react? What did she do? Forgive him? No. Not yet. Not that easy. "I've never suspected the brothers would be dangerous but sounds like you think they are."

31

"I have no evidence to suggest that. Only things I've heard them say. I do know they're not going to get caught and go to prison." He pushed off the wall and crossed his arms. He wore a short-sleeved shirt, and his tanned, muscular forearms looked like bronzed iron.

She forced her focus to his face, his wide jaw dark and covered with thick stubble. But it was his startling blue eyes that caught and held her attention.

He locked on and didn't so much as blink one of his long lashes. "I assume you or your guard caught on to the fact that the Contis are into something illegal."

She was staring like an idiot at the man's eyes, assessing his muscles, all in front of her old boss and Collier's boss. Talk about unprofessional. Not something she'd ever done on the job when she'd been a deputy or detective.

She took a breath and broke the hold. "Stolen antiquities, right?"

"That's right." His crisp nod was all business. "And we can't have you telling anyone about it."

"Too late," she fired back. "My sisters came to the warehouse right after you left. I alerted them to my location before I entered the building and told them if they didn't hear back from me in thirty minutes from my arrival, they were to respond. When I didn't answer their texts or calls, they came to my rescue. Of course I told them what happened and what I had heard. And Patrick—that's our guard—has his suspicions too."

"Then we'll have to allay his suspicions so this doesn't get around." Collier planted his feet. "Maybe reassign him in case he gets nosey."

"*We* allay?" she asked.

"That's why we asked you here," Gutierrez said, thankfully taking her attention. "We'd like to deputize you to help Agent Collier on his undercover assignment."

"Help you?" She shot Collier a look that she was certain held surprise. Shock too. And suspicion mixed with residual anger. "Over my dead body."

"I hope it doesn't come to that." He grinned at her, his mouth crooking up on one side and dimples revealing themselves.

Devastatingly handsome. She couldn't look away. She opened her mouth to fire off a smart retort, but stopped when Harris stood.

"We wouldn't ask if this wasn't urgent." She peered down on Teagan, a power position for sure. "Agent Collier has finally gotten the Contis to trust him, and he's close to finding the identity of their supplier. We have got to stop the route of stolen antiquities entering our country. The threat of angering Middle Eastern countries is great, and we don't want to fuel retaliation in terrorist attacks."

Now come on. Don't put me on the spot like this. She wanted to be mad at this guy. For tying her up. Even more so for the ridiculous way she was responding to him. Here she was a professional thirty-three-year-old woman, and she was acting like a teenager. She swallowed away the angst and took stock of the request.

How could she refuse to help protect the country from terrorist retaliation over the theft of precious antiquities?

She looked at Harris. "I'll do it."

"You will?" Collier gaped at her.

"I'm a patriot too. I don't want my fellow countrymen harmed by others. How could I refuse, even if it means part-nering with the guy who tied me up?"

He held her gaze, his expression somber. "I hope you can let that go."

She hoped so too. For her sake and for the sake of the investigation, but right now she couldn't guarantee how she would react around this man.

4

___

Not staring at Teagan was about as difficult as not staring at a pink elephant in the middle of the room, but Drew tried. What had brought about her sudden change? She was spitting mad and then, boom. Ms. Agreeable. Not that she'd changed her mind about her anger with him. She was still mad. He got that. He'd be the same. He'd gotten the drop on her. Embarrassing enough, but he followed it up by threatening her and her guard. Gagged her, tied her, and left the building without giving her a way to get free.

Lieutenant Gutierrez looked at Harris. "Steele will report to me and will be on equal footing with your guy or this is a no go."

"Fine." Harris's lip curled a fraction, but Drew recognized it as about the only sign she gave of her emotions.

Gutierrez nodded and after a lingering look Drew thought was meant to cement the lieutenant's position, he turned to Teagan. "Let me swear you in and work out the details, then you can sit down in the conference room with these agents to formulate a plan."

"Sounds good." Teagan smiled at her former boss.

Drew had his work cut out for him if he was ever to

receive such a smile. And oddly enough, when he should pin his entire attention on the investigation, he really wanted one directed his way. Had wanted one since he laid eyes on her at the Conti brothers' business months ago. What would she think if she knew he'd watched her for some time? Probably add that to the creep factor of sneaking up on her and taking her down. So those thoughts weren't coming out of his mouth if he could help it.

"Was good to meet you both." Gutierrez held out his hand to Harris. "Conference room is the first door on the left."

Obviously, the guy wanted some time alone with Teagan. To cover what, Drew didn't know, but he would try to find out. And he would use the time while waiting for her to join them to figure out how to get on her good side.

Harris shook hands with Gutierrez. "I'll be heading back to our office and leaving Collier to work out the details."

Drew also shook the lieutenant's hand and gave Teagan one last apologetic look. "See you in a few."

She nodded, but her attention had already shifted to her former supervisor.

Thinking about her working in this office, Drew stepped into the hallway. He could easily see her as a deputy. She didn't hesitate to slam him against the wall and show her authority. She regretted it. He could see that in her expression, but he also suspected it felt good. Would have for him if he were in her shoes.

Now visualizing her as a detective would have to wait until he witnessed her thought processes and logic in running an investigation. Undercover was different than finding a killer. It was live and fluid, and to do the job a person had to be quick-witted and have keen observation skills. She would've needed observation skills as a detective, but most of the time her life wouldn't depend on it like it would have while on patrol, and if she ever went undercover.

Harris turned to him. "Let's go as slow as you can on this. Read her in on the minimum she needs to know to not hinder the investigation."

Drew didn't answer. He didn't like his boss's tone and insinuation. Like they were using Teagan. Didn't sit well with him, and he would do what he believed was right, despite Harris's directions. Better to treat Teagan right whenever possible and ask for his supervisor's forgiveness later.

"Your assessment earlier was right on the money," Harris continued as if she assumed he would comply with her wishes. "The woman is good and mad at you. But turn on your charms and you should be fine."

"Charms?" he asked, bothered by the second time she mentioned this.

"Oh, come on, Collier. You know the ladies swoon around you, and you use it with female suspects all the time."

She was right. Partly. He didn't know about the swooning, but he did use it to his benefit in interrogations. He never flirted or tried to charm fellow law enforcement officers. Not unless he wanted it to go beyond a professional relationship, which he'd done a few times. None of them went very far. He never allowed anything to go beyond a few dates. He didn't plan to get married. Ever. Even *if* a woman who piqued his interest like Teagan Steele came along. He would never want to lead a woman on.

"I'll do my best to win her over," he said to appease his boss.

"We'll hold our usual check-in unless something comes up before that." She eyed him. "Try not to let anything come up."

He stepped back for her to pass, wishing he could say what he was thinking. He couldn't. Not when he'd gotten into hot water in the past for mouthing off. Best to keep his trap shut. He already had one woman he needed to placate. No point in making it two.

He entered the small conference room reeking of stale fast-food mixed with burnt coffee. The empty coffee pot on the small table in the corner had deep char marks. A long table dominated the middle of the room, and upholstered chairs lined the walls. A large television was mounted next to a whiteboard smeared with red marker residue.

Too antsy to sit, he circled the table, pausing to look out the door each time he reached that end of the room and glancing at the wall clock on each turn. Took Teagan fifteen minutes to show up at the door, where she paused. She'd been wearing a classic blue suit with a white blouse last night, but today she wore black slacks and a red knit top that clung to her curves and deepened her already nearly black hair. He didn't see a weapon, but she was a civilian when she'd come in today, and if she carried all the time, she'd likely had to check it at the front desk.

She looked him in the eye. "I'm going to get a cup of coffee. You want one?"

"Sure. Thanks. Black."

She nodded and departed. He wanted to take her kindness as a sign that her anger was melting, but maybe not. Maybe it was her faith in action. Her family was legendary in the law enforcement world. Not only for their fine service, but for the Christian values they held.

At least he hoped he hadn't been paired with a hotheaded person, just tempered for a moment. That personality didn't work well in an undercover situation.

She returned carrying two cardboard cups of steaming coffee. The nutty aroma trumped the foul smell lingering in the room. She set them both on the table and took a seat at the head. He dropped down next to her and cupped the warm cardboard. "Thank you for agreeing to work on this investigation."

She arched an eyebrow. "Really? I would think you'd be mad about me butting in when I'm probably not needed."

Interesting. "Why do you say that?"

"I figure you only asked as a way to ensure my silence. Sure, I could blab about the op once I was an officer too, but you probably think the chances are better that as a sworn officer I'll keep my mouth shut."

He could lie to her—Harris would probably want him to —but he reserved his lies for the undercover world. "Your assessment is accurate."

"I'll keep quiet. So will my sisters and our guard." She lifted her coffee cup and took a sip. "That said, do you want to cut and run?"

"No," he said, surprising himself. She'd given him the perfect out, and he should've taken it. But maybe she could be helpful. After all, she'd pegged him and Harris right off the bat, so she had skills.

She took a long sip of the coffee, black like his. "What's the plan?"

He almost hated to tell her and ruin the short truce. "Harris thinks it would be a good idea if we forged a fake relationship. I'll tell the brothers that I want to ask you out. Get their buy-in. Tell them in addition to that, it would be good to have an inside source to keep an eye on their business's security."

She didn't react. Not at all. Not a bat of her eyelashes. She simply set her cup on the table while continuing to stare at him. "Do you think they'll go for it?"

"Yeah, I do. You're not hard on the eyes, so selling being interested in you wouldn't be a stretch." Not at all. "Now all it will take is for you to forgive me for getting the jump on you last night. If not, it'll never work."

She let out a squeaky breath. "I'm sorry for attacking you in the office. I don't know what came over me. I'm usually much more in control."

"I get it—trust me. I'd be spitting mad if it happened to me."

"But like you said. You were just doing your job. And you didn't hurt me." She held up a bandaged finger. "My only injury is from slicing the zip tie. Now that I think about it, you were pretty kind, considering everything."

"Does that mean I'm forgiven?" He grinned at her. A grin that Harris would consider charming, but it was honestly generated from thinking that Teagan might let this go.

"Enough to do the job and convince the Contis I'm glad to be dating you." She gave a tight smile. "And as much as needed to not be holding something against another person. My faith wouldn't allow that, and I already had to ask for forgiveness for losing my cool and roughing you up."

He liked how she didn't hold back on talking about her faith. He once was an all-in kind of guy when it came to faith, but then his undercover days had eroded the strength of his convictions. Not attending worship every week and being surrounded by unscrupulous people had taken a toll on him.

She lifted her chin. "You look like you don't think my faith should be part of the workplace."

Uh-oh. Had he made her mad again? "I was actually thinking about how mine has eroded while undercover."

She lowered her chin. "I always wondered how people could go under like you have. Especially for a year. That's a long time."

"Which is a good reason for this op to wrap up."

"Do you plan to take another assignment after it does?"

39

"Can't. ICE rules won't allow it, but I might consider it if they did."

"So I guess you're not married or don't have a real girlfriend."

"No. You with anyone who'll object to our dates?" he asked, not really for the job. It wasn't fair to make her think it was.

She shook her head. "No time. My family depends on me to keep the business running. Not sure what I'll tell them if this assignment takes up too much time."

"You won't tell them about being sworn again, right?"

"Right. But I'll have to tell them about you, and I hate to mislead them." She sipped on her cup again, her expression filled with questions. "Where do we go from here?"

"The Contis are expecting me this morning. I'll head over to World of Crafts. It would be a good time for you to show up while I'm there. I can express my interest in you and get the Contis' blessing on dating."

"I can do a routine check on our guard like we often do, and it won't raise suspicions."

"Then let's get going." He started to rise.

She raised a hand. "What about filling me in on their operation?"

Ah yes, of course she would want to know that. And that was the kind of thing Harris didn't want him to share. "I don't want to keep the brothers waiting. Can we talk about it over dinner tonight? It'll be our first date."

She raised an eyebrow. "You really think you can sell them on the dating thing?"

"I persuaded them to let me into their inner circle. Means they trust me." And it won't be hard to convince them that he was into Teagan. Not when the more time he spent with her, the more his interest grew.

Teagan entered the Steele Guardians' office and took a deep breath of the pine scent coming from the fresh Christmas tree with twinkling multi-color lights. She'd put it up right after Thanksgiving and decorated it with gift tags for visitors to take and return with gifts for children in need.

She loved Christmas. How she loved it. Probably because of her birthday on the fifth of December. She embraced the whole month as her own. As a child, she'd once believed the fuss was all about her birthday until she understood the real meaning of Christmas, but by then she was hooked on Christmas. She always made a big deal of it. All except last year when her cousin Thomas had been murdered near Thanksgiving. The whole family had a low-key Christmas then.

Their receptionist, Gretchen, looked up from behind a long desk decked out with pine garland and twinkly white lights. She'd braided her hair the same shade of black as Teagan's, but the dyed color looked stark against her lighter complexion.

"Oh good." She pursed her lips coated in purple lipstick. "Glad you're finally here. Everyone's looking for you."

"Figured they would be." Teagan never arrived at work after seven and it was going on eleven now. She probably should've called to prevent worry. Couldn't even think of it though. Not after the call from Gutierrez, being deputized again, and seeing Drew.

Drew—not Dylan.

Teagan offered Gretchen an apologetic look. "I'll check in with everyone so they quit bugging you."

"Your family is never a bother." She rolled her eyes in a cheeky look, then laughed.

Teagan caught her good mood and laughed too as she

41

strode across the polished concrete floor. With all the former law enforcement officers in the family, they could each be a real pain. Driven. Forthright. And pushy.

Yep. That described them. And that Gretchen had put up with all of them for over two years spoke volumes about her abilities to handle anyone who walked through their doors. And the reason the family made sure she was well-compensated and had benefits even at times when family members went without full pay.

Teagan climbed the iron staircase with thick wood slab risers. She took them two at a time and paused at the landing to put her game face on. She would have to evade and redirect any questions without lying. And without raising suspicions. Her Uncle Gene would be tough to fool, but her dad would be the hardest one of all.

Her office was located right inside the door so she dropped off her backpack, ignoring the mound of paper-work waiting for her in her Inbox next to a carved miniature nativity set. The smell of fresh coffee beckoned her back into the hallway and into the break room. She filled her favorite mug, a British souvenir with a Royal Guard member painted on the side from her trip to England. What better mug for the COO of a company that provided guards?

Sipping the full-bodied coffee, she looked into Bristol's door holding a large evergreen wreath with a big plaid bow. Teagan's youngest cousin, who'd recently joined the company in a sales role, wasn't in. Good. One down. Four to go.

Teagan moved on to the next office belonging to Mackenzie.

Her sister looked up from her laptop. "So you *do* remember where you work."

"Sorry. Had an early meeting that I forgot about."

"Not like you to forget anything." Mackenzie tilted her

head, her blond hair worn straight and cascading over her shoulder. The only blond in the family, she took after their mother. In hair color, sure, but she was shorter like their mom too.

"Guess last night threw me off," Teagan admitted. No lie there.

"Any more thoughts on what's going on at WOC?"

"I plan to head over there in a few minutes to check in with our guard. See if they might know anything."

Mackenzie narrowed her grayish-blue eyes, also like their mom's color. "Wouldn't they have said something if they did?"

"If they knew what they were seeing, but maybe they witnessed something that they didn't know was important."

"It's a long shot."

"Yeah, but I have to do something."

"I get it. If some creep tied me up and gagged me, it would be my main focus until he was found and made to pay." As a former state police detective, Mackenzie's thoughts often mirrored Teagan's. Not that Mackenzie's personality was similar. Not at all. She was a deep thinker and philosophizer. She was nearly as driven as Teagan, but Teagan always figured that was due to middle child syndrome, where the middle child sought more attention because they felt neglected.

"Do you even know anything about antiquities to pick up on any leads?" Mackenzie asked.

"Nothing."

"Gran and Grandad's brains are filled with all kinds of things. Maybe check in with them."

"Sounds like it might be a good idea." One Teagan wouldn't follow. Her grandparents, more than anyone in the family, had a way of getting information out of their grand-children. Teagan would likely tell them about Drew. Not only couldn't she reveal his identity, but she didn't want them to notice the unwanted romantic vibes she would likely put out either.

"Go. Do your thing." Mackenzie waved her hands. "There's nothing urgent here."

"Thanks. I'll check in later." Teagan stepped down the hall to Peyton's office, saving the office her uncle and dad shared at the end of the hall for last. Peyton had a beautiful corner office overlooking Mount Hood. Mackenzie could've chosen this space, but she'd imagined herself staring over at the mountains, lost in thought instead of working.

Peyton was on the phone so Teagan simply waved and stopped at the end of the hallway to look out the window facing Mount Hood before going in to see her dad and uncle.

All she had to do was think about some of the looks Drew fired her way today, and her heart skipped a beat. Like this moment. Her attention should be on getting out of here without blowing his cover, but his ultra-blue eyes fixed only on her came to mind. Then those eyes relaxed into a soft blue lake as he tried to make up for last night. He'd smiled. Laughed.

Nice. So nice. She had it bad already, and she would betray herself all right.

"You always look at mountains that way?" her dad's voice came from his doorway.

He leaned against the doorjamb. He wore a green polo shirt, khaki pants, and he'd styled his thick hair the same color as hers with gel. She almost laughed when she remembered her mom making him learn to use gel and how he'd hated it at first. He'd wanted to keep the buzz cut he'd worn for the many years he'd been on the force, but their mom had encouraged him to make a change.

"Well?" His look grew more pointed, like one of the awls

he used in his leatherworking hobby that he'd started after he retired from the force.

She needed to play dumb. "What way?"

"Like you want to marry them."

"Dad. Really!" She erased Drew from her mind and gave her dad a playful punch to the shoulder. "You're letting your imagination go wild in your old age."

"Might be getting old, but I still know what I see." He eyed her. "You dating someone? Or thinking about it?"

She couldn't say no as hopefully, within an hour, she'd be scheduled to go on a date with Drew. "I need to get over to World of Crafts for an inspection. I don't have time to stand around. I have work to do."

He stood back and eyed her. "Uh-huh, so do we, but we answer the questions put to us."

She gave him a hug. "Love you, Dad. See you later."

She bolted to her office.

"This isn't over," he called after her.

Man, she failed. Failed big time. Reverted to her teenage behavior when she'd done something wrong and avoidance seemed like the best answer. It never was. In the end, he always demanded an answer, and she complied before taking her punishment.

But she wasn't a teenager anymore, and her undercover actions held life and death consequences—not only for her, but for Drew too.

She checked the guard schedule. Sandy Usher was on duty at WOC. A notation showed she was subbing for the daytime guard attending training. Might mean she wouldn't have a lot of information to share.

Wouldn't stop Teagan. No way.

She found a clipboard holding evaluation forms, grabbed her purse, and then fled the office before her dad came after her. She even sped through the misty rain and slick roads to WOC as if someone were chasing her. Or maybe she was in a hurry to help Drew find the antiquity suppliers, so she wouldn't have to sidestep her dad again.

In the lobby, Sandy stood in uniform by the warehouse door. Teagan tucked her clipboard under her arm and greeted Betty, the receptionist who'd been working with the company for years and ran its front end as if it were her own kingdom.

Teagan smiled at her. "Just here checking in with Sandy and the Contis. Are the brothers here by any chance?"

"In their office." The older woman with curly gray hair and thick glasses shifted her attention back to her computer screen.

Teagan crossed over to Sandy.

"Ms. Steele." Sandy pulled her shoulders back even further, almost standing at attention.

A former marine, Sandy insisted on formality, as did other guards who'd come up through the military. As much as Teagan wished they would use her first name, she loved the respect they had for authority.

Teagan crossed the space. Residual fear from last night tried to take hold. She took a breath and stopped next to Sandy. "Everything going okay on this location?"

"Nothing odd as far as I've seen." She stepped closer to Teagan. "Honestly, I've been here a few days, and I'm not even sure why they need security during the day. Not sure who would want to boost craft supplies." She grinned.

Teagan would've said the same thing yesterday. Not today. Today she knew the Contis were protecting very valuable antiquities in addition to their craft supplies. She wished she could simply request security footage from last night, but Drew said it could make the brothers suspicious and compromise his investigation.

Teagan smiled at her guard. "Other than boredom, how do you like the assignment?"

"Good." Sandy drew her eyebrows together. "It isn't nearly as interesting as the hospital. Fewer people to watch."

"We appreciate you being so flexible to cross-train here. We do like to keep the same people on the same assignments. Helps build familiarity with the surroundings, so they know when something is off, but we need relief staff familiar with the assignment too."

"I don't mind. Just saying I prefer my regular hospital gig, and I hope you all keep me on it."

"Duly noted." Teagan tapped the clipboard. "I need to go through this checklist with you. Is now a good time?"

"As good as any."

"Let's step into the warehouse so we don't bother Betty."

"Of course." Sandy pulled the door open.

Teagan started to smooth her hand over her hair. *No. Stop.* She was primping for Drew. No way she'd let him catch her doing that. She didn't want to be doing it at all. She had no real interest in dating. The company was her only boyfriend and would be that way until the business was performing solidly.

Could take quite a while as several companies started cutting back on their security during the day as Sandy mentioned. Losing this account when the brothers were arrested—and she would make sure if they were guilty of selling illegal antiquities that they would be arrested—wouldn't help the Steele Guardians' bottom line. Her work with Drew could hurt their company's financial status but would prevent a much bigger problem of their reputation being tainted.

The warehouse was bustling with staff filling baskets for orders, and she doubted the brothers were doing any illegal business right now. Still, she kept her eyes and ears open as

47

she ran down the checklist with Sandy and made crisp checkmarks in the boxes.

After the last box was neatly filled, she stowed her pen. "Anything you want to add?"

"Nothing other than I appreciate the recent raise, and I love my job."

"You're worth every penny." And more, but they couldn't go any higher and stay in business. "You can return to the lobby now, and thanks for taking the time to help me."

"Of course." She marched out as if on parade.

Teagan strolled down the aisle, passing the space where Drew had hauled her against his rock-solid chest and dragged her out of the main aisle. Dried blood dotted the floor and razor blades glinted in the light. A shiver ran down her back.

Was it from being grabbed so abruptly or from Drew doing the grabbing? At the time, she hadn't liked it one bit, but as she caught sight of him talking to Sal Conti now, she could easily imagine those strong arms holding her in a far less platonic way.

Stop. Now! Let it go right this minute. You are not falling for this handsome man when you have no time for him in your life. Act like the professional woman the Contis know you to be, or they might get suspicious.

Suspicions that could be cast onto Drew. She couldn't let that happen. She had to keep her guard up every moment or the pair of them could die.

5

_____

Drew spotted Teagan the second she entered the warehouse. He'd been waiting for her to arrive. Waiting to see if he reacted to her the same way he had earlier in her lieutenant's office. He did. Maybe more so.

"Like what you see?" Sal jabbed Drew in the side. "You're almost salivating."

Drew didn't like the man's tone. Nor the fact that he'd been caught gawking at Teagan. He should've told Harris no when she suggested he partner with Teagan. He knew she'd be a distraction. He didn't need a distraction. Not now. Not ever really.

But his unconscious behavior had given him the perfect opening. "I do. Like it a lot."

"Yeah, she's a looker. All the Steele women are. But I gotta warn you. She has a dad and uncle who'd put you down if you hurt a one of them."

What would they do when they found out Drew was working with her? Or if they learned he'd manhandled her last night? If they were in the know about his assignment and his real identity, would they object?

If Drew were the dad of a beautiful daughter, he sure

would. After all the losers he'd seen on the job, he might even consider locking his daughter away until she was eighty. He wouldn't want her anywhere near the horrible things he'd seen in his career. But then, Teagan was an experienced law enforcement officer, and she could handle herself.

Or could she? He'd managed to take her down last night and another man with ulterior motives could've done the same. Not something Drew liked to consider. Not one bit.

He shoved his hands into his pockets and waited for her to cross the room.

"Good to see you, Teagan." Sal held out a meaty hand. "What brings you here?"

She shook Sal's hand and looked him square in the eyes. "One of our surprise guard audits."

Sal nodded. "Always liked that practice since your dad put it into place. Shows integrity."

Integrity. Right. What did Sal know about integrity?

"We find it helps us, the guards, and the company we're working for too." She shifted her stance to look at Drew and hold out her hand. "Teagan Steele. Steele Guardians."

"Dylan Crane." He took her hand and held it a little too long. He hoped Sal thought it was due to Drew's interest in her, which it was. No need for acting here. "I work with Sal and his brothers."

She arched an eyebrow. Likely because he didn't say what he did or maybe at the mention of his fake name. She responded in a way that could be expected, but did Sal think it odd?

Drew glanced at him. He was too busy looking Teagan up and down to notice anything else.

The urge to punch the man for ogling her made Drew shove his hands back into his pockets.

Teagan looked at Sal. "Do you have a moment to fill out our questionnaire?"

"Sure. Sure."

She switched the papers on her clipboard and handed it and a pen to him.

Sal fixed his attention on the questionnaire.

"So you work with Steele Guardians," Drew said to Teagan.

She shot him a look, but then seemed to realize he was working up to asking her out.

"I do. I'm the COO."

"Chief Operating Officer. Wow!" Another point he didn't have to fake being impressed about. He couldn't manage to keep his checkbook balanced most of the time, much less run a company. "Top of the ranks. Been doing that long?"

"Two years, but I was a Clackamas County deputy and detective before that."

He raised his eyebrows, pretending to be surprised, and nodded at her jacket, where the bulge of a holster showed through the fabric. "I see you carry."

"That a problem?"

He liked a strong woman who wasn't afraid of guns, but in his role as Dylan, he should have a problem with that, so he gave her a concerned look. "Carry all the time?"

"Yes," she said.

He mocked a big gulp. "Even on dates?"

"Yes, but I might put it in my purse instead of wearing it on my hip." She grinned, giving him such a flirty look that he almost forgot his role.

"Don't suppose you're free tonight." He took tickets out of his pocket that he'd scored before coming to the warehouse. "A buddy just gave me two tickets to the Trailblazers tonight. You want to go with me?"

She took a step back. "I don't know anything about you."

Good. Good. She was making it appear real. At least he hoped this was how she reacted when some strange man asked her out—something he figured happened a lot—and she knew how to handle herself.

He relaxed his posture and made sure not to seem offended by her comment. "You know the Conti brothers and know they wouldn't associate with a loser, right?"

"He's right." Sal looked up and tapped the pen on the clipboard. "You can trust the guy."

Drew waved the tickets. "They're courtside."

She tilted her head, and her expression softened. "I *am* a big Blazer fan."

"Figured you might me."

She rested her hands on her very curvy hips "You think you know me, huh?"

"I'd like to." The words came out with such sincerity it surprised him. Was he really that interested in this woman already?

"Smooth, man. Real smooth." Sal chuckled and handed the clipboard and pen back to Teagan. "He's trying so hard, you should go out with him just for that. I mean, you're clearly out of his league, but what could one date hurt?"

"Hey, thanks, man." Drew socked Sal's arm but smiled at Teagan. "Will you take pity on a guy who's trying to date up the ladder to impossible status?"

She laughed, tossing her head back and revealing a creamy-looking neck. "I will."

She stopped laughing and met his eyes. That pull he'd felt between them from the very beginning strengthened. He wanted to draw her close. Badly. So badly. He nearly closed the distance to her. Nearly.

You're on the job, for Pete's sake. Remember that.

Not only to stay safe, but to remember she was agreeing

to a date because of the job. Not because she was really interested in him. The job.

Forget the immense attraction. Keep your mind in the game. Do your job and live to fight another day.

Teagan had changed into jeans and a well-worn Blazer jersey before arriving and securing a secluded table at one of her favorite restaurants where "Silent Night" played over the speakers. The southern cooking restaurant located near the Moda Center where the Blazers played boasted antique Christmas snow globes and rusty antiques. The shiplap walls were covered in old advertising signs. She loved the down-home recipes served here and had tried pretty much everything on the menu. The foods were all so very bad for her, but oh so good when she needed extra comfort in her life. Something she undeniably needed today.

The glass door swung open. Drew entered the space and heads turned. He wore black jeans and shrugged out of a leather jacket, revealing his black crew T-shirt that stretched tight over his broad chest and muscled arms. He looked more like he was going on a nighttime op instead of a date. Regardless, the sight of him kicked her heart beat up.

She put him at six-three, and his shoulders at the large-and-in-charge size. She'd always gone for men who pumped iron. She worked out most every day and appreciated fitness. Being tall herself, she often wondered if she only felt secure with a bigger guy. Regardless, he fit her kind of guy to a T, whatever that old saying actually meant.

He spotted her and when his gaze landed on her, she felt the intensity all the way to her bones. He crossed the room with that commanding cop swagger. Why didn't the Contis see that in him? Wonder about him?

Because most people saw what they wanted to see. What they were directed to see. Why didn't she want to see creepy Dylan striding toward her instead of a fine-looking man exuding appeal? That would be so very much easier to ignore.

Business, Teagan. This is all business.

"Collier," she said as he settled his big frame on one of the dainty vintage chairs.

He arched a dark eyebrow. "If we're going to date, you'll have to start calling me by my first name."

"Dylan, I assume."

"Yeah." His mouth curved down in disappointment.

"You don't like that?"

"I don't like living an assumed identity in the first place, and I don't like to extend it to people outside the op. But yeah. I'm Dylan to you."

She held up her menu. "Well, Dylan, we should order so we can get to the game on time."

"We can order, but we won't be going to the game." He casually opened his menu as if he hadn't dropped a bombshell that their date was off.

She wouldn't let him get away with it. "What do you mean won't be going to the game? I thought dating was our cover."

"It is." He peered at her over his menu. "Sal thinks we'll be attending the game, and that means I'll be tied up. So he's free to meet his contact—who he's kept a secret—without me tailing him. But he's wrong. I plan to be there to witness the meet and ID the guy."

She kept her attention pinned to Drew. "You mean *we'll* be there."

He dropped his menu, his eyes turning as dark as black iron. "I work alone."

"Not anymore." She crossed her arms. "You want me to

54

keep quiet and pretend to be your girlfriend, then you don't shut me out of the active work." She expected him to glare at her, but she caught a glimmer of respect in his expression.

He opened the menu. "I've never eaten here. What do you recommend?"

"Everything," she said, taking his change of subject as his agreement. If she got any hint that he'd made this move to avoid the subject, she would press him on it.

He cocked an eyebrow. "Everything?"

"Honestly. Everything. They make the best southern comfort foods."

"You were born and raised in the northwest, right? How do you know southern cooking?"

"I worked a three-month investigation as part of a task force in New Orleans. It was an awesome culinary experience, and we got the bad guys too." She laughed.

He smiled, broad and liquid, the potency melting any reserves she might have about him ditching her on tonight's op.

How fast she could change. Just a smile. A simple smile, and she forgot everything else. One thing was crystal clear. She wouldn't have to act with him. She could fall for him in a snap. Even after he manhandled her last night. What did that say about her? That she was willing to give him a fresh start, she supposed.

Dylan was the one who'd tied her up. She was sitting across from Drew.

The waitress with her bleached blond hair in a ponytail joined them, and she directed her attention to Drew first. "Decide what you want?"

He cast a fond smile at Teagan. "Honey, do you know what you want?"

She liked his manners in letting her order first. And she

liked being called *honey*. As if he really meant what he was saying.

"I'll have the seafood jambalaya." She could already taste the spicy seafood and rice. Not to mention the flaky buttermilk biscuit that went with it. "Can I get a side of coleslaw too and unsweetened tea?"

"Of course." The waitress scribbled on her pad and faced Drew.

"I'll have the fried chicken and the collard greens," Drew said. "Make my tea sweet."

"An excellent choice." The waitress jotted it all down and departed, her heels clicking on the distressed wooden floors.

Teagan put her napkin on her lap. "Okay, you ordered like a true southern boy. Where'd that come from?"

"I served in the marines before ICE, and my buddy Otis was from Alabama. On leave, we'd go to his family's house and work on restoring his 1955 F-150 truck. His mama fed us. That's where I got my love for the food and for restoring vintage cars." He leaned forward. "I don't know how I missed this place though. Glad to have found it."

She was about to mention that she restored cars with her father, but the waitress returned, first giving Drew his tea before setting down Teagan's glass without taking her eyes off Drew. She gave him a suggestive look and slowly backed away.

"She has a preference for you." Teagan took a sip of her drink.

"I got that."

"Does that happen often?"

"Enough."

"You don't seem to like it."

"You caught that, huh?" He took a long drink of his tea. "Tea's almost as good as Otis's mama makes."

A change of subject. Could he be shy about the way women responded to him?

"Why didn't you come home on leave? Or should I first ask where home is?"

"Minneapolis, Minnesota. Most of the time it's too dang cold to be there. Besides, nothing really to draw me home."

"No parents?"

"Yeah. Believe it or not I was born not hatched." He chuckled, but tension lurked underneath the good humor. "It's just my mom. When I got the assignment here, she moved to Portland. I call her when I have my regular check-ins with Harris. My mom hates that I'm UC and is looking forward to the end."

"What about you? Looking forward to the op ending?"

"I guess I am. I never really planned to do it in the first place. I'm the only one in the office who speaks Italian, which the Contis often resort to when they don't want anyone to know what they're saying. They have no idea I speak the language, so I've been able to learn valuable information."

"Italian's not a common language to learn. I don't think a lot of schools offer it, right?"

"My father was career Air Force, and when I was a kid, he was stationed at the Aviano Air Force Base. We lived in Aviano for six years." He shrugged. "I picked up the language."

She loved getting to know more about him. "Did you like living there?"

"It's a small sleepy town, so as a younger kid I liked it but then I wanted more." He frowned. "I got my wish, but in the worst way. Right before I turned ten, my dad died right in front of my eyes, and we moved back to the States."

"Oh no," she said. "I'm so sorry."

He shrugged and stared at his hands resting on the table, his jaw muscles working hard.

Clearly, he didn't want to talk about this painful loss. She really wanted to know more, but she would respect his privacy and move on. "My family would be all over me if I chose to go undercover for a long time."

He looked at her. "I read about your family on the Steele Guardians' website. Seems like you're close."

She shouldn't be surprised that he'd researched her background, but she was. "Very."

"Otis's big family was the same way, and I thought it was great. With just my mom and me, it's not such a big deal, but we have a solid connection. Especially with our faith. Though, like I said, since I've been UC it's been a struggle. I guess I need more Mom *and* God time."

She loved that he was a fellow believer, even if he was struggling. She'd been a Christian her entire life and knew there were times she relied on her faith less. In those times, she struggled to live her faith. But God always came through. Always. Often allowing something to happen in her life where only her faith could bring her through. Sort of like He'd sent the shepherd to find the lost sheep, He brought her back into the fold.

Please, God. Do the same thing for Drew.

He suddenly straightened his back, and his expression hardened. "We should talk about the operation. What I know about the Conti brothers and what to expect in these next few days."

"Okay." She leaned closer, trying to get the relaxed Drew back instead of the guy Dylan who looked like he'd taken over. She already missed Drew.

Oh girl. You are so in for a world of hurt here!

6

Drew chugged his tea and thankfully, Teagan stopped looking at him, her eyes sultry, suggestive. She likely didn't know she'd been doing it, but there was an interest between them for sure. Good for the op when she pretended to date him, not good for his sanity.

He swallowed and looked over her shoulder to get his head into the game. He needed to ask about her experience in undercover work and give her a fast primer on UC protocols. "You ever go undercover before?"

She shook her head. "I always thought it was interesting, but my family connections were too strong to consider it."

"Then why do you think you can do this now?"

"Most UC assignments at Clackamas were long-term. Six months or more. I couldn't commit to that. But you're finalizing things here, and I figure I can do it for a short time before my family starts to get too nosey for me to handle."

"I guess it's not like you'll be doing much more than dating me. That shouldn't raise too many questions."

She arched an eyebrow and gave him a pointed look. "First, you don't know my family. Nosey is a nice way of putting things. And second, I thought we were partners in the op."

"Partners?" He figured this might come up at some point but not before they even got started.

"You didn't say no when I said I would accompany you tonight."

"But I didn't agree to it either."

"Okay, I see." She leaned back and draped an arm over a chair, appearing relaxed but her steady gaze said she was anything but. "Look. I get it. You didn't know what to do with me. You want me to help in the least intrusive way and keep my mouth shut. But I'm here to say I want to be involved beyond dating, and I need you to figure out how to make that happen."

He leaned across the table, not taking his focus from her. "Going undercover isn't simple. It takes skills and practice. You have neither. I don't have time to babysit you or properly train you, and I can't have you screw this up."

"I won't. You can be assured of that. I can play the dumb girlfriend. But first, you have to tell me about what you're doing so we can figure out a way for me to fit in."

He wanted to sigh and at the same time congratulate her for her determination. She was the kind of woman who would keep him interested for life. He hardly knew her, but he knew that for sure. "You won't back down, will you?"

"Keeping our company safe from scandal is the most important thing to me right now. I won't tell anyone about you or what happened no matter what you decide to do, but let me help or I'll find a way to do it myself." She sat up, her rigid posture made of steel. Or Steele.

He had to work hard not to slam his fist on the table. He was equal parts irritated with her and impressed with her ability to stand up for herself. That trait would work well in the UC world. He should probably call Harris to tell her he planned to read Teagan in, but Harris would likely tell him to find a way around Teagan's demands. He could tell Teagan had her mind set, and he wouldn't change it. So better to ask Harris for forgiveness. Later. Much later.

He took a cue from the earlier calmer Teagan and sat back, feigning relaxation. "What do you know about stolen antiquities from Iraq?"

"Only that it's a big deal and both ICE and the FBI investigate it."

So nothing. "We're investigating items imported from Iraq. It became a problem in 2003 with the US invasion of the country and has continued to be a *big deal*. First, the Iraq Museum in Baghdad was looted. Some of the antiquities were recovered, but when security fell apart during our invasion, thieves also dug hundreds of holes into mounds where ancient cities are buried. Archeologists believe there are five thousand or more of these cities—tells—still to be properly excavated. The sites aren't protected in any way, and there are always people out to make money on the antiquities buried there."

"What a shame. Our attempt to help these people caused this problem." She turned her glass in circles, but kept her gaze trained on him. "I've always wondered what the difference is between artifacts and antiquities."

"Antiquities refer to ancient times, which is what we are dealing with here. Iraq itself is three thousand years old and some of these cities are four thousand."

The waitress approached carrying their food so Drew stopped the conversation and let her settle the plates on the table. He quickly told her they would like tea refills to encourage her to move on.

"Mind if I say grace?" he asked Teagan.

"Not at all." She held her hand out to him.

Not something he expected. He clasped it and the

warmth shot straight to his heart. Not in a romantic kind of way, but as if coming home. Belonging. Calm.

He offered a prayer for their food and for the operation that night. His mother and how he'd neglected her for the past year came to mind and his voice cracked. He cleared his throat and lifted his head, determined not to get personal with Teagan again. She was unearthing all sorts of things that should remain buried.

It felt good to talk to someone about his real life after being UC for so long. To pray aloud in a restaurant again, too. That was freeing and wonderful at the same time. Sure, he shouldn't have. The Contis could have someone watching him and Teagan, but he'd already scanned the room multiple times and didn't see anyone paying even the slightest hint of attention to them.

He chomped a bite of fried chicken and had to work hard not to grin in delight. He swallowed. "Otis's mama would be hard-pressed to make better chicken than this."

Teagan swallowed her bite and grinned. "Told you so. I will totally understand if you have to put our discussion on hold to eat."

"I can talk between bites." He took another one and savored the crispy skin and crunchy breading. "Our operation—Operation Oasis—began nearly a year ago. Started when a DEA agent working undercover in an international drug smuggling investigation caught wind of the Conti brothers, and the word on the street was that they were into antiquities too."

She paused, her fork of rice midway to her mouth. "They're into drugs?"

He nodded and stabbed a bite of his coleslaw but held his fork over his plate to continue the story. "Heroin from the Golden Crescent. It's one of Asia's two principal areas of illicit opium production. That includes Afghanistan,

Pakistan, and Iran. Almost three thousand tons of heroin is produced in Afghanistan, and a rough estimate says above a million people are involved in drug trafficking there."

"Wow." She dropped her fork and sat back. "Just wow. I had no idea it was such a huge problem in their country."

He tapped hot pepper sauce onto his collard greens. "Which means it's a problem here too, though most of our heroin comes from Mexico these days. But I digress. Our CI on the drug investigation brought the lead on antiquities to the agent's attention, and my SAC sent me undercover."

Teagan took a few bites of her rice while the waitress topped off their tea glasses, and he took his first bite of the greens. The tangy vinegar sauce melded with the greens, and he had to resist moaning again. He'd been eating so badly for the past year and having something that was similar to home cooking was special. He'd missed out on so much.

The waitress departed.

"This confidential informant you mentioned," Teagan said. "Is he reliable?"

"I mean, yeah, if you ignore our number one rule of undercover work. Never trust a CI." He laughed, but he was dead serious. If he wasn't, he could find himself dead. "The Contis are using their shipping connections and acting as a go-between. Importing drugs and antiquities for another person and taking a cut of the money. That's the person I'm after."

"And you're close to finding him or her?"

"Him. Getting closer. Our CI introduced me to the Contis and vouched for me, but it still took months of meeting with them. Shooting the breeze. Talking business. Letting them think I'm one of them."

"And how do you do that?" Her fork hung in the air, her rapt attention fixed on him.

63

"We created a bogus import/export business. Rented an office. Looped an agent in as the assistant for the business and arranged the backstopping."

"Backstopping?"

"A back story with false documents to support the UCO. We have offices in the front of the building and one-way glass in the back. Video monitors and listening devices behind it."

"Sounds like a big undercover operation."

"Actually, as far as the feds go, it's not. But I have a good case agent running it, and we're making progress. Recently, I gave each Conti brother a Rolex watch that I said I'd gotten from a contact with more of them that he wanted to move. I told them it was a token of my appreciation for taking me under their wing and making me a part of their crew. That finally made them warm up to me. Then this week I made the awkward jab."

She stabbed a large hunk of sausage covered with red sauce. "I have no idea what that means."

"Right, yeah, why would you? You mention an illegal subject and do it in a blunt, straightforward way. Get them off the fence and to commit. In addition to stopping the antiquities pipeline, our goal is to have them launder ICE funds. Reverse money laundering. To put them away for longer and close down the pipeline. I told Sal I had connections with an international heroin trafficker—a guy named Monty who is in reality our UCA."

"Undercover Agent," she clarified.

"That's right. Sal seemed interested, so I asked if he could help me launder the proceeds from my buddy's drug sales."

She leaned closer, eyes wide. "What happened?"

"He played dumb. Like he didn't have a clue what heroin was. Okay. Fine. I had to do more. I had a brick of heroin in my office for a prop. I got it out, telling Sal I was holding the stuff for Monty. Hoped that would solidify my relationship to Monty. Told Sal that Monty needed to avoid the DEA's scrutiny. Plus, paying taxes to the IRS? No way."

"And Sal went for it?"

He caught her enthusiasm for his story. "He did. Suggested we draw up a dummy contract between my fake company and another he would have his sellers form out of the country. I would wire the money to them to reroute through their overseas accounts, and then send the money to a second company in the United States that I would establish. He got a twenty percent commission, which would be outrageous if I really was in the business, but it was something he couldn't refuse and made getting him on money laundering possible."

"Then why haven't you brought him in?"

"The operation kept expanding as we went along. We want his antiquities supplier too. The big fish."

"So what's the plan?"

"I overheard him telling Aldo he had a meeting tonight and said something big was going down in two days. Then he asked if Aldo and Vito would run security for him. Figured if he needed security, they're involved in something I need to see. So I'm going to tail him."

"*We're* going to tail him."

He inwardly cringed at her comment. He knew she might argue, and he had no real reason to keep her out, but he did his best work alone. "I can't let you come along. It could be dangerous."

"I'm aware." She lifted her chin, her desire to look strong, he supposed, but it only made her look cuter.

"This is a job for one person."

"Why?"

He had no rebuttal to that. "Because that's the way I like it."

Her head tilted, and she studied him. "Maybe it's time you learn teamwork can make the dream work." She chuckled.

He appreciated her lightening the mood. Without a reason to tell her no and them needing to finish their meal and head out, he gave a sharp nod. "I don't suppose you have a vest in your car."

"Actually, I do. Habits die hard, and I still keep my go bag from deputy days. That always included an extra vest for the over ninety-degree days when the vest turned me into a sweat monster."

He couldn't imagine her being a sweat monster, but the vests were hot, so he totally got it. He kept an extra too, but it would be far too big for her.

He looked at his watch. "We better eat up. We have twenty minutes until go time."

"I'm almost too excited to eat, but we don't want my stomach growling and giving us away." Her eyes sparkled with excitement, and she grinned as she forked a slice of sausage.

That smile. Wow! Just wow!

He loved seeing her so relaxed and nearly reached across the table to take her hand. A woman who carried and shared his love for his line of work and at the same time fired off his interest in her as a woman. Not something he'd ever encountered. So appealing.

And so distracting.

Something he couldn't afford to let impact him while trailing dangerous criminals. Yet, she would be at his side, and he would have to make sure he achieved the op's goals, and at the same time, make sure she remained safe.

Double trouble to be sure...so why was he looking forward to it?

$\approx$

Teagan lowered the window in the passenger seat of Drew's car to listen for any danger in their surroundings, the cool and damp night air rolling in. Red and green Christmas lights strung on nearby buildings cast creepy shadows over the concrete and low-slung buildings. Normally Teagan would find the lights cheery, and they would raise her Christmas spirit, but tonight the colors seemed ominous. Sinister almost.

Note to self. Don't tail criminals during the holiday season or you'll never look at Christmas decorations the same way again.

Humor. Right. Odd time for it, but she needed something to ease the jitters building inside.

Drew had been following the Contis' vehicle at a distance for miles. Now they approached the warehouse driveway, and he hung back even more. He killed his headlights, plunging the road into darkness, and he stopped near the parking lot entrance. He lifted binoculars. Teagan strained to see but could just barely make out the men parked in front of one of the long buildings near the back of the lot. They slipped through the front door.

"See the name of the place they entered?" Drew asked.

She'd spotted it on the sign by the road. "Northwest Geo Instruments. I assume that's important."

"I ran across them on another investigation involving government corruption. They provide automated systems to monitor the safety and stability of many things. Buildings, bridges, roads, tunnels, dams. And..." He paused to look at her. "Excavations."

"Like at archeological digs," she said, catching on. "From where these antiquities could be stolen."

"Exactly." He lowered his binoculars, his eyes burning with excitement under the street light. "A match made in heaven. Export the equipment to Iraq and no one would think twice. Then maybe bring used equipment back to this country for repair and recalibrating and hide the antiquities in the crates."

"Might not even be a legit business."

"We can look into the company, but back when I ran across them, our analysts deemed them legit, and the company didn't raise any red flags."

Didn't mean they'd dug deep enough. Searched hard enough. Even had the skills to do it right. She sure didn't, anyway. "Can I make a suggestion?"

He kept his attention pointed out the windshield. "Sure."

"You ever heard of The Veritas Center?"

He nodded. A single bob of his head, sharp and crisp. "The private agency that processes crime scene evidence for law enforcement. What about them?"

He sounded skeptical but she wouldn't let that deter her. "Their computer guru, Nick Thorn, is a whiz. No one in the area like him. If we want to quickly locate information, he's our guy."

"I don't have that kind of money in the budget." He glanced at her. "Might've earlier on, but with only a few days to go, we're tapped out."

"I'm friends with some of the owners. I could see if Nick would help for a discount or no charge."

"Sounds like a plan. But first, we go in and learn what we can the old-fashioned way. With our ears." Drew pulled the vehicle forward and parked between two large shipping containers. "You ready?"

"Never more so." She quietly got out, closing the car door as silently as possible.

Drew opened the trunk and shoved a few items into his pockets. They hoofed it across the lot, darting in and out of objects under the full moon to hide their arrival. She palmed her Glock and crept behind Drew. They reached the correct building and slipped through shadows cast by the steel structure.

Their target? A black door at the rear of the building.

Drew raised a hand, and she stopped. He signaled his intent to move toward the door, and she was to stay put. She huffed out a sigh at being left behind, but nodded and was rewarded with a tight smile highlighted by the dim green bulb above.

He moved along the edge of the building, his steps fluid and smooth for such a large guy. He turned and waved her forward. She whispered along the building's siding, hugging it like a magnetic force drew her to the metal. Drew took out a handheld radar device about the size of a small walkie-talkie that he slid along the building. She'd seen SWAT teams use it in the past, but she'd never had the need for one on the job. It was designed to detect the smallest of movements with great accuracy. Even movements as minute as the rise and fall of a chest in breathing.

The screen lit up, casting a blue glow on Drew's face and displaying movement fifty feet away at the building's front entrance.

"Should be safe to enter." Drew pocketed the device. "Give me a minute to pick the lock. Hand signals only from here on out."

She nodded as if she were a pro at breaking and surveilling, but she'd never breached a building without first announcing herself as a law enforcement officer. And even then, it had only been a few times for domestic calls.

69

Despite the cool temps and brisk breeze bringing the stink of burning rubber, sweat beaded on her forehead. Thankfully, it was winter or she would be sweating through her vest as her heart thumped in her chest.

Drew gave her a long look and stowed his weapon. He was telling her to have his back. And she did. Searching the darkness for any foe. Watching through brush and tall grasses moving in the dark. Listening to the quiet hum of traffic in the distance. Praying no one tried to confront them.

He twisted the knob, and it turned under his hand. *Perfect.* They hadn't needed to break in. If they learned anything helpful inside, they could claim they thought the business was open and the information would be useable in court. A gray area for sure, but far better than breaking and entering.

She swiped the back of her hand over her forehead and noted a slight tremble in the hand holding her weapon. If only she were her cousin Bristol—a weapons guru—who had the ability to hit a target dead center most of the time. Teagan was proficient for sure, and she could protect Drew, but she sure wasn't a sharpshooter like her cousin.

Drew lifted his sidearm and gave her another pointed look before opening the door a crack. He peered in, then waved her on and signaled for her to stay close behind him.

They entered a storage room with giant racks of small boxes labeled resistivity meters, obviously one of the products the company sold. The boxes were too small to hold antiquities of any size.

Silent. Stealthy. They crept over the concrete floor until Drew flashed up a hand. She eased next to him and spotted the three Conti brothers in heavy coats standing next to two men dressed in casual attire. One man was flag pole thin with a shock of silvery hair. The other guy was beefy with

70

hair as dark as the night sky, and his hand rested on a sidearm.

"You trust this guy?" Flag Pole asked Sal.

"Dylan?" Sal asked. "Yeah. I've been stringing him along for nearly a year. He thinks I didn't know he was dealing all that time, but you know me. Careful. Besides I had him researched and followed for nearly two months. He's just a young guy who's coming up in the game and needs someone to clean money for a friend to gain his status."

Flag Pole scratched his pointy chin. "And you think we should be that someone?"

"I say we bring him in for a little. See how it goes. Maybe he can run some of the antiquities for us with his heroin imports."

"Not sure I want to go that far with him. We stick to some money wired to one of my accounts. He handles that well, we add on. I'll get the information to you."

Perfect! But when?

"Soon, I hope. I want to move forward. I suckered him for a twenty percent fee."

Aldo snorted. "Easiest money we'll ever make."

"Easy, sure," Flag Pole said. "But the risk is huge. So don't do a thing without me knowing about it. Got it?"

"Got it." Sal frowned.

Teagan knew Sal well enough to know he didn't like playing second fiddle to anyone. He must really need this guy—whoever he was.

Drew looked at Teagan and whispered, "Take pictures of these guys. Wouldn't be good if Dylan got caught with them on his phone."

Teagan got out her phone and opened the camera. She ensured that the flash was turned off, but she still held her breath. Tapped the screen. Waited for the telltale click to sound if she'd failed to correctly configure the settings.

Silence. No flash. The men didn't notice.

She let out a nervous breath but anxiety crawled up her back. They could still get caught and Flag Pole seemed like the kind of guy who would kill them. The thought fueled a pure adrenaline rush, and her whole body trembled.

Drew rested a hand on her shoulder. Nice. Supportive, but doing nothing to calm her nerves.

"And this Dylan guy," Flag Pole said, "you keep an eye on him. Even a hint of a problem, and he joins Smiley in his unmarked grave."

7

Unmarked grave.

Drew had to stow that thought to concentrate and get them safely out of there. He silently led Teagan to his vehicle and got on the road, his car pointed for the restaurant to pick up her car. They didn't speak while he navigated toward the freeway. Was Teagan too worked up to talk or did she respect that Drew still had a job to do to get them to a safe distance from the men?

She dug out her phone, her hands still trembling. Maybe fear was the answer. "I'm going to call Nick to get that information."

"Good." He gave her a quick smile but she was staring at her phone, her hand still shaking.

He concentrated on the drive, but caught snippets of her conversation with the tech expert, who sounded like he was onboard. He would not only look into the Contis, but also check out Northwest Geo Instruments and run the photos she'd just taken through facial recognition software.

He would also try to get a lead on the man these guys called Smiley. Most likely a nickname, but if they could find the ID of the skinny guy at the warehouse, they might be able to find a missing associate named Smiley.

Smiley. A dead missing associate. Not that Drew wanted anyone to be murdered, but if this Smiley fella was already dead, a murder charge would put the skinny guy behind bars even longer. At his age, probably life. A good thing—before he tried to take Drew out too.

Teagan said goodbye to Nick and swiveled to Drew. "He'll start on the research right away and get back to me the minute he has any information. No charge."

Drew shook his head. "How'd he agree to that?"

"All I had to say was our family business was on the line, and he agreed." She pressed her hands flat on her knees, maybe to stop the trembling. "Everyone at the center is great that way. My parents are longtime friends with the Byrd family—spelled B-Y-R-D—and Sierra Byrd, now Rice, is the center's trace evidence expert."

"I wish we could get her into that warehouse to lift some prints or DNA, but no way that's happening." Drew let residual energy from the warehouse surveillance out on a long breath. "Byrd. That's the last name of the guy who went to Harris on your behalf."

"That's right," she said. "Clay Byrd. He has four brothers, all former law enforcement officers. They own Nighthawk Security, a local investigative and protection agency."

"I remember hearing about them on the news. They protected a famous Olympic downhill skier, right?"

"Yes. Harper Young. She's now married to Aiden Byrd." A soft smile crossed Teagan's face, but her lips still trembled. "They fell in love while their team was protecting her."

Drew stopped at a light and peered at Teagan. "Dangerous to fall for someone under such a situation. Especially when someone's life is on the line."

"But I could see it happening when two people are

thrown together like they were pretty much twenty-four/seven."

"Can't happen on an undercover op," he said, making sure his tone was firm and didn't hold a hint of his hypocritical behavior when it came to the signals he'd been throwing out to her. "Could easily blow someone's cover. Get them killed."

"Don't worry, Drew." She grinned. "I'm planning to resist your charms if you ever show any."

"Ouch." He winced. "Don't think our date was typical. I can do much better when I'm not talking about someone involved in illegal smuggling."

Hoping to end the topic, he laughed, and the light turned green so he continued into the intersection, the wipers clearing off rain now falling at a solid clip. He'd made light of her comment, but it had actually stung. How crazy was that? He took barbs from people in his UC world all the time, but a tiny one said in jest from Teagan, and his feelings were hurt like he was some little girl.

"So what happens next?" Teagan asked.

Good. She changed the subject. He'd said a couple couldn't fall in love on an undercover op, but honestly, he could easily fall for this woman. Meant he had to be doubly, maybe even more, aware of his actions when around her. And the best answer was to limit his time with her. Starting now.

He turned onto the restaurant's street. "I drop you at your car, then you wait for me to call you for another date."

Her hands curled into fists. "Not happening."

"Has to happen." He pulled to the curb behind her small electric hybrid. "We can't risk Sal getting suspicious."

"Then what are you planning to do?"

"All depends on the information Nick Thorn provides." He shifted into park and looked at her. "I won't sit around

75

and wait on him, though. I'll do my own research and get an ICE analyst on it too."

"Then we should meet for breakfast." She clicked off her seat belt. "To review the information from Nick and set a plan."

She wasn't going to give up easily. He admired that, but his job was to bring these guys in, and now, also make sure she didn't get hurt in the process. "I told you you're out of this except for dates."

"You forget. Nick will give *me* the data, not you." She pulled on the door handle, slid out, but paused to look back at him, her expression deadly serious. "Be at my house at eight, and we'll go over Nick's report."

"Holding information hostage? Isn't that beneath you?"

"It won't hinder the investigation. At least not if you show up." She ran her gaze over him. "You should probably have guessed by now that my family is everything to me, and I'll stop at nothing to protect them."

Drew clutched the wheel, but his mother came to mind. He would do anything to protect her from harm or financial ruin. Maybe more if that was even possible. So why would he fault Teagan for wanting to do the same with her family's livelihood? Problem was, she was stubborn. Maybe too stubborn for her own good. She could get hurt. Drew didn't want that. Not at all. To that end, he would follow her home to be sure she got inside okay.

He could've hung back in the shadows but didn't make a secret of tailing her over the soggy but quiet streets. When she parked in front of a huge Victorian house with wide steps leading up to a wrap-around porch, he slid to the curb behind her and jumped out, ignoring the rain that had tapered off to a fine mist. He watched those long legs slide out of the driver's side of her vehicle and her body stretch to full height.

She shoved the straps from her purse and computer case onto her shoulder and threw her hair over it, frustration in her moves. "You didn't need to follow me home."

"I feel responsible for your safety."

"Why? I was the one who horned in on your investigation and wouldn't let it alone." She started for the sidewalk. "And I can take care of myself. I've been doing it for thirty-three years. Making sure I stay in prime physical shape in case I need to fight, and as you can see, I've survived just fine."

Oh, he could see it all right. Every little inch of how well she'd protected that fit body, but he wasn't going there.

Drew clamped his mouth closed and strode next to her up the sidewalk toward the big porch. He checked his surroundings as he walked. He would be lying if the not-so-veiled threat from the skinny guy in the warehouse didn't bother him. Undercover brought uneasiness most of the time, and he always knew his life was on the line if he was made, but having an obvious thug come right out and say they'd bury him was alarming, to say the least.

More importantly, it raised his concern for Teagan. The very reason why he'd followed her home and walked her to her door. Not that she liked it. She didn't. Arguing that she could take care of herself. But losing his dad so suddenly made him hyper-aware of protecting the people he cared about, and he was coming to care for this woman in such a short time.

They climbed the steps, and she unlocked the door and then pushed it open, the smell of freshly popped popcorn wafting out.

Did she plan to walk off without a word? Seemed like it.

His gut twisted with frustration—for her lack of interest in him *and* for her interest in him. He wanted her to feel the

77

same things he did, but he didn't want her to feel it *now*. Not when they could be in danger.

She clutched the knob and turned to look at him. "I'll see you at eight. Not a minute before or some of my sisters might still be here and we need to keep your identity quiet for now. I love to cook, so you can expect breakfast."

With that, she stepped in and closed the door in his face.

Bam. Just like that. Gone.

He had his work cut out for him. How did a man protect a woman from killers when she didn't think she needed protecting? Sure, fine, maybe she could take care of herself most of the time. But this situation was different. They were not only trying to bring down smugglers and money launderers, but if the conversation they'd overheard at the warehouse was true—murderers.

Teagan's sisters and cousins were still in the family room, gathered around a roaring fire and stringing popcorn for the tree. They'd decided on an old-fashioned Christmas theme this year, and since they worked long days, the décor had to be prepared at night. Teagan would love to stop in and help, but she was still amped up with adrenaline from the covert visit to the warehouse. She wouldn't be able to hide her shaky hands while stringing popcorn. No way. She could claim the injured finger, but her family knew that even with the cut she'd find a way to decorate.

She hung her jacket on a hook in the large foyer and rushed past the room.

"I'm hitting the hay early. Night," she called out as she rushed past the wide entrance.

Questions were fired back at her. Of course they were. Not only had she been gone most of the day, but she loved

Christmas and was willingly foregoing one of her favorite tasks. Still, she couldn't respond. Wouldn't respond.

She took the stairs to her room two at a time, like she was being chased by them as they'd done in childhood games on the farm where they'd all grown up. It wasn't hard to imagine their looks of confusion, followed by a quick discussion of the reason she ran past. Far better to let them wonder about her than to let them see her mood and start grilling her until she spilled information she was sworn to keep quiet.

She opened the door to her room and stepped in, locking it behind her. *No. No.* If they came to check on her, that would really make them wonder what was going on. She twisted the lock again and dropped her purse on the dresser. She dug for her new deputy shield to hide it under her socks. She couldn't risk anyone finding it. Not that her family would go through her purse, but it wasn't unheard of to look for someone's keys to move a car in the way.

When morning came, how could she lie to her family and get away with it? She sure wouldn't invite her dad or grandad over. They'd see right through her.

Voices sounded through the wall from Mackenzie's room. She was probably recording her podcast on faith and the Christian life for millennials. She basically talked about her life and how she overcame daily obstacles with her faith. If only Teagan could live her faith as completely as Mackenzie, but Teagan often fell short.

Sighing, she sank into the comfy armchair in the corner and ran her hands over the worn floral fabric. She'd gotten the chair from her gran, and they'd recovered it together in a color to match the soft blue on the walls of her room. Usually, Teagan felt cozy in the chair. Warm. Safe. Not tonight. Not after the encounter with Flag Pole. She hadn't let on to Drew, but she was very concerned.

"Stop dwelling on it," she muttered and opened her laptop to do a Google image search. She uploaded the best photo she'd taken of Flag Pole and waited as the search engine churned, looking for a match. Sure, Nick was doing the same thing with much more computing power, but she was too wired to sleep and had to do something constructive.

The photo returned quite a few matches. She took her time running through them. Nope. None of them were of their guy. Moving on, she entered Northwest Geo Instruments into the search engine and located their website. She checked the about page. A bust. Zero information about the owners or the person who founded or managed the company.

A soft knock sounded on the door. Company? Just what Teagan didn't want tonight. Maybe she shouldn't answer. No, she had to. Whoever was in the hall would see her light slipping under the door.

She closed her laptop and took a deep cleansing breath. "Come in."

The door opened, and Mackenzie poked her head in. "You're not stringing popcorn with the others?"

Teagan tapped her computer. "Doing some work."

Dressed in a fuzzy red pajama top and plaid flannel bottoms, Mackenzie stepped into the room and closed the door. She crossed to Teagan's bed and kicked off unicorn slippers, then folded her legs up under her. "Okay. What gives? It's not unusual for you to be working, but what *is* unusual is that you gave up a chance to do Christmas decorating and were AWOL for most of the day. You're usually glued to your desk. Where'd you disappear to today and tonight?"

"Working on a client thing." Teagan detected the near lie in her tone so Mackenzie had to have heard it too.

Mackenzie tilted her head and her hair slid over her shoulder. "Which client?"

"Does it matter?"

"Yeah, because you're never vague. You're more than willing to share details, so you're holding something back, and I want to know what it is."

"This one is private for now."

"Hmm." Mackenzie tapped the tiny cleft in her chin. "This have something to do with last night?"

Teagan couldn't trust her voice so she shrugged.

"Okay, so it does." Mackenzie eyed Teagan. "You're an awful liar. Like everyone in the family. We were taught too well to always tell the truth."

Memories of getting caught lying as a child came back, and Teagan shook her head. "Not that we didn't try it growing up. But the punishment was far too great to do it often."

"Then why are you trying to lie to me?"

Bingo. Right there. The question Teagan was trying to avoid. "I'm not. The opposite. I don't want to lie to you, but I have to keep this to myself."

"And you can't tell me where you were tonight?"

"Okay fine. I went on a date."

Mackenzie shot up. "You what? With who?"

"His name is Dylan. He works with the Conti brothers. We met this morning. I went over to the Conti's warehouse to decide what I wanted to do about last night." Nearly the truth—not the right name—and she'd officially met Drew at Clackamas County.

"And you went out with him just like that?" Mackenzie slid closer to Teagan. "There must be something extra special about this guy when no one has convinced you to date in ages."

"He's great," she said and left it at that.

"Good looking?"

Teagan conjured up Drew's face with the wide jaw covered in dark stubble. His broad chest and wide shoulders. His dark hair worn a little too long due to his UC op. Her mind went to mush, and a rush of warmth flooded her body.

"Ah, yeah. Yeah. Your look says it all." Mackenzie clapped her hands. "I can't wait to tell everyone."

"No!" Teagan shot out of her chair and grabbed Mackenzie's arm with the hand not holding her laptop. "Please. It's new. Very new. Don't say anything. I'll let them know if I think it might go somewhere."

Mackenzie mocked zipping her lips as she hopped off the bed. "Don't wait too long, or I might not be able to keep it to myself."

She strode to the door, and Teagan ran her hands through her hair. She doubted Mackenzie would ever have to tell the family. Not when the dating would be over as fast as it started, and Teagan would be right back to her normal life.

Exactly the way she liked it, right? So why did that thought make her incredibly sad tonight?

8

Drew parked behind Teagan's car and approached her large home. The sun beamed down on the brightly painted house on one of the few dry days they'd had this month. The forecasts called for rain tomorrow. Maybe even snow. Not a common event in the Portland metro area, but often occurring at least once a year.

He liked snow. Always had since he was a little kid when they would get the occasional snowfalls here and more snow when he lived in Italy while his dad was stationed at the Air Force base there, of course, Minnesota was a snowy state for sure. But they didn't need snow hampering his undercover work. Not when time was ticking down on ICE's deadline to close out the operation, and the Contis and their unknown associate were planning something big in two days. Maybe a day now.

And he didn't much like this morning's delay either. He should be working instead of meeting with Teagan and trying to stop her from insisting on participating in every aspect of the investigation.

Drew had spent hours last night searching the internet for the skinny guy from the warehouse. If he'd located anything he would've canceled this meeting with Teagan and tracked the guy down. Alone. But Drew's searches brought up a whole lot of nothing. Zip. Zilch. He needed Nick Thorn's findings, and Teagan was his go-between. Pretty smart on her behalf. Not so much on his.

He rang the doorbell and took a few breaths to clear away his irritation. Hurried footsteps clipped toward him, and the decorative wood door opened. Teagan had dressed in pale green slacks and a very tight-fitting ribbed top. She met his gaze and smiled. A soft, almost tender smile.

Poof. His irritation evaporated. Gone. A powerful emotion he couldn't put a name to flooded his body. He took an instinctual step back.

"Come in." She stood back, acting casually, as if she didn't see his reaction.

How could she miss it? Wasn't his heart thundering loud enough for her to hear?

He gulped in air and entered the home. The pungent aroma of fresh bread and savory bacon fought for his attention. Two smells that were guaranteed to make him stay no matter his other priorities or emotional distress. "Smells good."

"I made an egg breakfast casserole along with maple bacon. I make it for my dad every Father's Day so figured you'd like it too." She closed the door and headed into a wide opening to his right. "We can review the report from Nick while we eat."

He trailed after her, surprised by the more contemporary furnishings that he didn't expect with the home's traditional architecture. She stopped in a dining room holding a long table, and he counted twelve chairs. Two places were set near the wall that held a large painting.

"Have a seat, and the food will be right out." She went through a swinging door, her hips swaying.

He sat and looked around for a report that he wanted to start reading not only to get the information, but to pin his attention in the right area and not on her. He didn't spot a thing. She was keeping the details close to the vest. He didn't blame her. She wanted in on the action, and that meant not letting him see anything without her.

The door swung open, and she carried in a large wooden tray. She set it on the table and placed a plate with the egg casserole, bacon, and perfectly browned toast on the placemat in front of him, which already held silverware. She added a glass of orange juice and a bowl of fresh fruit.

He gave her a look of approval. "This looks amazing."

"Hope you like it." She set the same items on the other placemat. "I'll get the coffee, and we can get started on Nick's report."

He tracked her as she disappeared through the door again. She really was something. Made a meal like this and once faced down and apprehended bad guys, but now ran a large company. And of course, she was very pretty. Not the most important thing, but it sure didn't hurt.

She came back with the coffee pot in one hand and a folder tucked under her arm. She poured him a steaming cup, the earthy scent perking him up after little sleep last night. "I grind my own beans so I hope you like the blend."

"This smells and looks wonderful." He waited for her to sit. "Mind if we pray quickly so I can dig in?"

"Go ahead." She placed the folder on the table and offered her hand as she bowed her head.

He held on tightly and offered a sincere prayer for the meal then released her hand and looked up. "You don't know how nice it is to find another person of faith in law enforcement, even if formerly in law enforcement."

"Actually, I do. I guess I'd forgotten, though." She forked a piece of pineapple and held the fork over the bowl. "You said your faith was suffering since going undercover. You think that will fix itself when the op ends?"

Did he? "I honestly don't know. One thing about going under is you see some really ugly things. You see enough of it and you start wondering why God allows them. It always takes me back to when I lost my dad. He died of a brain aneurism right in front of me." Drew worked hard not to let the memories flood back and fall apart in front of Teagan. "I was helpless to do anything but call for help and kneel beside him as he died. It's the same thing while under. Doesn't impact me as much as losing my dad, but it still brings up the why question."

"I could see that." Teagan tilted her head, her hair softly falling over her shoulder as she studied his face. "I'm sorry you had to lose your dad at such a young age. And in that way. My cousin was murdered going on two years ago. That was so hard." She let out a long shaky breath. "Is still hard. But nothing like you must've suffered."

He took a moment to let go of his residual feelings from his father's death and compose his thoughts. "You can't measure loss that way. It's all hard and painful. And you also had to deal with the aftereffects of a violent crime. Doubly hard."

"What I remember so vividly at the time was just what you said. Asking why. Almost demanding answers. We all did." Her eyes glistened with unshed tears, but she took a breath and slowly let it out. "On the job, we've also seen the same things you mentioned. Criminals who hurt people and swindle others. It's hard to take when these creeps continue to live and some of them even flourish. And there was my cousin Thomas. An upstanding, Christian guy, running our company and doing a super job until he was murdered. Makes no sense. At least not to us."

"Yeah." Drew set down his fork, his appetite waning. "I'm

still wrestling with that after all these years. I don't know if my faith will recover. I want it to, but if I'm honest, I just don't know." He picked up his coffee cup and pointed at her folder before he took them even further off course and spilled his entire past to her. "Let's move on. Look into some of those bad guys and maybe try to even the score by putting them behind bars."

She set down her cup and went to the big picture on the nearby wall. She slid it back to reveal a whiteboard with information written in neat letters in blue and red ink.

He shook his head. "Wow. The Steeles don't mess around. A situation room right in your house."

"I told you we're a law enforcement family. Maybe to the extreme." She grinned, this one cute and playful, and her eyes sparkled. "But really, this is used for the business most of the time. We don't run into other obstacles all that often."

"I hear a but in your tone."

"But lately, my cousins had some tough things they needed help with. So we used the board for that too." A pensive look on her face, she returned to her seat. "I wish they could be here now. Helping. I know they would if we could let them."

"I'm sorry."

"Hey." She lifted a hand. "I get it. Your life could depend on me keeping my big mouth shut." She grinned again.

He caught her mood, and his appetite returned. "Tell me what we're looking at."

He stabbed his fork into the casserole and savored the bacon, egg, pepper, and onion mixture.

"So Flag Pole guy." She wrinkled her nose. "The name I gave to the skinny guy with white hair is Chauncey Rossi."

"I like Flag Pole guy better." Drew chuckled.

"Me too." She laughed as she handed a packet of papers to him. "Here's his background report, but I put the highlights on the board. He started Northwest Geo Instruments in 1982. He has a strong reputation and has expanded to ship equipment worldwide for the past twenty years. No hint of criminal activity. He's a father of two boys. Avid soccer fan. So avid, he even travels abroad to soccer matches, and he's been known to bet heavily on the teams, his favorite being Italy, of course."

"How about a connection to a guy named Smiley?"

"That's the good news. Nick located an associate from a single picture posted online with the name Smiley in the description. His real name is Lenny Spence. He's on page three of the report."

Drew flipped the papers and took in the man's built physique and a grimace on his wide face. "I'd bet he was once Rossi's muscle."

"Me too. He was listed as a company employee—no job description—starting at the time the business went international until 2016."

"Then what happened?"

She took a long sip of her orange juice. "Nothing. No missing person report. No interest from the police. He just seems to have disappeared."

Had to be their guy. "Looks like Rossi really killed him. Or had one of his flunkies kill him. Exactly like he hinted at last night. We need to figure out where he's buried. Try to prove murder and link it to Rossi. All in less than two days."

She set her glass down. "But how will that help with your undercover op?"

"It might not, but putting him away for murder should end the smuggling pipeline too." Drew flipped through the pages. "He's the sole owner of the company?"

"Yes, but he has two sons who could carry on the legal aspects of the business, and I assume the illegal ones if needed."

Their lone subject had turned into a party of three. "We have to not only nail him but shut down the business."

"And still, if the sons are involved, they could start up elsewhere."

Drew set down his fork, planted his hands on the table, and lifted his gaze to Teagan's. "Then if they're involved, we'll have to nail them too."

~

Drew honestly hated leaving Teagan behind. He half expected her to follow him, but he kept checking his rearview mirror and didn't see her car. Or any suspicious vehicles at all. He took a circuitous route to be sure no one was tailing him. That was as much of a part of his daily routine this past year as breathing was. It had to be if he wanted to keep breathing.

He pulled into the World of Crafts lot and sat for a moment to get his game face on. Changing to Dylan's personality wasn't usually hard, but today he struggled. He wanted to remain Drew, and he suspected Teagan played a big part in that. Too bad. He couldn't be Drew again until he wrapped up this investigation.

He took a fortifying breath and strode up to the door. The moment he pushed it open, he smiled at Betty, the longtime company receptionist. "Jingle Bells" played over the speakers and the space smelled like cinnamon from the basket of pinecones on the counter.

"Hey, good-looking," he offered his normal greeting.

She grinned, revealing a missing incisor. "Wondered if you'd be coming by today."

"Are you kidding?" He leaned on the counter. "Couldn't miss seeing my best girl."

89

She laughed and waved a hand. "Vito tells me you went to the ballgame with Teagan Steele."

Vito was a bigmouth, as were the other brothers to some extent. Not when it came to their illegal doings. For that, they were as tightlipped as a child refusing to take his medicine.

"Tell you a secret." Drew leaned closer to Betty. "We never made it to the game. I took her to dinner first, and we sat and talked until it was too late to go."

Betty watched him carefully as his mother might in this situation. "You like her, then?"

"I do." He glanced at the female guard who was trying hard to pretend not to listen. "How about you? What do you think of her?"

Betty's lips puckered. "She's polite enough but always focused on business. Vito says she works all the time. Not sure when she'll find the time to go out with you on a regular basis."

"Look at all of this, Betty!" He ran his hands over his body like Dylan would do. "What woman could resist?"

The guard snorted, but Betty laughed. Dylan was a larger-than-life personality so this behavior fell well within the parameters he set, but he could easily imagine he was turning the guard's stomach, and she might warn her boss to steer clear of him.

"The brothers in?" he asked.

"In the office last time I saw them. Go on back. I know they'll be glad to see you."

Dylan blew her a kiss and stepped past the guard. He caught a roll of her eyes. The woman looked like her radar for slimy guys was beeping. He should be offended, but her reaction only meant he was doing his job and doing it well.

He headed to the office in the back. The door was open, and Sal was talking. Drew came to a stop.

"You have it?" Sal asked. "You're not lying to me, are you? You have it? The real deal?"

If his words didn't convince Drew to stop and eavesdrop, Sal's tone would.

"I need to see it. Now!" Sal's tone had risen even higher, breaking like a middle school boy in puberty. "Fine. Let me know when the shipment arrives."

Quiet reigned for only a moment.

"Aldo," Sal called out. "I need you to prepare for a three-million-dollar purchase."

"Three million?" Aldo's voice squeaked. "We don't have that kind of liquid cash."

"Then we accelerate the money we get from Dylan. Use his cash until we can free ours up."

"He won't like that," Vito said, a warning in his voice.

"What he doesn't know won't hurt him." Sal's tone had turned deadly serious, putting a hitch in Drew's confidence.

"What about Rossi?" Vito challenged. "He said washing Dylan's money was a trial, and three mil is way beyond a trial."

"Let me worry about Rossi." Sal's confidence might be completely misplaced. At least that's what Drew thought when it came to the man he'd seen last night. He didn't seem to take kindly to not being listened to.

That could blow up in Drew's face. And what about the three mil? ICE would never cough up that kind of cash to give these guys to wash.

Drew needed a game plan.

He turned to leave.

No, stop. Betty knows you came back here.

She would say something to the brothers. They'd wonder where he went. Would start them questioning him. He had no choice. He had to go in and play things by ear.

Worse yet, he couldn't be caught eavesdropping. That could be the end right there.

He silently backed up, then stomped toward the door and pretended to be on a phone call to warn the brothers he was coming. Near the door, he said a fake goodbye into his phone and shoved it into his pocket before entering the office.

The place was set up with a desk for each brother, Sal's being the largest and nearest the door. His desk was neat and tidy as was Aldo's, but Vito's held piles of papers, and Sal was constantly on his brother's case to clean up. Drew figured that after he arrested the brothers, Vito would be the one to crack and flip on the others, and Drew planned to exploit the guy's weakness.

"Yo, Conti bros!" Drew called out, while he tried to figure out how to get the cash the men needed and might expect. "What's up?"

Sal's expression held a healthy measure of relief, but he quickly controlled it and faked boredom. "Wondered if you would show your ugly mug today."

Ah, so he wanted to play it cool. Drew could do the same thing. "Why would I come by to see your sorry face?"

Sal chuckled. "Pull up a seat."

Drew dropped into a large leather chair by Sal's desk and nodded at Aldo and Vito, who sat behind their own desks.

"How was the game last night?" Sal asked.

Drew forced a cat-that-ate-the-canary grin. "Dinner went long, and we didn't make it to the game."

"You got along, huh?" Sal tilted his head. "Wouldn't have predicted that."

Drew looked Sal in the eyes. "Never know what might happen."

"I suppose you're gonna see her again."

"Actually, just had breakfast with her. Not only is she a looker but she can cook." He patted his stomach. "Might have to change up my workout routine if I keep seeing her."

"I don't know why you waste time working out." Sal leaned back and stretched his arms overhead. "Find a woman who can put up with you, and you can forget all that junk and spend more time making money."

"You could be right. As I told you, I'm all about making the bucks." Drew leaned back too, mirroring Sal's relaxed vibe, to wait for the man to make his request.

Sal snapped his chair forward and pressed hands covered with dark age spots on the table. "I talked to my associate last night. We're in. We want to start off big."

"How big?"

"A mil a week."

Drew sat up. "Not happening, man. Monty doesn't know you from Adam. He won't trust you with that much cash. Not at first. I say we do twenty grand. Work up from there."

Sal swung his head side-to-side, his jowls shaking. "Doesn't work for me."

"Why not? It's not like you're hurting for cash, right? I mean you'll make a cool five grand for doing a couple of wire transfers. Can't ask for a better result than that."

Sal frowned. "I hate to disappoint my associate."

Vito snorted.

Sal fired a testy look at his youngest brother. "Don't you have something better to do besides sit here and backseat quarterback me?"

Vito shook his head. "Not when you're a riot to watch. You really should be on TikTok. You'd rake in the followers."

Sal glared until his brother wilted, then Sal turned back to Drew. "We'll start your way, but only if we have a rapid escalation of numbers."

"I'll talk to Monty. See if he wants to speed things up. But remember we have to stay under the Fed's ten grand radar so the deposits will be small."

"No skin off my nose. We can do the work."

"You mean I have to do it," Aldo said. "Half the time you don't even know where our money's located."

"Your skills don't need supervision, unlike someone else." Sal gave Vito a pointed look. "As long as the dough's there when I need it—that's all I need to know. And don't let Vito get his hands on it."

Yeah, Vito would be the one to press for information and flip on the others once Drew had these guys in handcuffs.

The minute Sal accepted cash that he believed came from Monty's drug-trafficking business was the minute he would be legally cooked.

9

Teagan opened the door to Posh Nails, a salon frequented by wealthy clients. Drew had left her behind, telling her that dinner was her next job in the op. So what? That didn't mean she couldn't follow up on some of the information that Nick had discovered. She would never purposefully step on Drew's toes and interfere in his undercover assignment. His life was far too important to do that. But she could begin unearthing details that might be helpful.

Starting with Chauncey Rossi's wife. She was a frequent flyer at this salon, and Teagan used a bit of subterfuge to find out that the woman had an appointment at two o'clock. Teagan quickly booked her own appointment at the same time. Mani-pedi sessions were known to cause loose lips and provide lots of gossip.

Not that Teagan had participated in a session in a long time. She could already see the stink eye she would get when the technician took a look at Teagan's hands. Cooking often dried them out because she washed so frequently.

She stepped into the swanky place and acrylic nail glue and polish odor hit her hard. She searched the expensive leather chairs and immediately recognized Lauralee Rossi from her social media pictures. The older woman had bleached blond hair worn long and straight and batted thick false lashes with caked-on black mascara. Her makeup seeped into the wrinkles on her face, making her appear older. She wore designer casual clothes in bright pink and black that seemed more fitting for a teenager than a woman over sixty.

Keeping eyes and ears open, Teagan registered and crossed the room to select a polish color at the array of colorful bottles in plastic racks on the wall. Lauralee chatted about clothing and moved on to discussing her high cork platform flip-flops. Nick's dossier put the woman at sixty-two, and Teagan wondered how safe such shoes were for Lauralee to be wearing.

Teagan settled on a pale pink color that would go with everything and cupped the bottle, thankful that her hand wasn't trembling during her little subterfuge.

"Teagan." A cute Asian technician stood and waved a delicate hand.

"Here." Teagan rushed down the aisle to the smiling girl, glad to see she'd scored the station right next to Chauncey's wife.

Lauralee looked up. Teagan smiled and nodded as she took a seat in a soft leather chair. The older woman responded with a broad smile. She seemed a pleasant enough woman and very chatty. Could mean Teagan would gain valuable information.

"I'm Angie," the technician said as she plunged both of Teagan's hands into a small water bowl to soak. "Did you select a polish color?"

Teagan stifled a gasp at the pain in her injured finger, but wouldn't draw attention to it and looked at Lauralee. "Honestly, I really like your color. Would you mind if I copied you?"

"Of course not." The other woman flashed another smile, her even white teeth perfectly spaced. "When a young beauty like you wants to look like me, I have to be flattered."

"You're too kind." Heat rose up Teagan's neck and flushed into her face.

The technicians exchanged the nail polish information.

"Be right back." Angie went to get another bottle of the color called Bubble Bath.

Teagan looked at Lauralee. "Are you getting a manicure for a special occasion?"

"Special? Hmm." Lauralee's perfectly plucked eyebrows drew together. "Could be, I suppose. It's my birthday, and I'm getting something I've dreamed of my entire life."

"Happy Birthday," Teagan said with enthusiasm. "Sounds exciting."

"It is." Lauralee leaned closer as if she had a secret. "My husband owns his own business, and my oldest son, Oliver, is taking over. Ollie has a big, I mean huge, deal going down this month, and we will finally have enough money for me to buy the villa in Italy that I've been dreaming of since I was a little girl."

"Oh, how wonderful." Teagan didn't have to pretend as it *would* be wonderful to be able to afford such a thing, but who dreamed of a villa when they were a kid? Kind of odd. "What kind of business is he in?"

"International geological equipment sales." She waved her hand with its freshly polished nails, the sparkly lacquer flashing in the overhead light. "Don't ask me to tell you more than that. I have no idea of the business details. I stay as far away from them as I can, only getting involved if they need me to sign something. And then I put my name where they ask."

"So you must own part of the company," Teagan said.

"Some legal thing about shares or something like that." Her gaze intensified. "Sounds like you're interested in business."

"Not really." Teagan turned away to hide her lie and held out her hand to Angie, who'd returned with the bottle.

Angie tsked. "Been a while since your last manicure, I see."

"Yeah. You know how it goes these days. Always busy."

Lauralee's eyes ringed with heavy liner widened. "First and foremost, you have to take care of yourself. You don't want your man looking in other directions."

She really didn't know what to say in response to that, so she didn't speak and watched as Angie dried one of Teagan's hands.

"Are you married or involved?" Lauralee asked.

"No." Teagan winced. Not at the question, but at Angie's forceful nipping at Teagan's cuticles.

"That's a shame." Lauralee put her hand in the nail dryer. "I always made it a practice not to be without a man, and it's served me well for over forty years. Never had to work a day in my life."

"Do you have only one son?" Teagan asked, changing the subject before she said something that might make Lauralee mad.

"We have two boys, but the youngest has gone off to California trying to find himself." She shook her head, but her hair remained stiff and in place. "Why a man in his thirties has to find himself, I'll never know, but he's always been a bit flighty. Not solid and dependable like Oliver. Maybe he takes after me." She laughed, a light tinkling sounding more like a young girl than an older woman.

"Sounds like Oliver is invaluable to the company."

"He is." She stared off into the distance. "I mean, this

latest deal that will help me realize my dreams is beyond amazing. It's almost too good to be true."

"I guess he sold a lot of geological equipment." Teagan got more obvious with her fishing expedition and held her breath that it didn't put Lauralee off.

"As I said, I try to tune out my hubby and Oliver when they talk business. But I've heard enough to realize that Oliver bought something that he'll resell for a huge profit. Like millions of dollars of profit."

"Oh, wow. Must be something special."

She shrugged and giggled. "Since I don't really listen, I don't really know. Just show me the money."

Teagan didn't want to press this line of questioning anymore as she would seem too obvious. "When will you begin looking for this villa or have you already picked one out?"

"Chauncey—that's my husband—says I have to wait until the money's in the bank."

"That must be hard." Teagan tried to sound sympathetic but struggled. She was trying to keep the family business afloat and pay basic wages to her family members, let alone buy an Italian villa.

"Not really. He said the deal will be concluded in the next few days. I've waited my whole life for this villa. What's a few more days?" She leaned closer again. "Between you and me, I already picked a place out and inquired with the real estate agent listing the property. I'm waiting to hear back."

So the deal, whatever it was, was going down soon. Maybe the deal she'd overheard them mention. Teagan needed more information. "How much time will you spend at your villa?"

"Just for vacations at first, and we'll rent it out when we're not there. But Chauncey said this big score will set us

99

up for retirement, and he'll retire soon. We'll have so very much more time then." She frowned.

"Why the frown? Don't you want him to retire?"

"Honestly? I doubt he'll ever fully retire. He's always after the next big score. Once this one is done, I can see him searching for something to top Ollie's deal."

No. No he won't. We'll be arresting him soon enough.

Of course Teagan didn't say that. She nodded and couldn't wait to tell Drew what she'd learned.

"But maybe I'm wrong." Lauralee took her other hand out of the soaking gel. "Oliver really wants his independence from his father."

"Is that what you want?"

"Yes, not only so Chauncey retires, but so Oliver can spread his wings. And I want him to find a nice young woman to settle down with." Her eyes flashed open. "Say, you seem like a nice young lady, and you're not with someone. Maybe I could arrange for the two of you to meet."

Teagan didn't answer right away. Should she play this out? Try to meet Oliver? What would Drew say? He would probably tell her to back off.

"I can see you're hesitant. This isn't a typical mom fix-up for an unfortunate-looking son. My Ollie is very attractive, and the only reason he's not married yet is because he devotes all of his time to the business." Lauralee jerked her hand free, picked up her phone from the table, and tapped it to reveal a picture of a man with sleeked-back dark hair, a toned body, and Lauralee's gorgeous smile.

"He *is* quite good looking," Teagan said, though he did nothing for her. Not like Drew.

"So give me your number. It's only one date. Or maybe a cup of coffee." Lauralee held out her phone. "Go ahead. Put your number in. What do you have to lose?"

Only my life.

Drew's blood boiled as he pushed past a shocked Teagan and into her house.

"What are you doing here?" she whispered, her tone frantic.

"We need to talk. In private." He made sure his tone removed any question she might have that he would talk to her right now, no matter what she wanted.

"Follow me." She marched down the hall in a saucy walk that captured his imagination and tried to interrupt his anger from their earlier phone call.

She'd been so excited to tell him she had a lunch date with Oliver Rossi tomorrow. Not Drew. He'd seen red. Bright bull-fighting, blistering red that lingered, and he rushed right over here.

He kept up with her quick strides, vaguely aware of people sitting in the family room and the smell of onions and beef roasting. His mouth had the good sense to water at the tempting aroma, but he ignored how his stomach rumbled in response.

She turned. "Go ahead and have a seat."

Bookshelves loaded with law enforcement books covered two walls, and they'd located two comfy-looking leather club chairs that held the marks of being well-used nearby.

He took a seat in one of them and took a hearty breath to come across calmer. "Why on earth would you try to make contact with anyone in the Rossi family?"

She closed the door. "I was trying to help."

"One of the first rules of law enforcement, as I know you know, is always make sure someone knows where you are. You could've been putting yourself in danger."

"Um, Drew." A smile flickered on her face as she sat next

to him. "I was in a nail salon. What could Lauralee do to me there? Slit my throat with a nail file?"

"Don't make light of this." He fisted his hands but held his tongue, but it was hard. She'd gone rogue, scheduled a date with Oliver Rossi, and Drew didn't like it. Not only from his UC point of view, but as a man who was seriously interested in her. He didn't want another man to sit across the table and flirt with her. He didn't want another man even considering flirting with her.

She crossed her long legs. She'd changed into black leggings and an oversized T-shirt that hid all of her curves, and she still looked amazing. What would she wear tomorrow to the lunch date? A lunch date with another man. He could barely keep from demanding to know.

She let her foot encased in camo slippers swing. "I won't go if you don't want me to, but I might be able to get Oliver to brag about himself and find out what they've bought. It could be the thing Sal Conti needs three mil for."

Her point was valid. If Drew shared this information with his supervisor, Harris would be all over encouraging Teagan to attend this lunch date. He should be too. He was letting his personal feelings get in the way when he had limited time to put his op to bed.

He had to control his emotions. He had no claim on her. Would never have a claim on her. Despite his feelings. He would fight them. He could never get involved only to walk away and hurt her.

But at all costs—he had to be sure she was safe. "If I let you go, you'll have to be careful. Not only because we don't know what kind of guy Oliver Rossi is, but because you can't be seen by the Contis or that could blow up my op. "

She eyed him. "First off, you won't *let* me go. It's my decision. And second, lots of women date two men at a time."

"Sure, but no way the Contis would think it was a coincidence that you're dating me and the son of their supplier too."

Her gaze softened. "I suppose you're right."

"Did you give Mrs. Rossi your real name?"

She shook her head. "I told her I was Meg Jacobs."

A small victory. "And how did that name come to you?"

"It's the main character's name in a book I'm reading. And I didn't give her my phone number either. Made up a story about my phone being stolen and was getting a new one after the manicure. So I got her and Oliver's numbers and said I would text him when I had the new phone. Figured that would give me a chance to get a prepaid phone issued."

"And she bought the story?"

"Hook, line, and sinker, as my grandad would say." Teagan grinned. "All I need is the new phone."

"If we do this, you could take on the character's other background and job if it works. Would be easier to remember that way."

"It works. I'd be a sous chef between jobs. I quit in a fit over differences with the head chef and recently moved back to Portland after being away."

A knock sounded on the door. Teagan cast a wary eye at it. "Yeah."

The door opened and a stylish woman with long silvery hair and a round face entered. Drew put the woman in her mid to late fifties. She carried a tray holding two steaming mugs and eyed Teagan. "Thought you might be too busy to offer your guest a refreshment, so I made some hot cocoa for this cold day."

Teagan seemed to deflate.

Interesting.

"I'm Teagan's mother." The woman shifted the tray to

one hand and held out the other, her fingernail polish powder blue. "Ruby Steele."

Drew started to rise to shake hands.

Ruby waved him off, then clutched his hand firmly. "No need to stand on my account."

"Dr—Dylan Crane." At her forceful stare, he almost forgot he was UC and blurted out his real name. This was a woman to be reckoned with, and she'd produced an equally strong daughter.

"Are you a friend or business acquaintance of Teagan's?" Ruby asked.

"Umm—"

"We went on a date last night," Teagan said, her tone flat.

Ruby shot a surprised look at her daughter, who shook her head. "It was only one date, Mom. No need to make a big deal of it or go running in to tell everyone."

She swung her focus back to Dylan. "I get all the girls together during the week for dinner or they don't take care of themselves. They skip meals and never take any downtime." She shifted her attention to her daughter. "Dinner will be on the table in ten minutes. Have you invited Dylan?"

Teagan's face paled. "No."

Ruby turned to Drew. "Then, Dylan, I insist that you stay, and I won't take no for an answer. I made a nice beef stew for this cold night. My mother-in-law contributed several loaves of her famous crusty bread and a rich chocolate chip cheesecake."

His stomach grumbled, and he gave Teagan a sheepish look. "It's been a while since I've had a real home-cooked dinner."

"It's settled." Ruby clapped her hands, an elated look on her face, and faced Teagan. "Finish up here, and I'll see you both at the table in ten minutes." She marched out and closed the door.

Teagan let out a long breath. "As you can see, my mom likes to take charge."

"You're like that too, you know. In fact, I recently had that same thought. You stand your ground."

"Yeah, I've been told that. Funny how it drives me crazy in her, but I act the same way." She looked like she wanted to sigh but held it in. "You can ignore her, though, and take off if you want to." She reached for her mug, her pink nails glittering in the light.

Was she trying to get rid of him? If so, he didn't like it. Maybe he should leave, but the smell coming from the kitchen was enticing. And he would like to have a meal with good people for once.

That was decided. He would stay. "I'm glad for the meal, but we'll need to get a few things straight about our dating life and who I am before I sit at a table with your family."

"I already told Mackenzie that you work with the Conti brothers, and we met yesterday morning when I went over to World of Crafts to decide what I wanted to do about what happened in the warehouse." She sipped the cocoa, leaving a hint of it on her upper lip.

He had to work hard to ignore it. "Does she know I'm the one who restrained you that night?"

"No. No one knows that. My cousins and parents don't know about the incident at all, and I would like to leave it that way."

"Me too. I could see your mother kicking my behind out the door." He chuckled.

Teagan laughed with him. He loved how she'd relaxed, and he could easily imagine really dating her and being here with her. Chilling out. Maybe reading a book. Just enjoying the quiet together.

She looked at her watch. "Almost time to eat so we need to hammer out my lunch date for tomorrow."

Right. She had to bring *that* back up. "If we do this, and I'm not saying I approve yet, you'll be wired, and I'll be watching."

She frowned. "I'm good with that as long as you're sure he doesn't see you."

He sat forward. "Give me some credit for being undercover for nearly a year and not being made."

"Sorry. You're right. I just want this to work." She set the mug down. "I hate that the Contis have been playing us. Using our company to provide security for stolen goods is not okay with me and wouldn't be okay with my family if they knew."

He couldn't fault her for wanting to protect her family. He would do the same for his mother. "Fine. You meet Oliver tomorrow. We'll need a code word to tell me you're in trouble and to come in."

She tapped her chin. "I've got the perfect word. Sweat."

"Sweat? Odd choice."

"In cooking, it means to gently heat vegetables in a little oil. You stir and turn them frequently to ensure liquid evaporates." She paused and took a breath. "And in real life, if I have to use the codeword, sweating is what I'll be doing. Profusely. So it won't be easy to forget the word even if I *am* stressed to the max."

10

Teagan's family sat around the table studying Drew like he was some criminal they were planning to arrest. Teagan wasn't surprised. Not at all. So she jumped in to introduce everyone, starting with her cousins. Londyn, Peyton, and Bristol sat together on the far side of the table. They'd taken chairs in the oldest to youngest order as they'd done since childhood.

Both Bristol and Londyn had chocolatey brown hair, but Peyton took after their gran with flaming red hair. On the other side of the table, Teagan's sister, Ryleigh had skipped two chairs where Teagan and Mackenzie would normally sit, but Mackenzie was missing—an absence she would have to answer to their mom for.

Their mom stood on one end of the long table, dishing out the hearty beef stew filling the air with the savory scent of garlic fighting to win over the tantalizing aroma of the freshly baked bread. Her mother had arrived hours earlier today to let the dough mixed by Teagan's gran rise for the final time and bake. Her mom had tried baking bread from scratch. Many times. Each time she'd said she couldn't make the same quality of dough as Gran made.

Teagan's dad got up from his seat at the other end of the table and held out his hand to Drew. "Hugh Steele. Father and uncle to this fine group of young ladies."

Teagan's mom was the force that kept the family moving forward. Her dad was the strong one in the business, but a real softie when it came to the girls. Teagan always marveled at how he could be two different men. But then, all of them put on a tough exterior when they worked in law enforcement. That had carried over to Steele Guardians too.

Drew clasped her dad's hand and looked him in the eye. "Dylan Crane."

"Ruby says you and Teagan went on a date last night." Her dad carefully watched Dylan as if he were a suspect under detention.

"Yes, sir. We went to dinner." Drew extracted his hand. "We were supposed to go to the game, but we got to talking and lost track of time."

Her dad pulled out the chair nearest to his. "Go ahead and sit here. We can get to know each other during dinner."

"I'd rather he sit next to me." Teagan clutched Drew's forearm and led him away. "Since Mac isn't here, he can take her seat."

Her father flashed an irritated look but nodded. "Guess I can ask questions with him sitting down the way too. Did it often enough when you girls were up to no good."

"I'm not up to no good, sir." Drew met her father's gaze head on. "Just dating your daughter."

Drew pulled out Teagan's chair for her, earning huge brownie points with her and likely with her parents too, as they respected good manners.

A grumpy harrumph escaped from her dad's mouth as he sat to pass a large salad bowl to Drew. "Dig into the healthy things Ruby insists we eat while she dishes out the good stuff."

Drew laughed, and it sounded sincere. He mounded a huge helping of salad in the chilled bowl and took several pieces of the crusty bread when her dad passed that too. Drew sure wasn't shy in serving himself, and Teagan liked that about him. He seemed as if he fit right in and wasn't at all intimidated by her dad's evil eye, which he kept casting at Drew. No guy she'd ever brought home had escaped the third-degree, so she didn't consider it a negative.

Or maybe Drew was the kind of guy who didn't care what a woman's father thought of him. She'd caught the vibe that after a year undercover he had a bit of the bad boy in him—lived on the edge, was street smart and potentially volatile. And she liked that about him too.

Her mother set a bowl of stew in front of Drew and one in front of Teagan's dad. "Eat Hugh, it'll make you less grumpy, and you'll give Dylan a chance."

Her dad grabbed her hand and lifted it to his mouth to kiss the back. "What would I do without such a fine woman at my side?"

Her mother rolled her eyes and laughed. "No need to flatter me when I call you out."

Her dad smiled then cast a pointed look at Drew. "We'll pray as soon as my lovely wife finishes dishing out the stew."

The salad came back to her dad, and he took a modest helping, but added several pieces of the bread and started slathering it with butter. He was a meat and potatoes kind of guy, and despite her mother's coaxing, he didn't willingly eat healthy foods.

"Let's pray." He reached out for Bristol's hand, but couldn't reach Drew.

She clasped Drew's hand. Warm and no perspiration at all. Of course not. He'd lived undercover for a year. When your life had been on the line twenty-four/seven for a year, a surly father wouldn't be a challenge at all.

She listened to her father's genuine prayer, thanking God for their many blessings, and the group joined in on the Amen.

Teagan glanced around the table. Around the room. She didn't often take enough time to appreciate the richness of their lives. Troubles often assailed them, but they had everything. Basic needs of food on the table. A roof over their heads. A beautiful family, even if they did lose her cousin Thomas in a violent stabbing. They also had their wants of nice clothing, cars, and hobbies they could afford.

It took concerted effort to provide this lifestyle for everyone by keeping the company running, but seeing her family thrive because of her work blessed her beyond anything else. What would it feel like to provide for her own children? To bring them into this loving family?

She could only imagine and was starting to want to see it happen.

Drew dug into the stew and savored the bite. "Good. So good. Thank you for inviting me."

"You're welcome." Her mother smiled, looking quite happy to have Drew at the table. She'd been hinting since Teagan's recent birthday, that she might slow down and start dating. A potential husband at the table? Score for her mom.

"So, Dylan," her mother said. "Tell us about yourself."

Drew finished chewing slowly and swallowed, as if buying time to decide what to say.

"Don't put him on the spot, Mom," Teagan said. "Let him enjoy his meal and let everyone else update us on what's going on in their lives." She looked at her older cousin. "Like you, Londyn. How are the wedding plans coming along?"

Londyn shared a knowing look with Teagan and shook her head. "Maybe you should ask Mom about that. She's busy coming up with so many ideas my head is spinning."

"That's what mothers are for," Teagan's mom said. "Let her have this time."

"I'm doing my best, but some things like releasing doves at the ceremony are way beyond my wish list."

Peyton snorted. "She really wants doves?"

"I'm not sure if she really wants them, but she did suggest it. Gran helped me veto it. She told Mom if God wanted doves at a wedding it would be in the Bible." Londyn laughed. "So now I mention that for things like ice sculptures too, and Mom backs down."

Bristol shook her head. "I'm glad you're paving the way for Peyton and me so we don't have as many things to veto. Jared says he wants a simple wedding, so we'll have to work extra hard to keep it that way."

"If I promise not to be a pushy mother-of-the-bride." Teagan's mom shared a desperate glance between Ryleigh and Teagan. "Would that help one of you get engaged?"

Teagan looked at her sister, and they both groaned.

"Um, Aunt Ruby," Londyn said. "If you wanted to scare Dylan off, that might've been the right thing to say."

"I don't have a problem with that." Teagan's dad set down his bread. "I'm not ready for my girls to get hitched. I'm simply not old enough to be father-of-the-bride."

That brought a laugh from everyone and a discussion with many voices fighting to be heard over the other.

Drew looked at Teagan and leaned closer to whisper, "I like your family, but seems like it'll be hard for them, especially your mother, when they find out who I am and that we're not dating."

Teagan started to reply when the front door opened. Mackenzie rushed into the room in jeans and sneakers with rain dripping from her already soaked jacket. She tore it off as she came charging in, sending water flying in all directions.

"Sorry I'm late. Teagan, I—" Mackenzie searched the room, and her gaze landed on Drew. "Oh, you. You're the guy Teagan told me about, right?"

"Right," Teagan said.

"Then you'll *both* be interested in what I have to say." She jerked a thumb over her shoulder. "In private."

"If it's about the business, you can say it right here." Her dad clamped his hands on the edge of the table.

"Sorry, Dad." Mackenzie kissed their dad on the head. "Not this time."

She spun and marched across the hall.

Drew stood and pulled out Teagan's chair for her. She liked his manners, but there were times she wanted to shove her chair back and rush out of the room. This was one of them.

They hurried across the hall to Mackenzie, who was pacing the floor in front of the large fireplace.

When they entered the room, she stopped and met their gazes. "You won't believe what I just learned."

Drew stood back as Mackenzie closed the heavy wood pocket doors to the room, the brackets grating along the old metal tracks piercing the quiet. The space closed in around Drew as he studied Mackenzie and tried to place which parent she resembled. She didn't look like her sisters or her cousins. Her hair looked to be a natural blond, which probably came from their mom.

Teagan joined him, and he held his breath, waiting for Mackenzie's explanation of the item so urgent that she pulled them away from their family and into this secluded space. Looked like Teagan was doing the same thing.

Mackenzie turned from the door. "Nick Thorn stopped

by the office. He said he was trying to call you, but you weren't answering, and he knew you would want this info right away."

"You know phones are forbidden at the dinner table, so I left it in here on silent." Teagan grabbed her phone from the coffee table. "Yeah, he texted me to call him right away."

Drew's interest shifted into overdrive. "What did he say?"

"First of all, he figured I knew what was going on and who a guy named Smiley was and that he'd been murdered." Mackenzie eyed her sister. "Murdered? Really? Who is he?"

Drew kept his focus pinned on Mackenzie. "Teagan said that you and Ryleigh know about the Conti's illegal smuggling. Smiley's related to that."

Makenzie's right eyebrow rose in a perfect arch. "And your role in all of this is what?"

Teagan crossed her arms. "Let's say he's helping me investigate the Contis and leave it at that."

Mackenzie lowered her eyebrow and stared at Drew. "I don't know about all of this cloak and dagger business, but I trust Teagan, so fine. I'll move on. According to Nick, this Smiley guy owns a plot of rural land with a double-wide trailer on it. He shows zero income since 2016, and he hasn't filed income taxes since the prior year. His property taxes continue to be paid every year, but utilities have been cut off. Seems like he's vanished and no one has reported him missing."

"So if he's dead, someone is still paying his taxes." Drew looked at Teagan. "Maybe paid by someone who buried him on his land and doesn't want anyone to find him."

"Sounds like a good possibility." Teagan's eyes widened. "We need to check out his place as soon as possible."

"Our probable cause for a warrant to search his property is pretty sketchy," Drew said.

"Ah-hah." Mackenzie's gaze landed on Drew again. "You're law enforcement."

Drat. Really? Drew had let the whole family atmosphere at dinner and this warm, loving family go to his head, and he'd forgotten himself. A year undercover was seeming to evaporate right before him. The more people who knew about his status, the more likely his cover would be blown.

He eyed Mackenzie. "I'd appreciate you keeping your suspicions between us. Your family doesn't need to be speculating too."

"Please." Teagan grabbed her sister's arm. "I need your support here. The whole circle of trust thing we have going on. You'll cover for me here, and you won't throw me under the bus no matter our parental or other family pressures."

"Yeah. I get it, but we're talking about potential murder —not sneaking out at night to make out with your latest crush."

Teagan continued to hold her sister's arm, her eyes pleading. "If I believed telling them would help, I would find a way to do it. But in this case, it could get someone killed."

Drew hated to admit it, but he admired Teagan for thinking about not outing him even though she really wanted to loop her family in. She'd clearly given this some consideration, and he was starting to see she had an analytical mind. A good thing for running her family company. Perhaps a not-so-good thing for keeping Drew's secrets.

Mackenzie faced Drew. "Get someone killed, like you, whoever you really are?"

"Like me." He clenched his hands before he said something he might regret. He really did respect this family and didn't want them to think badly of him. *Odd.* It was the first time in years he cared about what anyone other than his mother thought of him. Even his supervisors. He figured he did the very best work he could, and if they didn't see it, that was their problem. So far it hadn't been an issue. But maybe if he didn't get a warrant and went rogue to search Smiley's property, it might come back to bite him.

Mackenzie removed her sister's hand from her arm. "We're not law enforcement anymore, so we could take a look at it."

"No!" The word erupted from Teagan's mouth.

Crazy strong reaction. Had he been wrong? Was she not well-suited to undercover work?

Mackenzie's facial muscles tightened and for the first time, he saw her resemblance to Teagan. That stubborn set of her jaw. Her slightly raised chin. A challenge issued with her narrow stare. "What are you not telling me?"

"It's nothing really. I promised Dylan I wouldn't overstep on this investigation. If he can't go there, neither can I."

Mackenzie's assessing expression worried Drew. "Please don't claim sister privilege again."

"Sorry," Teagan said. "I have to. So if you don't have anything else from Nick, I need to talk to Dylan. Alone."

Mackenzie continued to stare at them for an uncomfortable moment, then she grabbed the jacket she'd hung on the back of a chair and pulled out a packet of papers. "His official report with the address."

"Thanks." Teagan took it. "One more promise."

"What?" Mackenzie's tone had turned testy.

"Don't go near this property." Teagan locked gazes with her sister. "You could ruin things, and as we said, lives are at stake here."

11

Shock of all shocks, Drew had gotten the warrant for Smiley's property that morning. He shoved it in his pocket as he climbed out of his vehicle, while the sun crept over the trees at the back of the property. Teagan parked next to him and stepped out of her car too. Drew hadn't expected Harris to agree to the warrant request, but she'd wanted to conclude the investigation on a win. The more wins she had in her column, the more likely she would get promoted up the ranks, the thing that drove her to be an overachiever.

She had a judge she knew who would see what they needed him to see. Not an unusual thing. Most law enforcement supervisors had favorite or go-to judges. With this one, Harris had emphasized the UC details and Rossi's statement that Drew had directly overheard.

Could come back to bite them now that the warrant was granted. A lawyer could try to argue that the business was closed when Drew and Teagan overheard Rossi. Rossi had expected privacy and would make the overheard comment inadmissible. But then this was where the judge they chose that leaned in law enforcement's direction was utilized. Also, since they believed Smiley to be deceased, who except the Contis or Rossi would bring in a lawyer? If Smiley had indeed been murdered, those guys wouldn't want to connect themselves to potential murder charges being brought against them.

Drew slipped into his vest from the back of his vehicle and secured the Velcro. Teagan had already put hers on under a rain jacket. A light mist fell, and Drew clamped a ball cap over his head to ward off the rain and hopefully keep anyone from his UC world from recognizing him should they show up. Rain or not, he would let nothing irritate him when he might have the best lead of his investigation on this desolate property. He slipped into his worn leather jacket, tugged on the zipper, and looked at Teagan.

She tugged her jacket closed and pulled up her hood, not noticing his study of her. She looked straight ahead at the double-wide trailer with tall grasses and vines growing over dented and rusty sides.

She gave Drew a quick look before turning back to the property. "Place isn't in great shape, but then I didn't expect it would be. Especially after seeing the satellite pictures in Nick's report."

"He's a great resource," Drew said. "Nice to have a guy with his skills on the right side of the law."

"Agreed." She tugged the front of her hood lower. "I've seen and heard about him finding things many others have failed to locate. I'd hate to be on the wrong side of him."

Drew nodded his agreement. "I don't expect to find anything inside, but let's start there while we wait for your forensic anthropologist to arrive with her GPR equipment."

Drew was banking on the forensic anthropologist, Kelsey Dunbar, from the Veritas Center and her ground penetrating radar to locate Smiley's remains.

Teagan started tromping over dried knee-high grass, mowing it down with her tactical boots that she'd paired with khaki tactical pants. He'd seen all sides of her now. Her corporate side, her casual side, and today, the law enforcement side. He didn't know her well enough to know which he liked best, but he could see this woman tossing on his baseball cap and hanging with him and the guys.

She looked over her shoulder at him. "Actually, Kelsey first uses a drone to find bodies."

He caught up to her. "You're serious? She uses a drone."

"Don't ask me how it works. Kelsey can explain when she gets here." Teagan marched straight for the door and pounded on it.

Drew lifted his jacket and clamped a hand on his sidearm as did Teagan. He doubted anyone would answer, but things could go sideways in a flash, and he always believed in being prepared.

She counted under her breath, her voice cool and calm, but he spotted the tension in her shoulders. The woman in front of him was not the woman he'd seen with her family yesterday. And what a family. He already liked them and hated lying to them through the rest of dinner.

She reached the count of fifty and glanced back at him. "We go in."

"Roger that," he said and wished he'd arrived first to breach the door.

He admired women in law enforcement and considered them equals, but losing his father at such a young age had made him overly protective of his mother, and that translated to other women. He didn't want to see another woman ever go through the pain his mom had experienced.

And yet wives of male law enforcement officers lived with that risk every day. Which was why he would never marry. Never let a woman nearly suffer a breakdown over his loss like his mother experienced at the death of his father.

Teagan got out her Maglite, as did he, the beam shining bright in their paths. She wrenched the door open, the metal groaning as if giving up its life. She drew her weapon.

"Police!" She charged inside.

He lifted his sidearm from the holster and trailed her into the dark, dank, and smelly tin box of a house. Clutter filled the small space. Newspapers. Beer cans. Dirty dishes on the table as if Smiley had walked out during a meal and didn't return. The side window was shattered, the glass still scattered on the stained carpet as if the Conti brothers had simply sprinkled some of their glitter.

She stepped through the combined living and dining area, batting at spiderwebs as she moved and blazing a bug-free trail for him. She took a quick glance into a bathroom, and they moved on, reaching the single bedroom, the covers crumpled and dirty. Mold crawled down the wall in the corner from a leaky roof, looking like it was hungry for food and had devoured most of an open newspaper.

"Clear." She holstered her weapon and nodded at an open closet filled with clothing and shoes. "Looks like he went out one day and never came back."

"Could further cement our theory that he was murdered." Drew slid his sidearm into the holster. "Let's give this place a better look."

He turned back to the hallway and headed for the kitchen. He put on disposable gloves and thumbed through the piles of paperwork sitting in a precarious pile on the end of the counter.

Gloves already on, Teagan stepped into the family room and began tossing things around.

"Last mail here is dated in August of 2016. All utility bills," he said. "Which is about when Mackenzie said Smiley had disappeared."

Teagan nodded and dug under sofa cushions. "Nothing except dirt."

"Let's check the shed out back. Might find something there." He marched to the door, and she followed.

He jumped down, bypassing the two sketchy-looking wooden steps and waited at the base for Teagan. He would much rather look at her, but he continued to survey the area. He doubted the Contis or Rossi had anyone watching the place after all these years, but he couldn't be too careful. Not only with his life, but he was responsible for Teagan too. He might have formed an unwilling alliance with her, but they were partners in this investigation, and he always had his partner's back.

They picked their way through the grass and past several stands of huge rhododendrons that grew so well in Oregon's naturally acidic soil. Neither spoke, but the silence wasn't awkward. Surprising, especially for as little time as they'd known each other or from the difficult way they'd first met.

Now that was something. Would be a great story to tell his kids someday. *Whoa.* No. He didn't plan to have kids. Not that he didn't want them. He did. But he needed a wife to have kids. So no kids.

He pulled open the door that clung on life support to the rusty hinges. "No electricity."

They both shone their flashlights into the space. Garden tools including a wooden handled shovel caked with gray Oregon clay soil and a rusty metal spade hung upside down on wooden pegs. A lawnmower covered in inches of greasy dirt and debris sat by the door next to old woven and aluminum lawn chairs. Once bright primary colors, they'd faded to sickly pastels.

He glanced at Teagan. "Shovel looks like the only thing that's been used in recent years."

"Maybe used to dig Smiley's grave." Teagan's enthusiastic tone gave him hope for finding a lead. "Of course the killer probably wore gloves, but it could still tell us something, I suppose."

A vehicle engine and tires crunching over gravel sounded outside. Drew spun to look behind them. A white van with the Veritas Center logo on its side turned onto the property and parked next to his car.

"Looks like our expert is here," he said. "Doesn't look like anything we can use in here. Let's go meet her."

"Right behind you."

They followed the mowed-down path they'd created on the way in as law enforcement protocol would suggest to minimize the trampling of any evidence.

A woman with curly black hair slid out of the passenger side of the van. She wore a frilly blouse and black pants. The skinny guy with her had his hair pulled back in a man-bun and wore a polo shirt with the center's logo embroidered on the chest. He went to the back of the van and returned carrying a protective suit and rubber boots along with a blue backpack. He dropped the boots and backpack next to the woman and shook out the suit before handing it to her.

She smiled at him, but it was wan and uninspired, and he turned to go back to the rear of the van. Her skin had lost color since she'd stepped out, and she held on to the side of the van with her free hand.

"What's wrong, Kelsey?" Teagan stepped over to the other woman and put a hand on her shoulder.

"Morning sickness."

"You're expecting?" Teagan's eyes brightened. "How wonderful."

"It will be once I get over this sickness. I didn't have it with Sophia so it's taking me by surprise." She wrinkled her nose and looked at Drew. "Not something you needed to know. I'm Kelsey Dunbar."

"Dr. Kelsey Dunbar." Teagan lowered her hand. "She's not one to brag, so we have to do it for her."

Kelsey shook hands with Drew, her fingers slender and delicate. "I like my work to speak for itself."

Drew shook but held back and didn't put his all into the handshake. She seemed petite to begin with, and he didn't want to jostle her when she felt queasy.

"ICE Agent Drew Collier." He used his real identity as he didn't want this event to be connected with his UC work and get back to the Contis or Rossi.

"Let me get into these coveralls." Kelsey shook out her suit. "Any idea at all of where we might find this victim?"

"No," Drew said. "He could still be alive for all we know, but the facts point to the opposite."

Kelsey leaned on the van and tugged off a short boot and slid her leg into the coveralls, then into one of the rubber boots.

Her assistant returned with a drone. She looked at him. "Please go ahead and mark the property boundaries for the drone while I get set up."

"On it." The young guy left the drone next to the backpack and disappeared behind the van again then came out holding stakes and an iPad. His face pinned to the screen, he trudged off.

Drew turned his attention back to Kelsey. "Teagan told me you can find buried bodies with a drone, but I can't begin to see how."

"That's why they pay me the big bucks." She laughed, a tiny tinkling sound, and she removed the other boot and then looked at them. "Seriously, the drone uses infrared imaging to detect bodies. It works both above and below the ground. And even if someone moved the body, the technology can also find where a corpse had been buried and removed up to two years after the removal."

"That's amazing," Drew said.

"Saves me a lot of time. Before technology, I could walk right past a clandestine body without knowing it was there. Sure, I can look for other markers and use GPR, but the drone doubles my chance of finding the body."

He wanted to offer to help with getting her last boot on, but she managed it with the ease of someone who often precariously balanced against a van. "I'm fascinated with forensic science. Are you free to share how it actually works?"

"Sure. It's not often others want to know." She tugged up the top of her suit. "The first thing you need to know is that bodies release carbon and nitrogen into the soil as they decay. That, in turn, decreases the amount of light the soil reflects. Initially, the flood of chemicals kills plants, traveling distances where vegetation roots absorb it, but that changes as time passes."

She paused for a long breath and pulled on her suit's zipper. "It soon disperses into the soil around the body and becomes a fertilizer that reflects a ton of light. It'll also make the vegetation nice and lush and is often a telltale sign that we can also use to locate remains."

"Okay, you send this drone up, then what?" he asked.

"Once I have a hit, I'll pass over the ground using GPR to confirm if I think it's needed, and then I start digging. It's a precise process, and we won't be tromping around and digging holes all over the place like you see on TV and in the movies."

She grabbed the controller. "Ready?"

"Can't wait to see it in action." Drew's enthusiasm was over the top, and he needed to cool it. He was beginning to sound like a fangirl.

She launched the drone, and the buzzing motor spiraled the device into the cold air filled only with a fine mist. "I'll do a grid search following the property lines."

Drew tracked the drone's progress up and down the large open area. After six passes that covered the nearby area, Kelsey stepped to the end of the grid marked off by her assistant and started again. Each pass without locating anything made Drew's heart sink more, and his gut gnarled into a knot like the roots of these massive trees.

She made these precise sweeps three more times until they had one grid left at the back end of the property.

"Looks like we might strike out," Drew said to Teagan.

"We still have one more grid to go. Besides, if I was going to bury someone, I'd do it as far away from the road as possible so no one saw me, and that's the section she has left to do."

"Good point." He watched the drone sweep back and forth like a soaring hawk, a hint of hope holding on in his heart when it was seeming more hopeless.

On the third pass, Kelsey let the drone settle into an overgrown area near bushes on the back side of the lot. "We have a hit."

"Yes!" Drew fist bumped Teagan and caught her wide beaming smile.

Kelsey didn't celebrate, but shrugged off her backpack and started unzipping the pocket as she walked to the location where she'd landed the drone. Drew and Teagan hurried after her.

She pulled stakes and a mallet from her backpack. Her assistant joined her. Without a word, they pounded the stakes into the ground, forming the shape of a human grave.

"Oh, oh," she said and hurried over an overgrown shrub on the far edge of the markers. "I didn't expect this."

"What is it?" Not sure if he should follow her, Drew remained in place.

"A skull. Partially buried."

"A human skull?" Drew asked.

"No question in my mind." She looked up, the gravity of the situation lodged in her tight expression. "We've located human remains."

At the discovery of the skull, Teagan wanted to take a moment to process. Acknowledge that a person had lost their life here. Respect the dead. Maybe get her head around the fact that she was staring at a skull.

Drew took it in stride. Or at least he seemed to. He'd been in law enforcement longer than she had, but she'd likely seen more homicide victims in her career. Never had she seen a skeletonized body, though. Or a skull peering up at her from the ground.

Had he become too jaded while undercover to be shocked at this? If so, what had he seen? And could he ever reenter life again or would his past year haunt him?

Kelsey seemed detached too. Maybe not inwardly but on the outside. She would have to be. Her job involved recovering skeletonized bodies all the time. She'd taken over and ground everything to a halt, telling her assistant to call Ainslie Houston, the Veritas photographer, then start toting needed tools from the van for an excavation.

Kelsey looked at Teagan and Drew. "We have to document the scene before we do anything, and Ainslie's our crime scene photographer."

"Is she available?" Drew asked.

"Murder trumps most everything else, so she'll make herself available. I can begin taking photographs now, but she'll take over when I start to excavate the remains." Kelsey got out her phone. "We'll also need the ME on scene as well as notify the local law enforcement agency."

"That would be Clackamas County." Teagan stepped back from the skull. "No need to call them. I've been sworn again to handle this investigation, and I can represent their interests. My family doesn't know that, so I would appreciate it if you kept it between us."

Kelsey raised an eyebrow but said nothing and made the phone call to the ME, who promised to come straight away.

Kelsey's assistant returned with a camera dangling from his skinny neck, several small trowels and brushes, and two blue tarps.

Kelsey helped him shake out the first tarp but looked at Drew and Teagan before placing it on the ground. "The prep work and dig will take some time so you might not want to hang around."

"Time, like a couple of hours?" Drew asked.

Kelsey shook her head. "Likely all day. I have to remove the soil layer by layer so I can sample each layer and then put it on a tarp to be screened for evidence."

"Layers?" Teagan asked, as she'd never seen this process unfold.

"Soil is made up of layers or horizons." Kelsey pinned down the corners of the tarp. "I won't bore you with the details. Just know a grave will have distinct layers on the edges, but the person who dug the grave will have mixed up the fill soil."

From Drew's questions so far, Teagan figured he wouldn't mind if Kelsey did bore him with the details.

"The layers show me the edges of the grave," Kelsey continued. "If I know the boundaries, I won't miss any evidence."

"But the skull is on the surface," Drew said. "How can that be?"

Kelsey peered at the ground. "Looks like this area was washed away during all of our recent rain, exposing a portion of the skull. We're lucky scavengers didn't carry it off or we might not be able to identity this body."

"You mentioned evidence," Drew said. "If the body has been here since 2016, can you still recover any useful evidence?"

Kelsey unfurled the second tarp on the other side of the staked space. "Some evidence doesn't degrade so if any exists, we'll be able to capture it. The soil is unique too. Like a fingerprint. We can hire a soil scientist if needed. They can compare the soil to a shovel or any soil found on a potential suspect's shoes, in his car, his house, et cetera. That will place them not only on this property but specifically in this grave."

"Would that be useful after so many years?" Teagan asked.

"You'd be surprised at what we still find. Killers who used a shovel only once. Dropped their shoes or boots in their trunk and never vacuumed it out. Toss boots in a garage. Things like that. So we have hope for finding and convicting this killer. It could take some time, though." She turned away and put her attention on her work.

Teagan took this as a dismissal and looked at Drew. "Now what?"

His forehead furrowed. "As much as I would like to watch Kelsey's process, there's really no point in hanging out here all day when we have so little time left to bring my op to a conclusion."

"We'll need a deputy or agent to babysit the location as the officer of record." Teagan got out her phone. "I'll ask Gutierrez to assign someone."

"And I'll notify Harris of the discovery."

She dialed, and he stepped away, pulling out his phone as he moved. He continued to exude that masculine confidence. The power that radiated from his stride. She tried to ignore it. Should ignore it. She knew better than to let it get to her, but it was there in each step as he strode away as if he owned the ground he walked on.

Gutierrez answered on the first ring, and she had to look at the ground to concentrate.

"We have a body." She brought Gutierrez up to date. "Do you want me to work the investigation or do you want to assign one of your permanent detectives?"

"It's related to your investigation so you take it. You were the best record keeper ever on the squad, and we can always reassign it later if need be."

Her shoulders automatically lifted at his compliment. He gave them, but not often, and they had to be well-earned. "Kelsey says this will be a time-consuming process. We'll need deputies to man the site."

He grumbled. "You know we're running lean and mean right now. I'll send someone over as soon as I can free them up."

She thanked him and disconnected. Drew was still on his phone, his hand clamped on the back of his neck that was still bronze from the summer. She couldn't help but wonder how he got the tan. She doubted Dylan engaged in any sports with the Contis. So did he have any free time or was he stuck in the role of Dylan all the time?

He shoved his phone into his pocket and marched back. "Harris thanks you for arranging an officer of record, but she wants to be sure you know we're working this potential murder investigation together."

"I think we're past potential, but we don't have a cause of

death so I'll let it go." She grinned at him. "A deputy will be dispatched, and yes, I know we work it together."

"I figured as much, but it had to be stated."

She got it. Some detectives would claim jurisdiction and give the feds the cold shoulder. But as far as she was concerned, this was a joint operation all the way. "So now what? I mean after the deputy arrives?"

"Time for Dylan to deposit some cash in the Contis' bank account."

"Then what?" Teagan asked.

"We'll have to play it by ear." He shoved his phone into his pocket. "Undercover work is a slow, tedious process sometimes. You have to be careful not to seem too eager and tip off the subjects. I'll make the deposit, and meet up with the brothers to be sure they know I did it."

"And what do you want me to do? Other than go home and get ready for my lunch date with Oliver?"

Drew gritted his teeth.

"What?"

He shoved his hands into his pockets. "I still don't like this date, but Harris agrees with it, so we're a go. You'll wait for me to signal that I'm in place to monitor things before you arrive."

He was being pushy again, but this was different. She could see he was worried about her. Maybe on a personal level, so she would let it go. "Of course I will."

"Good. Thank you." He gave her a tight smile. "As to other tasks, do you think Nick's reports on the Contis and Rossi are complete, or is there more research that could be done?"

"Complete for the amount of time we gave him," she said. "He's still running a few algorithms that could turn something up."

"But a lay person like one of us wouldn't likely find anything?"

"Not likely. But I can review Nick's report again. Maybe see something we missed when we first looked at it."

"Other than that, I can't think of anything you can do to help at the moment. I'll head out to talk to the Conti brothers. Then I'll observe your lunch, and we can meet up again for a dinner date."

She didn't like his answer, but he might be right. There might not be anything else she could do right now. Still, she had to do *something*. She would figure out exactly what that something might be on the drive back to the city.

Other than the big date with Oliver.

12

Not sure how he was feeling about the morning's developments, Drew parked outside his bogus business office. They'd found Smiley. Or at least Drew believed they had. And the discovery had caused Teagan pain. Man, he had hated seeing that. She tried to hide it, but she didn't manage it well. Her face had lost color, and her eyes were tight until she made the call to her lieutenant. Then she'd moved into her law enforcement mode and either coped or managed to hide the anguish better.

And what did Drew do? He'd frustrated her with his answer on what she could do to help. Basically, a whole lot of nothing. He understood her disappointment. He wouldn't like being put on the shelf either. He half expected her to follow him to the office, and he'd kept watching in his rearview mirror for her vehicle. Her law enforcement training had taught her how to tail a suspect unseen, but she would have to be nearly invisible to succeed.

He'd made several left turns in a row as was usual when leaving his real life to move into his UC life. Was the easiest way to see if someone tailed him. But no vehicle made the turns with him. Not a single one.

He had to assume she was home primping for a date with another man. His gut clenched. Worse, in a few hours, he had to sit and listen to her flirt with the guy—and the guy come on to her, as he most certainly would the minute he got a look at her.

Drew groaned and shoved that thought away. He had the Contis to deal with before he could agonize over the date. He got out and stopped on the sidewalk to look through the big storefront window. The small room faced the road and held two desks and signs advertising the business.

The female agent playing his receptionist sat behind the front desk trying to look busy. The Conti brothers sat next to his desk. He pushed inside and found them arguing over how to price glitter. Here they were antiquities smugglers, heroin suppliers, and potentially killers, and they were fighting over a fifty-cent price difference.

Drew greeted his assistant. "Go ahead and take a break."

She knew he was going to have a talk with the Contis that the guys wouldn't want her to hear, so she grabbed her purse and hurried out the door.

Drew approached the men. "Never knew glitter pricing was so complicated."

Sal swiveled to look at Drew. "You move the number of units we do online, and the price becomes critical. Got to mark it up enough to pay for handling the goods and not price ourselves out of the market, what with the Zon under-cutting everything."

Drew wasn't an online shopper, but he knew Sal was referring to Amazon. Even if the brothers didn't make most of their living off their craft business, it was important to their operation to be able to move illegal goods. Their truck fleet was instrumental in delivering products along the West Coast.

"Thanks for coming." Drew dropped into the chair

behind his desk. "Made my first deposit on the way over here."

Aldo lifted his head from staring at his smartphone. "I'll just look that up."

"Hey, man," Drew said. "I thought we'd developed some trust."

"Not when it extends to money." Aldo tapped his cell phone.

Drew's fingers itched to grab that phone and run. The device had to hold information that could indict these men for their illegal actions. Drew shoved his hands into his pockets. He had to bide his time. Like he told Teagan. Slow and methodical. That's what worked.

"You think any more about speeding up your deposits?" Sal asked.

"Thought about it." Drew leaned back but connected gazes with Sal. "No offense, my friend, but how do I know you're not playing me and Monty? Taking his money and running?"

"Don't see as how you have a choice if he wants us to clean his dough." Sal leaned forward and steepled his fingers together on the desk, looking bored by the conversation, but there was a sharp edge to his gaze.

Drew heard the man's foot tapping on the other side of the desk. His tell. This was important to him. Meant Drew had to care even less and get Sal to beg for the money. Then maybe he could get him to let Drew move product too and bring the brothers up on drug charges before the antiquities investigation concluded. Worst case, he had them on money laundering now. Every word of this conversation was being recorded, and if Drew ran out of time before the op came to a close, he could leverage the recording to get them to flip on Rossi on the antiquities.

"Here's the thing," Drew said, playing it cool. "We really

need you to have some skin in this game too. Something major to use as collateral."

Aldo snapped his chair forward. "We're carrying all the risk. Sure, you might be out some cash, but we're the ones breaking the law."

Nice! Admit it here in front of the cameras.

"Put yourself in my shoes." Drew had to work hard to sound legitimately offended. "I ask you to put a mil in my account with no guarantee of return? You say no for sure."

"I would." Aldo glanced at his brothers. "Not sure about them. They like to take more risks."

Drew relaxed back. "So what say you give me some product as assurance that the money will come back to us?"

"You want some glitter?" Sal cocked a smile.

His sarcastic tone crawled up Drew's back, and he fisted his hands under the desk but made sure not to give away his irritation in any visible way.

"That'd be a lot of glitter." Vito laughed and his brothers joined in, their deep voices booming through the small room.

Drew faked a laugh. "I was thinking more like glitter for the veins or nose."

The brothers' smiles fell.

Sal's eyes narrowed. "What makes you think we can provide that?"

"Come on, man," Drew said, letting that frustration into his voice. "We've been dancing around this for a year. You've got product. I need assurance. We know each other now, and it's time for you to ante up if you want to wash more of Monty's money. Your cut is highway robbery. You know it. We know it. But we want to clean the cash. Let's get this deal done so I can bring Monty fully onboard and you can make some coin."

Sal picked at the cuticle on his thumb and glanced at

Vito. They both nodded, though Aldo's expression was more reserved.

"Okay, fine," Sal said, not bothering to consult with Vito. "We set up a meet for tonight. Our warehouse. One a.m. when the guard is snoozing and doesn't notice me looping old footage in the security feed."

"Sounds like you've done this before," Drew said, finally having proof that they modified the video on other nights like when Drew had restrained Teagan and her guard.

"Of course." Sal grinned. "How do you think we move things without Steele Guardians getting wind of it? We need guards on site due to theft in the area, but they only know so much."

More than you think. At least Patrick did. But then he was a sub, so maybe the regular guards were asleep on the job or looked the other way. Drew doubted the company would tolerate that, but how would they know without surveilling their own staff in the night?

"One a.m. then." Drew stood and marched to the door to open it for the brothers, feeling their eyes boring into him like drill bits as they crossed the room.

Had Drew's pushiness made them suspect him? Made them want to get rid of him the way they ended Smiley's life?

Maybe.

He had to let Harris know of the meet tonight and the potential danger. He hoped she approved the meet despite the risk. He wanted—no, he needed—to end this investigation with arrests and convictions. Otherwise he'd wasted the last year of his life.

~

After showering and dressing for her date, Teagan went to Steele Guardians to keep her family from asking too many questions about all of her sudden absences. Once behind her desk, she forced her mind onto her typical daily tasks. She wanted to think about anything and everything to do with the investigation instead. She shouldn't.

She had to remember her family was counting on her to keep the Conti situation from hurting Steele Guardians—at least they would be if she could tell them about it. They were also counting on her to keep the business running in general.

After Thomas had been murdered, she'd taken over the reins of the company that he'd managed flawlessly. She'd had to. His parents and sisters were so distraught they couldn't think straight. But did Teagan follow in his very successful footsteps?

No, she fumbled to find her footing and promptly lost the company's biggest client. That sent doubts reverberating through the family. At least with her dad, who was trying to hold things together. Nearly two years later, she was still trying to prove her worth. Something most eldest children of a family felt an unreasonable need to do. She'd fallen prey to that syndrome big time.

She tried to focus on a contract. Read a page. Digested none of it. Read it again. Nothing.

Fine. She would set it aside for a minute. Read Nick's report again. Just quickly. Then get back to work.

She opened it on her computer and clicked on the first link, a recent article about Chauncey Rossi receiving an award for coaching youth soccer for second through eighth grade kids. He'd coached since his sons were young. They'd long ago outgrown the league, but he still coached. Quotes from parents filled the article about how selfless and generous he'd been. He had a warm smile in the picture and sure wasn't the cold, calculating man she'd seen when he'd threatened Drew's life.

He was not only generous with the soccer league, but other stories mentioned how his business supported other local charities, and he appeared to be a pillar of the community. Appeared. She knew better. Knew he could be a killer or at least a man who ordered another man killed.

She moved on, scrolling through social media photos posted by his wife. Would she be shocked when she learned of his activities? Maybe not. When someone was engaged in criminal activities, the spouse often knew something was off. They simply turned a blind eye.

The last story told of his service as an elder in a local Catholic church and Christian school. Of course, he sponsored their soccer team and was an assistant coach there too. That was the last straw. Living a life of faith on the surface, but engaging in illegal activities. Teagan was more determined than ever to prove his illegal actions.

But how?

She leaned back in her chair to think, the metal squeaking. She'd been meaning to lubricate it for months, but time was always too precious. Like now. She was missing something. Maybe something right in front of her face.

So Rossi, what don't I know? Maybe could ask Oliver about?

She obviously couldn't march into Rossi's work or home and ask to talk to him. And she'd already played the manicure card with his wife. Even if Teagan was soon leaving for a date with Oliver, she could hardly grill the guy right off the bat. Too bad she couldn't pretend to be a reporter and interview Oliver's dad. She figured he was the kind of guy who liked to brag and would talk, but she couldn't risk it. Not with having met with his wife and being scheduled for lunch with Oliver.

"C'mon think." She pounded a fist on the desk.

Her desk phone chimed. Seeing their receptionist, Gretchen's, name on the ID , Teagan answered.

"There's a Dylan Crane here to see you."

"He's here? But..." Her mind flew over the possible reasons Drew would come here while undercover. Or when he would see her in a short while at the lunch. Wasn't he risking his cover? She supposed he could come here without being under suspicion with the Contis as they believed he was dating her.

"You there, Teagan?" Gretchen asked.

"Yeah. Send him up. I'll meet him at the door." Teagan stood and released the quick ponytail she'd sleeked her hair into to keep it out of her face as she worked. She finger-combed through it and smoothed the peach-colored dress she'd chosen for the date. It had a fitted bodice and flared skirt and showed a bit of cleavage. The most feminine thing she owned, but she planned to cover it with a jacket.

"Stop primping," she muttered as she walked to the locked entrance door.

"You talking to yourself?" Mackenzie's voice came from behind.

Teagan jumped. "Don't sneak up on me like that."

"Not sneaking. Something has your full attention, and girl, you are dressed to impress. Maybe even attract a guy. So spill."

"Nothing. Simply going to meet a visitor."

"I was on my way out to do an interview for my podcast. I can let your guest in for you."

"Podcast. That's it." Mackenzie could interview Rossi. She would have to be read in on Drew's undercover investigation, and he would have to approve it, but maybe it could work.

Mackenzie tilted her head. "That's what?"

"Nothing." Teagan stepped away. "I need to see to my visitor."

"Fine," Mackenzie called out. "Be like that."

Teagan knew she'd sounded defensive or at the very least like she was hiding something, but she kept going and hoped Mackenzie was headed for the back exit leading to the lot where they parked their cars.

Teagan reached for the door and took a long breath before pulling it open.

Drew stood, strong and broad-shouldered on the other side. He ran his gaze over her, and his smile disappeared. Not the reaction she expected.

He curled his fingers into fists. "That Oliver creep doesn't deserve the effort you put into your appearance."

"No real effort other than a shower." She kept looking at him, trying to figure out the reason for his frustration.

"Well, you look amazing." His irritation vanished, and he gave her an appreciative look.

A warm feeling swam in her chest.

Could he tell how glad she was to see him? To see his admiring look directed at her?

A flush stole up her neck. If he hadn't known, he did now. She couldn't think of anything to say, so she stood back.

"Ah-hah. That's why you're so distracted," Mackenzie said, stepping past Teagan and eyeing Drew. "Looks like you're monopolizing my sister's time."

"That a problem?" Drew asked, honestly sounding interested in the answer.

"She could use a guy in her life so not necessarily bad." Mackenzie kept her former detective appraising look on Drew. "If you're a good guy, that is."

"Ignore her. She was just leaving." Teagan fired her sister

a warning look, pushed Mackenzie toward the door, and closed it firmly behind her. "We can go to my office."

She rushed away, taking deep breaths and letting them out to clear her brain of the personal feelings making her lightheaded.

He fell into step beside her. "Do you like working with your family?"

"Most of the time."

"Translated not times like this when one of them tries to fix you up." He grinned.

"Exactly." Teagan stepped into her office to retreat behind her desk. She felt safer there. Not physically but mentally safe from her budding feelings for this guy.

She expected him to take a seat in a chair across the desk, but he came to perch on the edge of her desk, only a few feet away. She scooted her chair back to put more space between them and earned a raise of his eyebrow.

"I had an idea," she blurted out.

"Okay." His smile flattened a bit as he searched her face, seeking some sort of answer, but she didn't know what he wanted.

She told him about the articles she'd just read. "I was thinking we need to pretend to be reporters and interview Rossi to get more info on his coaching to see if that might tell us something. Obviously, you can't do that, and I can't since I talked to his wife and have the date with Oliver. Too risky."

"Agreed."

"What if we sent Mackenzie to interview him?"

"Mackenzie?"

"She's really good at doing interviews. She has a podcast about millennials and faith."

"And that applies to Rossi, how?"

"One of the articles quoted him as saying he was active

in his church and in coaching youth soccer there. Mackenzie could say she wants to get his take on the millennials he's worked with and how he sees faith combining with sports."

He frowned. "If I'm Rossi, I'd be asking of all the people in the world who are involved in sports, why does this woman want to talk to me?"

"Yeah, good question, but you know how many people in the Pacific Northwest aren't churched, so she could say she did an internet search and his name came up."

"And what? She has an urgent request to talk to him? These things usually take time to arrange."

"She could say she had a cancellation for her show and ask if he could fill in. We'd have to read her in on the investigation, but I guarantee she wouldn't tell anyone."

"Sorry. I don't think it's a good idea. She won't likely learn anything helpful in the interview. She could even raise his suspicions. I just got a meet scheduled with him, and I need him to remain complacent." Drew planted his hands on his thighs. "I don't think the reward is worth the risk."

Teagan didn't want to admit it, but he had valid points. "You could be right. Maybe it's not a good idea. I just want to help. Usually, I have my family to run these kinds of ideas against, but being without their support and direction is hard."

"Trust me. I get it. That's one of the most difficult parts of undercover work. No one to bounce ideas off and having to act quickly much of the time." He got a faraway look on his face.

"And no one you love there to support you."

"Yeah, that too."

She wanted to take his hand and hold it. Not good. She focused on his broad chest instead. "So why did you come by?"

"Couple of things. As I mentioned, Sal is arranging for me to meet with his source tonight to ask for heroin as collateral to hold while he washes my money. Since the source for the money laundering is Rossi, he's got to be behind the drugs too."

She looked up. "Your meeting with the Conti brothers went well, then?"

"On the surface, it looks like it. We'll see what happens tonight. Our meet is set for one a.m."

"Anything I can do?" she asked hopefully.

"Actually, there might be. Once I get the drugs, I'll need them analyzed right away. Our labs are way too backlogged to do it on a timely basis."

"You want me to get someone at Veritas to analyze it?"

"Could you?"

"Let me call Maya Lane. She's their toxicology and controlled substance expert." Teagan got out her phone, dialed Maya's cell phone. The call connected right away.

"Maya, hi. Teagan Steele. I need a favor." Teagan described the situation, added that an ICE agent needed the results immediately, but they wouldn't have the sample until after one a.m.

"No worries. I've got plenty of work to keep me at the lab until then. Just call me when you have it, and I'll tell our guard to expect you."

"Thank you, Maya. I'll owe you big time." Teagan ended the call. "She's a go. We call her when you have the drugs, and she'll tell the night guard to expect us."

"You're going to the lab with me?"

"Unless you don't want me to."

"I'll be glad for your company."

"That's settled then. What else did you need?"

He pulled a microphone and battery from his pocket. "I

wanted to be sure you're ready for this date and that starts with wiring you up."

"Good. This is better than trying to get ready in a car. Otherwise I'm ready. Unless you think the dress is too much." She ran her hands over her dress.

His nostrils flared. "Not too much. Any guy would be a fool not to want to go on this date with you."

"What about you?"

"Me?" He gaped at her.

She'd caught him off guard, and she loved that. He's been so controlled. In charge. Bossy. But now she had the upper hand, and she would relish it for a moment. "Would you like to date for real?"

"I don't... I can't."

"If you're thinking you can claim being UC as a reason not to, that's going to end soon."

"It's not that."

"I think I'm falling for you, Drew," she admitted before she chickened out.

He jumped to his feet. "I don't want you to fall for me. It's not good for you."

"Why on earth not?"

"Because I can't give you what you want. What your family wants."

Interesting. "What exactly do you think I want, and what does my family have to do with this?"

"They want to see you married with children. Happy. Fulfilled. And you want the same thing."

"So? You're not going undercover again. Why can't I have that with you?"

"You just can't, okay?" He marched to the door. "Time to head to the restaurant. Get this annoying date over with."

Turning his back to her felt like a physical slap to the face, and it would take some time for her to recover, if ever.

13

Phone to her ear, Teagan adjusted the wire she'd hidden under her dress before leaving the office and walked toward the Italian restaurant. She scanned the area for Oliver's arrival, but didn't see a guy who looked like the pictures his mother had shared.

"I'm sorry." Drew's repentant voice came over her phone. "I shouldn't have blown up on you like that. Don't take your anger at me into lunch with you. You won't be your best, and I don't want you to be off your game."

"I'm good," she said, but she was far from good. She didn't know what he had against dating, but it was a hot button for sure. And she was mad at herself for admitting to him that she was falling for him. For caring what he thought after she'd confessed her feelings. For being less than the professional she always strived to be.

She'd let the man's intimate smile sucker her in, and she suddenly wanted what he said she wanted more than she'd ever known. Could she have been saying she didn't want to get serious with a guy because she'd never found a guy who liked her for who she was? Who didn't think she was too pushy and straightforward?

Drew didn't seem to have a problem with that. Not even when she'd shoved him against a wall. He appreciated her strength. But Drew wasn't the right guy, now was he? Totally not. He'd just told her that he was as interested in dating as he was in taking a bullet to the chest. Maybe the bullet enticed him more.

"Remember I'm right here," he said, his tone soothing. "If you say *sweat*, I'll come barging in."

"I got it, Drew. See you on the other side." She ended her call and stowed her phone in her purse to enter the restaurant.

She was immediately hit with the enticing aroma of garlic, onions, and oregano. With such a tantalizing smell, she should plan on gaining twenty pounds at lunch today. If her nerves let her eat.

She stopped at the unmanned podium inside the door and scanned the room decorated in rust and yellow with big booths and mismatched chairs around worn tables. A darkly handsome guy matching Lauralee's photo stood and waved at her. His navy suit with white shirt fit his trim shape as if custom made, and he'd paired it with a pale turquoise tie.

She approached his table, and he let his gaze roam over her. When it landed back on her face, his even white teeth flashed in a broad smile. She didn't like his study, but she faked a smile to hide her true feelings. He had a close-cut beard and big eyes with dark lashes. He was, in a word, *handsome*—but he did nothing for her. Nothing at all. Still, she had to pretend.

"Oliver Rossi." He held out his hand. "And I'm seriously hoping you are Meg Jacobs."

"Guilty as charged." She took his warm, slender, and smooth hand, comparing it to Drew's rougher, thicker hand. No reaction. Nothing. Not like the charge she felt with Drew.

Oliver placed his other hand over hers. "Glad to meet you, Meg Jacobs. For once I'm thankful for my mother's interference."

Teagan faked a laugh and extricated her hand.

He pulled out a chair for her.

She dropped onto it and scooted close to the table.

He sat across from her, his eyes roving over her again as if taking mental photographs. "I've come here with my family since I was a toddler, so took the liberty of ordering the best meal for you. I hope that's okay."

No, it's not okay. I'm a grown woman and can order my own food. "Of course. You know the place better than I do. But I have to warn you. I'm a sous chef and will likely end up critiquing the meal."

"A chef. That's wonderful. A guy would be lucky to have a gorgeous woman like you who can cook too."

Okay. Not five minutes in, and he proved he was a chauvinist. "And what do you do, Oliver?"

He shook out his napkin. "I'm an executive at Northwest Geo Instruments. We provide automated systems to monitor the safety and stability of things like bridges and buildings."

He started describing his work in detail, mentioning resistivity meters, which she had no idea about except for seeing the boxes in their warehouse, and she had to work hard to keep her expression from glazing over.

"Sorry for going on like that." He frowned. "You look bored."

"No offense, but I've always found corporate jobs kind of boring."

He raised an eyebrow that she could swear he had waxed or plucked into a perfect shape. "Some corporate jobs are, but this one has many perks to spice things up."

She leaned closer, feigning real interest. "When does it get spicy?"

He bent forward, his gaze raptly pinned to her. "We provide equipment for archeological digs."

"Oh, that *is* interesting. Tell me more about *that*." She took a sip of her water, trying to make him work hard to impress her. He struck her as the kind of guy who liked to brag, and that was the best way to get information from him.

"We don't do the digging." He made a sour face. "Too hot and dusty for my liking. But sometimes, I personally deliver the equipment and get a first-hand tour of the digs."

Yeah, she couldn't see this guy getting dirty. Especially if his manicured nails told her anything. If she hadn't gotten the manicure with his mother, his hands and nails would be in better shape than Teagan's.

"I would agree. I don't like to get dirty." Such a lie. She was the first one in the family to step into messy projects. "Then how is that interesting to you?"

He cupped his fingers around his water glass and turned it in circles on the table. "I really can't say."

"Too bad," she said, trying to put a healthy measure of disappointment in her tone. "I was beginning to warm up to your profession and you."

"It's just..." He glanced around. "It's highly confidential information on a need-to-know basis."

"And I don't need to know." She stared at him. "I get it, but I honestly don't like it."

"I like how direct you are."

"And I don't like how evasive you are." She let her gaze linger on him, then she looked away, glad to see the server was coming forward with plates piled high with food before Teagan pushed this guy too hard, too soon.

She wouldn't let this topic drop, but would continue to question Oliver during the meal. He might shut down even more. Or she might get him to open up. Either way, she had to try. With something illegal going down soon, she couldn't relent.

~

Drew gritted his teeth and stared through his binoculars as he watched and listened to Teagan flirt with another guy. She was doing an excellent job of playing Oliver. Too excellent. Good for the UC sting. Bad for Drew's emotions. He had to force himself from bursting through that door and claiming her as his. A thought as shocking as Oliver just admitting he had an antiquity coming in tonight that would change his and his family's life forever.

Seriously. The guy spilled the beans and told Teagan about a limestone relief of a Persian guard being delivered at three a.m. to the docks, and all he had to do was go pick it up. He declared the value at five million dollars, and he only paid two million for it. He already had a buyer lined up, and he would make a nice profit.

Not if Drew could help it. He was sure Harris would want them to stake out the dock but let Oliver take possession of the antiquity and then nab the person he sold it to as well.

"That is so exciting," Teagan said. "I could tell right up front that you were the dangerous type, not some tedious corporate stooge."

"And you like that, don't you?" He reached across the table and laid his hand on Teagan's.

She didn't flinch, but Drew caught a flash of revulsion in her expression. Yes! She was disgusted by this guy, and Drew had nothing to worry about.

Listen to him. Nothing to worry about. He didn't intend to get involved with her so why would he have anything to worry about to begin with?

She batted her lashes at Oliver. "Do you think I could come with you to the dock?"

He shook his head hard. "Not possible. Not with the kind of guys I'll be meeting. Too dangerous for such a pretty thing like you."

She didn't flinch at his description of her as a pretty thing, but Drew knew she would hate that.

She pressed her free hand over Oliver's. "Will you bring it back to your company warehouse?"

He nodded.

"Could we get together tomorrow, and I could see it then?" She beamed a smile across the table that no man could resist. "Please. This could really be the start of a good thing between us. Don't you want that to happen?" She linked her fingers with the creep's. "I do. Very much so."

"Of course. Yes. Yes." He lifted her hand to his lips and kissed it. "I'll try to arrange something for the morning. I plan to keep growing this side of our business, and with your avid interest, we'd make a fine team."

"I agree. Will you text me when I can see it?"

"Nothing could get in my way."

Drew would have to get ahold of Harris to put surveillance on Oliver tonight. Drew would like to do it himself but couldn't. He didn't want any chance that Rossi would somehow track him to the port and blow his UC status. Drew would, however, be watching when the guy met with Teagan. Drew would make sure that the meeting with Teagan didn't happen in their warehouse but occurred in a public place.

Oliver went into full-blown date mode and kept complimenting Teagan.

Drew wished she would jerk her hand free. As if his wish came true, her phone rang from where she'd placed it face down on the table.

"Sorry. I usually don't take calls on a date, but I have a few prospects for a new job, and I don't want to miss them."

"No worries." He reached for his water glass, his attention remaining firmly attached to Teagan's every more.

She looked at the screen. "Yes. It's a call I have to take. Excuse me for a minute."

She stood and crossed the busy room to a quiet corner where Drew suspected she could still see Oliver but be out of earshot.

Teagan lifted her phone to her ear. "Kelsey, hi. Drew's listening in. So what's up?"

"I need you to come back here," Kelsey said.

Her raised tone set Drew's heart plummeting.

"What happened?" If Teagan was concerned, her tone didn't show it.

"I demonstrated the drone for our new intern when she arrived. I wanted to show her what a negative result looked like, so I did a sweep over the final grid area that I didn't look at with you. But what we found almost knocked me off my feet. So I finished searching the rest of the property."

Drew didn't like the sound of where this was going.

"What did you find?" Teagan's voice held a good measure of concern this time.

Kelsey cleared her throat. "Three additional graves, and they're arranged in a very suspicious pattern that you have to see for yourselves."

14

———

Light rain spit from the sky over Smiley's property, and Teagan grabbed a ball cap and windbreaker from her law enforcement go bag in her trunk. She'd told Oliver she had a business emergency, but flashed him a flirty smile and reminded him to call her about the antiquity. He was disappointed but agreed.

She shrugged the Clackamas County jacket over her dress and slipped into boots. She wound her hair into a ponytail and tugged it through the back of her cap. On the way to join Drew, who was just pulling down the drive, she passed Kelsey's van and two police vehicles. Drew parked behind a second Veritas van that Ainslie must have driven to the site. To maintain his cover and hers with Oliver, they'd departed the restaurant separately, taking different routes.

On the car ride, she'd called her lieutenant, and he agreed to get to the scene as soon as possible. Teagan didn't want to handle a multiple murder investigation without first notifying him. Not that she required his help, but he needed to know that things had escalated to serial murder as defined by the FBI. They declared it the unlawful killing of two or more victims by the same offender in separate events.

If the graves had been discovered before she'd left the force, she would be all over taking lead on such an investigation, but nothing was normal here. She was a member of the team only due to unusual circumstances.

Unusual and now very deadly circumstances.

Drew climbed out, settling a camo version of the Seattle Seahawks football team cap on his head. He looked amazing without a cap, but with one, he carried a dangerous and intense vibe. If they weren't at a multiple murder scene, and if he hadn't already smacked down her interest in him, she might comment on it.

Multiple murders. Serial murders. Wow! Those words made her shudder. Her job had really escalated to working a serial killer investigation. Unbelievable.

Under past circumstances, her department would call in the state and the FBI for assistance, but with a federal team already on the task force, she doubted that Harris would allow that to happen. It was a wait-and-see thing. Who would triumph and take charge? Gutierrez or Harris?

Drew tugged his cap lower. "Ready to get details from Kelsey?"

Teagan nodded.

"Then let's do this." Drew started toward the back of the property where the skull had been located.

Teagan hurried to match his longer strides and fell into step beside him.

He glanced at her. "Good job at lunch. You had Oliver eating out of your hands."

She resisted shuddering. "He's a slimy one. No wonder he's still single."

Drew cocked a sideways grin. "That's what I thought and figured you did too. After all, if you're wanting to date me, you have to have good taste."

She laughed, likely his intention to lighten a mood that hung like a dark shadow in the air as they approached Kelsey and the four graves she'd marked off with stakes and string. Her team had also placed tarps near the stakes and raised a portable white canopy over each grave to keep out the rain. Dirt mounded the tarp next to the original grave where no one worked at the moment. Kelsey had moved to the grave next to it. She knelt on the tarp and held a small trowel in her hand, lifting tiny scoops of soil and dumping the dirt onto an anchored tarp.

Her assistant and a young woman knelt by the other marked graves and were using similar trowels to dig out the soil. So far, they'd removed soil about a foot deep in each grave.

Moving between the two graves Kelsie wasn't working, Ainslie held her camera, the clicking sound as she snapped photos the only sound in the area. Her shoulder-length auburn hair was pulled back in a ponytail that swung as she stepped between graves. She wore a white Tyvek suit like the others, but she had a very advanced baby bump straining the zipper on her suit.

Teagan had heard that she and Grady were joining the other Veritas partners in having children. The only holdout on the partner list at this point was Maya and her husband, Hunter. They'd gotten married after the other five partners so maybe they would be announcing a pregnancy soon too.

Soft rain wetted Teagan's body, and she was glad to step under the canopy covering Kelsey. As glad as a person could be to step closer to an unmarked grave. Ainslie glanced up, and Teagan waved. She nodded in acknowledgment and went right back to work. She and Kelsey both had such grim jobs, but they didn't seem to let the horror bother them, and they were two of the sweetest people Teagan knew.

Drew stopped next to Teagan. "What do you know so far?"

Kelsey sat back. "I excavated the grave where we found the skull to about a foot deep. I'm calling it grave one. If you step over there, you can see I revealed various upper torso bones, and I can confirm there is indeed a body buried there. But then, as I told you, our intern arrived, and I took a break to show her the drone. That's when I discovered the other graves."

"And do we know if the remains in each location are human?" Drew asked.

Kelsey nodded. "That's why we started on each of the graves instead of finishing the first one. Confirming the presence of human remains will more quickly let you all know what we're looking at here. We should have enough excavated to give you more details soon."

"You sound confident that you won't have to dig very deep," Teagan said.

Kelsey's eyes narrowed. "Experience tells me that most clandestine graves are shallow."

"Why's that?" Teagan asked.

She sat back and laid down her trowel. "First, digging in our Willamette Valley clay soil is hard work and the person digging gets tired. But then, killers are also eager to get their victims buried before they're discovered, so they clear a spot just deep enough to cover the body. They don't realize that shallow graves like this are often scavenged by predators and that leads to discovery."

"Makes sense," Drew said. "So how do we proceed from here?"

"We keep digging, but I also took the liberty of calling Sierra Rice, our trace evidence expert, to process the area, the house, and the shed. She's on her way."

"That's great, thanks," Teagan said.

Drew frowned. "I appreciate the expertise, but we'll have to figure who will pay for all of this."

Kelsey waved a hand. "No worries. We'll work it out. If neither of your agencies can pay our going rate, we'll write off the balance due."

"No offense," Drew said. "We're grateful for sure, but seems like a bad way to run a business."

Kelsey took a long breath. "We're running a business, yes, and we all like to get our salaries to pay our bills. But sometimes finding a killer and restoring the dignity of their victims so casually discarded like this trumps everything else."

Teagan's respect for Kelsey grew exponentially. "I'll do my best to get my LT on board with at least some payment."

Kelsey gave a tight smile and gestured at the grave in front of her that ran perpendicular to the first grave. "This is grave two. My assistant is working number three and our intern number four. We've already determined that graves three and four appear to be the last ones dug and these victims retained enough flesh that I can tell they are both males. Due to the remaining flesh, I have called in the ME. She will likely take charge of those bodies for autopsy."

"Please tell me it's Dr. Albertson," Teagan said.

"It is." Kelsey rested a hand on her knee. "I take it you know her."

"I do. She's great to work with. Very law enforcement friendly."

"Yes, and willing to come right away." Kelsey ripped off her gloves. "Ainslie is trying to keep up with all the photos as we progress, but I've had to start taking my own shots while she shoots the other two. This is slowing me down, and I don't have as many details for you as I would normally have before calling. But I wanted you to take a look at the drone view of the area. I know you'll find it interesting."

"Can we see it now?" Drew asked.

"Of course." Kelsey stood to take an iPad from her nearby backpack. "I shot this video after we marked the corners of the graves and before we erected the canopies."

She started the footage playing. The drone rose into the sky and hovered over the four graves.

Teagan peered at the screen. "They're laid out to form the shape of a cross."

Drew looked at her. "I wonder if that's significant or simply where the killer decided to bury the victims."

"I think the killer is really the only one who can answer that, but they seem to be too precisely placed for coincidence," Kelsey said. "Maybe religion has a part in this murder."

Drew glanced at Teagan, telling her in unspoken words that they would wait to discuss this new development until they were alone.

"Like I said," Kelsey put the iPad away, "we should have more details soon. You might want to be here for that."

"We do," Drew said. "We'll get out of your way so you can get back to work."

"Thank you. I'll let you know the minute we have information to share." Kelsey slipped on a fresh pair of gloves and dropped down to the tarp.

Drew stepped to a box of booties and gloves that Kelsey had placed near the graves. He put on a pair of each and moved to the open area in the center of the graves that formed the middle of the cross.

He looked at Teagan. "Once Kelsey has more to go on, I'll ask Harris to run a missing person's report."

"Hopefully these victims aren't like Smiley and have been reported missing."

"Most missing people are reported, so odds are likely in our favor here." He knelt in the middle area of the cross and gently brushed crumbly rust-colored leaves out of the center.

Teagan put on booties and gloves to join him. "Should we be touching anything before Sierra gets here?"

He stared down at his feet. Frowned. "I can't stand around and do nothing. Not with four people dead. We'll document everything as we go."

Teagan squatted next to him. "You think we'll find evidence here after all these years?"

"Odds aren't good for Smiley, but if the victims aren't skeletonized, they might not have been here long." He continued to gently move the leaves.

She started helping him, carefully setting leaves aside as she looked for anything out of the ordinary. Bricks pressed into the soil came into view. She stopped and sat back. "Look at this."

Drew scooted closer his eyes lighting up. "Let's keep clearing this space."

He moved faster now. His hands carefully sliding over the bricks until they'd revealed the entire area. He looked at Teagan. "Bricks form a circle. Or at least part of a circle."

Four arcs of bricks were arranged in a circular shape, but space had been left between them. It was as if something belonged in the open spaces but wasn't added or had gone missing.

He rubbed in the dirt near the middle of the circle. "What's this?"

He brushed harder to reveal a two-inch-wide strip of black steel. He kept brushing dirt, tracking the steel to the inside edges of the circle.

"Not sure what this means." He stood. "I can't have any

pictures on my phone. Can you snap a few pics to document this before we move on?"

She got out her phone, and he scooted out of the way. The sound on her phone was turned on, and her clicks with each picture fought with Ainslie's to disturb the peace.

Teagan's heart started beating harder, but she remained in place and continued shooting pictures until she'd covered the entire area. She lowered her phone. "Something obviously belongs where the spaces are. We should clear the area in every direction between the graves. Maybe we'll see something that's supposed to intersect with them."

"Sounds good."

"Just don't disturb anything within my boundaries or on the tarps," Kelsey warned without looking at them.

"We won't," Drew assured her.

"I'll go this way, you go that way." Teagan pointed in the two directions and started moving leaves horizontally from the circle opening. She brushed aside the leaves, pine needles and twigs, uncovering nothing but clay soil. She moved toward the horizontal grave ahead of her, scraping aside the tree litter and debris. She reached it without locating any leads. She scooted back to the center. "Anything?"

Drew shook his head. "Let's try the vertical spaces."

He started moving down the shape, and she headed upward. Two feet in, she discovered the metal piece in the circle continued. Her heart rate kicked into gear as she cleared it all the way to inside the circle. "I've got something here."

"Me too. Metal plate continues outside the circle."

She kept clearing until what looked like a large hilt to a sword became obvious. "What do you have?"

"Looks like a tip of a very rudimentary spear or sword."

"It's a sword." She stood to study the area she'd revealed. "I have the hilt on the top."

He joined her, staring at the ground. "So we have a circle with a sword going through it. Mean anything to you?"

Teagan tried to place it in context with their investigation but drew a blank. "Not at all."

Drew turned to Kelsey. "Can you get that drone in the air again and get a video of the area we cleared? Even with the graves covered by the canopies, it should still give us a better view of what we're looking at here."

"Absolutely." Clutching her back, Kelsey stood and picked her way carefully through the area to the storage box holding the drone.

"This could be it." Teagan looked at Drew. "The lead we need to solve these murders."

"Could be," he said, his gaze shifting to Kelsey. "But what in the world does a sword in a circle have to do with Smiley or Rossi?"

"Let's sit in my car," Drew said, but didn't wait for Teagan to agree before he started hoofing it across the property, his mind filled with their discovery. Kelsey had filmed the video of the sword and circle and forwarded it to Teagan's phone. Then Kelsey shooed them out of her way, but urged them to stay close as she'd revealed more of the skull in grave number two before they'd interrupted her to shoot the video.

He climbed behind the wheel, and Teagan joined him inside.

He faced her. "You want some heat to chase out the damp chill?"

"I'm good, but feel free to turn it on if you want."

He cranked the engine and pumped the heat. He wasn't overly cold, but he figured she could be, and she didn't want to be considered a prima donna. She would've learned early on in law enforcement that she had to go out of her way not to appear soft around her male co-workers. They needed to know that she had their backs, and she would've made sure not to even hint at needing special treatment because she was a woman.

He took off his cap to scratch his head. "The sword and circle could be a religious thing, I suppose. I know the Contis go to mass every week at St Michael's Catholic Church in Portland. It was originally founded by Italians, so maybe their family has always attended there. Rossi could be a member too, for all I know."

"I'll ask Nick to look into it. I'll send the pictures and video for him to investigate too." She took out her phone.

She concentrated on her screen, the light cutting though the shadows of the hazy day. The tip of her tongue poked out the left side of her mouth, and she looked as adorable as a cute puppy. He felt a chill inside from finding the graves, circle, and sword that the heater would never warm, but seeing her adorable look helped. And seeing her dangly earrings with tiny Christmas tree lights reminded him of the real Christmas and to trust God in this and every situation.

"There." She tapped the screen and looked up. "Sent."

"I wish everyone in law enforcement could afford Nick's services."

"He would be stretched way too thin, and then you'd have the same problems of delays as you already face."

"Yeah, it's just." He shrugged. "Like so many professions right now, law enforcement is struggling to find qualified workers."

"Makes me feel guilty that I left, but I had no choice after Thomas was murdered. As the oldest, I was the most likely one to take over the company. Not that Londyn is much younger. But she loves being a detective, and I didn't love it as much."

Her phone sounded a sharp ding. "It's Nick. He's on it."

Drew nodded. "We can't leave this up to him. We have to try to figure it out too. We have four graves. A sword. A circle. Maybe the burial has something to do with the Contis' and Rossi's Italian background."

She swiveled to face Drew. "Italy's still mostly Catholic, right? So wouldn't funerals be the same as in the States?"

"Pretty much." Memories from his childhood came back in vivid clarity. "When I lived there as a kid, I saw a lot of funerals. Or at least I saw the mourners walking behind the caskets to the grave site. Which, by the way, are nothing like ours."

"How so?"

He let his mind wander back to the first day he'd trailed mourners at a distance with his buddy Jamie. "The country has a space issue, so when a person dies, they aren't embalmed. Helps the body decompose faster. They're laid to rest in the family mausoleum and stay there for seven to ten years. Then their casket is opened, and if their bodies are sufficiently decayed, their bones are transferred into a small bone box and placed in a smaller porthole."

"Wait, what?" She gaped at him, her long lashes blinking fast. "They take the bones out of the casket and put them in a smaller place? Really?"

He nodded. "I know it sounds odd, but it's part of their culture."

"You mentioned being decayed enough." She shuddered. "What if they haven't?"

"The coffin is resealed, and they're left for another three to five years. The process is then repeated, and a small service is held for the family at each instance."

Teagan shook her head. "Sounds so odd. Can you see how that has anything to do with our situation?"

"Not really," he said.

She pursed her lips. "What if the circle has to do with the antiquities?"

"We'll have to check that out for sure." He looked out over the field, thinking of their next move. "Gutierrez should be here soon. After we meet with him, we should go to dinner to further cement our dating relationship for the Contis. I'm not going to let them or Rossi get away with murder."

Her eyes widened. "Food is one of the last things I want to think about, but I can fake it."

A movement ahead caught his attention, but it was only Ainslie lumbering toward her van. He couldn't imagine doing her job, and doing it while so pregnant? That took dedication. Would Teagan work while pregnant or afterwards?

So much he didn't know about her, but he wanted to learn more.

He turned back to her. "After dinner, we'll have time to look into the circle and cross before my meet-up with Rossi. We could search the internet at your place. If the Contis are watching me, they'll just think you invited me in. That is, if it's okay with you. You might not want me around your family, and I totally get that."

"We'll have to dodge some questions from whoever's home, but I'm fine with it."

"Great." He wanted to search for leads, but he also liked the idea of spending time with Teagan at her house. Even if it meant he had to try not to go off on personal tangents all the time.

Her phone chimed. "Text is from Kelsey. She's ready to see us."

"Don't have to tell me twice." Drew turned off the engine and climbed out of his vehicle. He stood near the hood in the cool breeze and soft mist to wait for Teagan. The air smelled of fresh rain, belying the ugly site waiting for him. For them.

He took a long look at her to assess her mood. "Ready for this?"

She peered deep into his eyes. "Is anyone ever ready to see man's inhumanity to man?"

"No." The deep anguish in her eyes cut into his heart, and he had to look away. He wanted to absorb all of her pain somehow. Take it on and set her free. Sadly, he had room for it. He was less distressed than he might've been a year ago. Sure, he hadn't seen men killed in his year UC, but he'd seen the underbelly of society flourishing.

Had it left him too jaded to be shocked by anything? Even four potential murders? A serial killer?

God help me if it has.

Fearing for his mental health, he stormed toward the graves, trying to eliminate his other question. Had he also become too jaded to have a normal relationship with another person if he chose to do so? A relationship with a good, decent, and strong woman like Teagan?

His gut ached, and he fired a tight look at Kelsey that fairly demanded an update. *Stop.* She was doing a great job, and he was taking his own fears out on her. He softened his gaze. "What did you find?"

"We have another set of remains for sure." She pointed at a fully revealed skull. "I'm reasonably certain it's another male, so we are looking at four males. And I should have more information like race, age, and stature soon."

"Any way you can estimate the time of death for a skeleton like this?" he asked, keeping his tone controlled.

"I can, and with newer tests available, the best choice will be to use his teeth."

"Teeth?" Teagan blinked a few times. "Really?"

Kelsey nodded. "I can use aspartic acid racemization analysis of tooth crown dentin and radiocarbon dating of enamel to determine many things like date of birth, age of deceased, nutrition, diet, and even date of death."

"Okay, I'm pretending I understand all of that." Teagan gave a nervous chuckle.

"Sorry." Kelsey wrinkled her nose. "I sometimes get wrapped up in forensic speak. But teeth are so fascinating. Maybe this will help. Twice a year tiny, distinct fibers anchor teeth to the gums. Depending on where you live, a bright line is laid in the spring or summer and a dark line in the fall or winter. I can count the bands and use the color and width of the outermost ring to estimate the person's age at death. It also narrows the time of death window too."

"Fascinating." He cast an approving look Kelsey's direction. "I can't thank you enough for helping with this investigation. We might not get such detailed information if someone else was doing the recovery."

"You definitely wouldn't," Teagan said.

Kelsey offered a weak smile. "We try to stay on the cutting edge and are also often asked to test potential forensic breakthroughs."

Drew might be pushing it, but he had to ask. "Any way to tell if this could be our missing guy, Smiley?"

"Not at the moment. DNA is the best way to confirm ID. I *can* say that the skull is larger than a typical female, and the eye sockets have a slightly blunter surface, which is common in a male and how I made my early determination." Kelsey brushed the back of her hand over her forehead, leaving a smear of dirt behind. "On average, males also have greater muscle development and more rugged muscle attachments. This skull says a lot already, but the best way to confirm gender is by looking at the pelvic bones, which are obviously not revealed yet."

"Then we'll wait for more," Drew said.

"Now that you know the victims are all males, I wouldn't wait for the other details if I were you. We'll be at it all day and into the night before we unearth additional details. I can call or text you with any definitive information once I have it."

"Is there anything we can do to help?" Teagan asked.

Kelsey looked at the sky. "Actually, there is. You could put up lights for us. That'll let all of us continue to excavate as late as needed."

"Of course," Drew said. "Just point us to them."

"In the back of my van. You won't miss them. We have our own generator for once it gets dark."

"You should eat too," Teagan said. "Especially with you and Ainslie being pregnant."

"We'll go get some food," Drew said. "Put some sandwiches and drinks in a cooler for later for you and your workers."

"That would be perfect." Kelsey aimed a bright smile at Drew. "You're so thoughtful."

Heat raced up his neck to his face under her praise. "We'll get to the lights."

Kelsey grinned. "I always think it's so cute when big strapping law enforcement guys like you get embarrassed over a simple compliment."

The heat intensified, and he wanted to bolt but planted his feet instead.

Teagan nodded. "I saw it often on the job."

Kelsey cocked her head. "I heard you'd retired, so what's with you being back on the force?"

"Special assignment for this one investigation."

"Then it must be an important one."

Drew held his breath, hoping she wouldn't give away any details.

"Let's say time is of the essence," Teagan said, and Drew let out his breath.

Kelsey's head bobbed in a serious nod. "Then I'll quit jabbering and get to helping you learn the identity of these four unfortunate victims."

15

After the day they'd had, Drew really didn't want to be in a restaurant. He wanted to chill at Teagan's house, maybe in front of the fire, and just *be*. Something he hadn't done in a very long time. Maybe hadn't done since his dad died. He'd immediately taken over caring for his mother, and he still felt responsible for her. Would that ever go away? No. She needed him, and he needed her.

But he would do his job. He'd done a lot of UC things he didn't want to do, and he only had a short time left as Dylan Crane. At least the meal came with the chance to sit across a secluded table in a comfy booth from Teagan in his favorite Chinese restaurant. Even if she was here because of the op and not because he'd legitimately asked her out.

A teenage server with a serious case of acne and slicked back hair the color of carrots dropped off their spring roll appetizers. He set a plate in front of Teagan, and she flashed him a smile. He offered a flustered grin in return, then hurriedly dropped Drew's plate and fled.

Great. She was flirting with a teenager. Okay, fine—not flirting—just being kind. Drew was jealous. Despite his earlier objection he'd made about dating, he'd fallen for her. How could he fall for her so fast and hard?

Because she was everything he ever wanted in a woman and more. Or at least it seemed like it, based on what he knew about her.

She shifted in her chair and nudged her holster to the side under her soft-looking suit jacket in a warm lime green that she'd changed into before dinner. Another thing he liked. A woman who could handle a gun was his kind of woman. Very appealing.

She dipped a spring roll in sweet and sour sauce. "I wish Nick would get back to us."

"About the sword and circle?" he asked.

"Mostly that, but about anything, actually. I know it'll take Kelsey some time to get the remains back to her bone lab to analyze, and Dr. Albertson won't autopsy the other two bodies until tomorrow. So we're really at a standstill on learning the victim's identities."

He took a long sip of his soda. "I'm hoping tonight's meeting will reveal something."

"Like what?"

He shrugged. "It'll be my first foray into the Conti's drug smuggling, and I hope it'll shed light on the antiquities."

"You really think Rossi is behind both?" She chomped off a crunchy bite of the spring roll.

He grabbed one too and plunged the end into the sweet sauce. "I think the brothers use the same shipping containers and routes for both. The US might not get most of its heroin from Iran anymore, but we still import a lot, and the robbing of these sites is done by terrorists to fund their efforts. Same with the drugs. I suspect it's the same people behind both."

"Stop one and you stop the other."

"Exactly."

They fell silent and finished their appetizers. The waiter arrived with a steaming plate of mushroom chicken for Teagan and spicy General Tso's chicken for Drew. The guy quickly backed away.

Drew spooned a big helping of the crispy chicken covered in sauce onto his plate. "Want to share entrees?"

"I was hoping you would ask." She looked at him. "Would save me from grabbing your food without permission."

"You planned a sneak attack, huh?" He laughed, and it felt good.

"Hey, we need to look like we're dating for real, and that's what I would do when I felt comfortable with the person I'm dating."

"Was it a plan to make us look good to any observer or because you feel comfortable with me?"

"Comfortable." She spooned a large chunk of his crispy chicken and plopped it on her plate next to a giant mushroom. She picked up her chopsticks and broke them apart. "What I'm not comfortable with are these things, so don't judge me."

"I wouldn't think of it." He grabbed his own sticks, separated them, and pinched a large chunk of chicken.

She pointed at his hands. "I see you're a pro with them."

"I don't cook for myself often. I'm a frequent flyer here."

"I figured that out when they greeted you at the door." She grabbed that big mushroom. "I always make time to cook. It's my way to relax. Problem is, then I have to find time to work off all the calories."

He let his gaze rove over her. "Looks like you're doing a fine job of it."

Her face turned crimson.

He retrieved a crispy chunk of chicken, the sauce dripping. "That embarrasses you?"

She set down her chopsticks and rested her hands on the table next to her plate. "I've never been good at accepting compliments. It's odd. I'm very outspoken. Some would say pushy and a leap-before-I-look kind of person. But a compliment leaves me tongue-tied."

"I'll have to remember that." He shoved the chicken into his mouth and had to fight not to sneeze at the extreme spice level he'd ordered.

"And what?" Humor flickered in her eyes. "Use it to shut me up when needed?"

"Could be." He laughed again.

She joined in. Gone were his misgivings about the day, replaced with a genuine peace and joy in their meal together. He dug into his food with gusto, and so did she.

Her phone rang from where she'd placed it on the table. "It's Kelsey."

Teagan looked around. "Place isn't too crowded and we should be fine to put her on speaker." Teagan tapped her phone and set it in the middle of the table. "Go ahead, Kelsey. It's on speaker, and Drew is here."

"Sorry to disturb, but I'm back at my lab and have some findings to share. I thought it would be good if you could come by for a face-to-face update."

"Now?" Drew asked, surprised the woman was still working after her long day.

"Would that be a problem?"

Teagan glanced at Drew, and he gave her a thumbs up. "We're finishing dinner and will be right over."

"I'll tell our night guard to expect you." Kelsey ended the call.

Teagan took her phone back and looked at Drew. "What say we get this to go? My appetite's gone, and I can hardly wait to know what she found."

Gone was the fun. The date-like atmosphere. The peace.

But Drew didn't mind. Not if heading out to the Veritas Center brought them one step closer to finding a serial killer.

$\sim$

Teagan stared out of the front window from the passenger seat in Drew's car. She'd been to the Veritas Center before, but never at night, and it was a sight to behold. The two towers connected at the base with a lobby and at the top with a skybridge. Lights glowed inside and sparkled into the dark night.

"Wow," Drew said. "This place isn't at all like I expected. Doesn't look like a lab in the least."

"Looks pretty fancy, but it's a real working lab. Maya Lane inherited the building from her grandfather. She's one of the partners. The right tower is all condos and many of the partners live there as do the owners of Nighthawk Security. She had the other tower built out in labs and Nighthawk has offices on the top floor."

"Must've cost a pretty penny to do."

"They funded it through DNA work for private individuals. It still helps pay for pro bono work."

"Which we are benefitting from." He parked in an empty space by the front door. "This visit will give me the lay of the land, so when I come here with drugs from my meet tonight, their guard will recognize me."

They got out and the cold moisture in the air seeped into her pores making the brightly lit building seem more appealing. They started for the main entrance together. A short, stocky guard with a gray buzz cut met them at the door. His nametag read *Pete Vincent*.

"Welcome." He offered a friendly smile. "Dr. Dunbar told me to expect you. Also heard from Dr. Lane that you'll be joining us again later tonight. I'll need to see some ID, and I can get you registered."

Drew paused for a moment, looking unsure for the first time since Teagan had known him. "Sorry, no ID."

"I can vouch for him," Teagan said quickly. She should've remembered the tight security at the lab, and she knew Drew didn't carry his real ID while undercover. He couldn't very well display his Dylan Crane driver's license for Pete.

"No can do, Ms. Steele." Pete sounded honestly apologetic. "Kelsey will have to be the one to vouch for you. Wait here."

They were left standing outside in the covered area as Pete headed in to the front desk to make the call.

Teagan gave Drew an apologetic look. "I should've told you about the security here. With all the law enforcement work they do, they take security of evidence very seriously. Pete's a former patrol officer, so he's a stickler for procedure."

"No worries. Kelsey will take care of it, and we'll get in to talk to her." He tapped his foot and stared through the glass door until Kelsey entered the lobby through the back door

"I'll vouch for them both, Pete," she called out. "Let them in."

Pete stepped back. "Come on over to the desk, and we'll get your visitor passes issued."

They trailed him to the reception desk, where they filled out a form on an iPad, and Pete issued security passes clipped on lanyards. Teagan hung hers around her neck and took off after Kelsey, who was moving at a much faster clip than that morning. She led them to a stairwell and jogged down as if she'd taken this route many times per day.

At the end of a brightly lit hallway, she pressed her

fingers onto a keypad outside a door labeled *Osteology Unit*, and the door snapped open.

A display of labeled animal bones filled the main wall ahead. That was upsetting enough, but when Teagan caught sight of the human skeleton filling one of the long stainless steel tables, her dinner threatened to come up.

Kelsey waved a hand at the bones. "Victim from the first grave."

Drew didn't seem fazed but went closer to the table and turned to look around the clinically clean room. "No offense, but your lab is smaller than I thought it would be."

"No offense taken. This is only my dry lab." She jerked a thumb over her shoulder. "My wet lab is on the other side of the glass door."

She pointed at a glass-and-metal door sealed tight. "You can look inside but don't open the door. You'll release a very unpleasant odor if you do."

Teagan might be feeling queasy, but she had to take a look in the other room. The larger space held a pair of the same metal tables but were placed against the wall and connected to large stainless sinks. On the other wall, she spotted a huge burner and large pots. Another wall held tools. Some she recognized, like trowels, others she didn't.

She looked back at Kelsey. "I can only imagine why you need a wet lab."

"For the most obnoxious part of the job unless you don't consider maggots obnoxious." Kelsey chuckled.

"I do. Especially at a murder scene." Drew shuddered.

"So what do you do in there?" Teagan asked, half afraid to know the answer.

"The remains almost always must be macerated or boiled to remove flesh and connective tissue clinging to the bones so we can better examine them." She lifted a hand. "The smell is awful, which is why we have an industrial air handling system installed. We're currently cleaning the bones for the male found in grave two."

Teagan couldn't really connect this delicate and petite woman to such a gruesome job, but as a law enforcement officer, Teagan had learned people weren't always what they appeared to be.

"And what are the tools used for?" Teagan asked.

"For recovering remains like we did today. We sterilize them in the wet lab as well."

Drew tilted his head. "You sterilize digging tools?"

Kelsey nodded. "Like any other crime scene, we don't want to contaminate it with soil or debris from a past scene."

"Of course," Drew said. "Guess I don't think of digging in dirt as something that could cause contamination."

"Most people don't." She nodded at the skeleton. "I believe this is the man, Smiley, who you're looking for. Nothing official, mind you, but I have given a DNA sample to Emory for all four victims. Sierra has taken a toothbrush from Smiley's home for comparison. The process will take twenty-four hours. I'll have my assistant try to hunt down his dental records first thing in the morning."

"But you're positive it's a male now?" Teagan asked.

"Most definitely. I estimate he was thirty-seven when he died, and he died in 2016. He was also five-foot-nine and Caucasian."

"All of which fits Smiley," Drew said. "No ID with the body, then?"

"We recovered a wallet, but the driver's license was too badly degraded to make out and no other cards. Sierra's people are working on the license, but she said not to hold out any hope for improvement. Victim two didn't have a wallet or any ID." Kelsey leaned against the table. "We should have bones ready to review for this victim in the morning."

"And the persons in graves three and four?" Teagan asked. "Did Dr. Albertson take control of those bodies?"

"Yes. She agreed that the victims retained enough flesh and internal organs for a full autopsy. She will conduct them in the morning." Kelsey dug in her pocket and pulled out a business card. "She gave me this to have you call her regarding the schedule."

Drew took the card. "Is this why you wanted us to stop by?"

"No. I wanted you to see this." She pushed off the table to pick up one of Smiley's ribs and display it. "As you can see, there are sharp cuts to this bone." She ran her fingers over gouges then set down the rib and lifted two sections of the middle part of the spine and pointed at a deep notch in the bone. "An even deeper corresponding cut in the thoracic spine."

Teagan leaned in closer. "And that tells you what?"

Kelsey set down the sections of the spine and went to the desk in the corner where she removed a long sword. "Grady Houston, our weapons expert, provided this." She held the blade parallel to the floor. "Several of the rib cuts show the victim had been slashed across his chest at this angle. The injuries are consistent with a sword of this size."

"His cause of death?" Drew asked.

"No. Those were just superficial strikes." Kelsey held out the sword to Drew and took a bigger bone from the chest area. "The sternum has a similar slash mark, but it's also fractured near his heart."

Drew stared at the sword in his hands. "Which means what?"

Kelsey tapped the table. "This man was stabbed in the heart with a blade of similar size to the one you're holding."

"A sword fight. Or at least an attack." Drew turned the

metal in his hand and studied it. "Gives new meaning to the sword we found in the middle of the circle."

"Symbolically," Kelsey said. "But that one is much too large to be the murder weapon."

"I didn't see a sword at Smiley's place," Teagan said. "But then I wouldn't expect to find the murder weapon left behind."

"That would be odd," Kelsey said. "Sierra also didn't locate any weapon that could account for these injuries."

"Do you know if she located anything of interest?" Teagan asked.

"Not that she told me, but when I left the scene, she was still working inside the house." Kelsey set down the bone. "She could be back and still in her lab tonight if you want me to check."

"Would you?" Teagan asked.

"Of course." Kelsey went to the desk in the corner. She grabbed the handset for the desk phone and punched a button. "Oh good. You're still at work. Drew and Teagan are here. Do you have anything that you want to share with them?"

Kelsey tapped her finger on the desk and tilted her head. "Oh, okay. I'll bring them right up."

"She find something?" Drew asked, sounding desperate for a lead.

Kelsey's eyes glinted in the overhead light. "She did indeed, and she's glad you're here to tell you about it."

16

Drew looked in the glass windows as Kelsey escorted them to the door for Sierra Rice's trace evidence lab on the front half of the fourth floor. She pressed her fingers on the wall-mounted reader, and the door popped open with a decisive snap. She stepped back.

Drew smiled at Kelsey. "Thanks for the escort."

"No worries. It's good to get out of the basement." She chuckled. "Actually, I like working down there. It's quiet. No one wants to come down because of what I do, and they don't happen to pass by. Limits my interruptions."

This woman had so many layers, Drew doubted anyone could ever fully uncover them all. "You don't seem the type who likes to avoid people."

"Oh, I don't. But with two kids and another on the way, I have to make every minute of my workday count. So to that end, I'll say goodnight." She mocked a bow and took off.

Drew held the door for Teagan. "I suppose you've been to this lab before."

She nodded. "Quite the place. Top-notch equipment and experts just like all the other labs here."

He stopped inside the door to take a good look at the

room. Machines that he couldn't put a name to ringed the walls, and the center of the room held stainless steel tables that matched the ones in Kelsey's lab.

Sierra stood behind the last table that she'd covered with white paper. She still had her hair in a ponytail from when he'd met her at the crime scene, but strands had fallen out since he'd talked to her at Smiley's place. Instead of a protective suit, she wore a pristine white lab coat.

She glanced up and waved them over. "Glad you're here. I don't have a lot to discuss, but there are two things I want to review with you."

Teagan hurried to the table, and Drew followed. For once, his surroundings captured his interest over watching her walk.

Sierra perched on a stool. "The first bit of news is what I didn't find. No blood or even a trace of blood in the house or shed."

"None of these victims were killed inside?" Drew took a seat on a stool next to Teagan on the other side of the table. "Assuming the other three were killed in a manner that involved loss of blood."

"Yes, assuming that." Sierra rested her gloved hands on the table. "There weren't any other postmortem body fluids either, so if they *were* killed inside by a non-bloodletting method, they were immediately removed from the house."

"What about outside on the property?" Teagan shifted on the stool, moving closer to Drew, and he caught her sweet scent of vanilla over the lab's antiseptic smell.

"That I can't rule out. My team and I didn't locate any pools of blood, but depending on how much time has passed since these victims were murdered, that wouldn't be unusual. Rain and weather will assimilate the blood into the ground."

Sierra paused and took a long breath. "Blood is a good

source of nitrogen. It's why gardeners use blood meal for fertilizer. There could be areas in the landscape that are flourishing from it, but the property is so large we would need a massive team to test it all. If we'd gotten to the site sooner, we would likely have found scavengers or flies that would lead us to the bloody areas if the murders had occurred on site."

Very much in agreement with what Kelsey had told them about the nitrogen.

"Is it wrong to be glad I don't do your job?" Teagan gave a nervous laugh.

"Not at all." Sierra smiled. "My job isn't often glamorous, but I love it. Of course if you find other evidence to suggest the victims were murdered on the property, we can try to find samples of blood in the soil."

Drew didn't know how that might happen, but he was thankful for her offer. "We'll let you know."

Sierra gave a sharp nod. "Did Kelsey tell you the wallet was a bust on victim one?"

"She did," Drew said.

"I have my best person trying to enhance the driver's license enough to get any information, but don't expect miracles."

"Do you find it odd that he didn't have other ID?" Drew asked.

"Not really. A lot of people deal only in cash and some are paranoid about identity theft so they carry very little that can ID them. Then people involved in criminal activities often leave their ID home. And then some people don't carry cards because they use their phones to pay. And before you ask, no phones located with the bodies."

Drew nodded. "From what we know about victim one, I could see him being a cash-only person. And we don't know enough on victim two to even speculate."

"If it helps, victim two was wearing pricey Italian cycling gear and shoes," Sierra said. "This guy wasn't penniless by any means."

"A cycler, huh?" Drew looked at Teagan to see if this news connected with something in her brain, but she shrugged.

"I also wanted to mention that my team will be comparing the soil on the shovel we found in the shed with the soil Kelsey unearthed at the graves," Sierra said. "By visual analysis alone, I suspect this is the tool used to dig the graves. I lifted prints from the shovel handle, but only from one person. They match many of the prints lifted in Smiley's house, so I suspect they belong to him and not the person who dug the grave."

Drew didn't see how this would help find the killer but investigating a murder was like putting together a jigsaw puzzle. At first, a piece didn't seem to fit, but after putting a few other pieces in place, it suddenly fit to create a clear picture.

"Was this the other reason you wanted to see us?" he asked.

Sierra shook her head, those strands of hair moving. "I found a flash drive in an air vent. A small one that could've dropped from the killer's pocket or belonged to Smiley. I gave it to Nick, who quickly imaged the drive for prosecution purposes and made a copy of the contents for me."

Now they were getting somewhere. "What was on it?"

"Let me show you." Sierra stood and stripped off her gloves. "We can use the computer on my desk, and I'll text Nick to join us so he can answer any questions."

"Do you guys ever sleep?" Drew asked.

"No, we're vampires." Sierra laughed and dumped her gloves in a biohazard bin. "Some of us get more shuteye than others. But Nick always works this late, and his lab is right below here so he'll probably come up."

She crossed the space to a neat desk in the corner and settled into a black ergonomic chair. She sent a text then woke her computer, the monitor displaying a video file. "This is the only file on the drive. It could lend credence to Smiley having died on his property."

She clicked play.

"No. No." Smiley faced the camera in his living room, his face contorted in fear as he backed away. The camera caught the tip of a shiny silver sword pointed in his direction. "Let me try again. I'll do better this time. Honest."

"Run for your life," the person filming the scene said in an altered voice. "I'm right behind you."

The video went dark. A shiver ran over Drew's body.

Teagan wrapped her arms around her stomach. "That's awful."

Drew agreed, but he would watch it over and over again to find a solid lead. "Run it one more time."

Sierra clicked play, but the clip lasted for only thirty-six seconds and there was nothing obvious other than the sword.

Drew gritted his teeth and tried to wrap his head around what it must've been like to be Smiley, the other man waving a large sword at him and telling him to run for his life. Fleeing outside. Being tracked. Horrific. "He was hunted like an animal."

Sierra looked up, her expression troubled. "Looks like it."

Teagan's hands were clutched in tight balls on the table. "This helps confirm Kelsey's finding that Smiley was likely killed with a sword. Were there prints on the flash drive that can help in the investigation?"

Sierra shook her head. "Which is why I think the killer wore gloves and dropped it."

"Dropped it," Drew said. "But why wouldn't he come back for it?"

Sierra leaned back and crossed her leg. "He might have for all we know and couldn't find it. Like I said, we located it wedged in a floor vent. Maybe he didn't think to lift the vent like we did. He might've thought the video couldn't incriminate him."

The door clicked open, and Nick strode in. Drew gave the guy who'd been helping them for days a thorough once over. He didn't look like the computer geek that Drew had expected. The man was built, around six feet tall, and had brown hair and a matching close-cut beard. He strode across the room.

"Good to see you again, Teagan." He smiled at her but thrust out his hand to Drew. "Nick Thorn."

"Drew Collier. ICE." He shook hands. "Thanks for joining us."

"I wish I had additional updates on the searches I'm running for you but nothing yet. We'll keep them running, and we're bound to turn something up." He leaned against the table behind him and crossed his feet at the ankles. "I added the local Catholic church and the circle and sword to my search, but nothing relevant on either of them yet."

"Thanks for all your help." Teagan cast a thankful look at Nick. "We appreciate you taking this on so quickly, and your information has been instrumental to get us to where we are in the investigation."

Nick planted his hands on the table behind him. "Looks like it's a good thing we got started when we did. What with four victims and all."

"We were looking at the video found at the crime scene,"

Drew said. "I can't see how it'll help yet. Unless we can unscramble the voice."

"I can improve the quality some, but it won't clean up enough to use for voice recognition." Nick moved his hands to rest on his hips. "But I did recover metadata on the file. I know it was shot on an iPhone on August 18, 2016 at 8:07 p.m."

"Could fit Smiley's time of death but otherwise, how will it help?" Drew asked. "The killer could very well have gotten a new phone by now."

"You're probably right," Nick said. "But they could still have the old one and not use it."

"I keep at least the last model when I upgrade," Teagan said.

"Me too," Sierra said. "And I know from our forensic property searches that it's not uncommon to find old phones stashed in a drawer or cupboard."

"Yeah." Nick groaned. "I waste a whole lot of time imaging them only to find nothing to help."

"Question," Teagan said. "If the video was found on a flash drive, how did that come from a phone?"

"You just need the right kind of connector for the phone to access a flash drive. Or the suspect could've connected to his computer to move it to a drive, though I didn't see that transfer protocol in the file."

"No computer in the house." Sierra leaned back. "But he could've brought a laptop with him or Smiley's computer was removed after he died."

"Were these adapters available when he was killed?" Drew asked.

"Yeah," Nick said. "They were around back then."

Drew really wished he could get excited about this lead, but so far he didn't see how it helped. "Still, it's a long shot at best that we find this phone."

"Agreed," Nick said. "If you do find it, I have another new tool that could help."

"What is it?" Teagan sounded far more eager than Drew felt.

Nick pushed off the table and planted his feet. "Let me explain. If I get too much into technobabble let me know, and I'll dumb it down." He chuckled. "So every camera has embedded sensors. Noise is produced in these sensors that's invisible to the naked eye. Not noise as in irritating sound like you think of as noise, but imperfections. This noise or these imperfections are unique to the camera. You with me so far?"

"Yep," Drew said, though he really didn't understand how this noise could be visualized.

"Good." Nick gave a tight smile. "The next part I know you'll understand. These imperfections are as unique as specific grooves on a fired bullet. As you know, these grooves allow the bullet to be matched to the gun that fired it. In a similar way, I can match the video to the camera that filmed it."

"*If* we can find the phone," Drew said.

"Yes, well there's the catch." Nick's eyebrows drew together. "Especially since Kelsey said Smiley was murdered so many years ago."

Drew liked that the guy was not only a geek, but he also seemed to understand criminal investigations. "What if our suspect knew about this whole noise thing and got rid of his phone?"

"Not likely he's even heard of it." Nick shoved his hands in his pockets. "Technology to match the noise to the phone was only developed a few months ago. It isn't even commercially available yet."

"So he really couldn't know we might have this information," Teagan said.

Nick shook his head. "Highly unlikely."

Drew still didn't get why the killer didn't look in the air duct, but maybe something or someone interrupted him, and he had to flee. Still, he could've come back or if he killed the other victims at the same location, he could've looked then. Maybe he thought it fell into the duct and disappeared down the vent.

Only one explanation to Drew. "Sounds like the killer is thinking he's in the clear and that if he couldn't find the drive, no one was going to."

Teagan looked at Drew. "All he has to do now to know he could be in jeopardy is go to Smiley's place and see the excavated graves."

"Yeah, that's a problem there's no solution to," Drew said. "Which means we have to work even faster to find him before he discovers we're on to him and goes to ground."

Teagan led Drew straight past her family room and into the dining room, her mind still filled with details from Nick and thoughts of a sword as the murder weapon. Who in today's world would use a sword to murder someone? Drew had dropped her at the restaurant to get her car, but she wished they'd ridden together so they could've discussed the findings from the Veritas partners. On a positive note, it gave them a chance to process the information before talking about it.

Her sisters sitting in the family room looked up, but Teagan lifted her laptop and pointed at the one Drew carried as if that explained everything. She hoped it told them to back off. Fat chance of that. At least not for long. They would try to heed her request for privacy, but one of them might crack and just happen to be passing. Teagan surely didn't want them to hear about the graves. As an added measure, she pulled the sliding doors closed behind them.

She gestured for Drew to take a seat at the far end of the table, and she moved the picture to reveal the whiteboard that they'd cleaned off after their last session here. She drew a quick sketch of the layout for the graves and the circle with the sword cross in the middle.

She turned to him. "So the sword used to murder Smiley fits with the theme of the circle and sword, but why use a sword in the first place, and what does it mean?"

"That's our biggest question to answer right now." He set his computer on the table and draped a long arm over the chair next to him where he'd hung his jacket. "And we need to focus our search on it. Could fit as related to the Rossi's connection to the Catholic church or to his connection to Iraq due to the stolen antiquities."

"Sounds about right," she said. "We can divide the search. Which one do you want?"

"Since I spent time in Italy, I'll take the church." He swiveled to open his computer.

"Then Iraq it is." She sat behind her computer and typed sword and circle into a search engine. A large number of images populated the screen.

"FYI," Drew said without looking at her. "I called Dr. Albertson on the way over here and the autopsies are at nine a.m."

Just the thought made Teagan's stomach turn. Was bad enough to attend an autopsy where the body wasn't severely decomposed, but the bodies found at Smiley's place? That was going to be tough to take. Still, she had a job to do, and she wouldn't shirk her responsibilities.

She swallowed. "We'll be attending, right?"

He looked up, his expression tight. "Yes, if you think you can handle it."

"I've gone to a few autopsies in my day. Not something I like to do, but I'm eager to discover the cause of death for our other two victims."

"Then yes. We'll both go." He held her gaze. "But know that if you decide not to do it, I won't judge you."

She firmed her shoulders. "I won't change my mind. It's my job, and I can do it."

"A job I got you involved in again."

"Don't worry about me, Drew. I'm a big girl and can handle it."

"I get that. I just wish you didn't have to."

She smiled at him. "I appreciate your concern."

She turned her attention back to her screen to keep from thinking about the gruesome scene awaiting them in the morning. Most of the pictures displayed in front of her belonged to companies that sold images. Two photos similar to the symbols they found were listed midway down the page. The first was for a group in Indiana who met to engage in sword fighting, and the second, a group in North Carolina who taught people how to use swords. She checked out the links but saw no connection to their investigation. Still, she made note of it in her file.

She added the word church to her search and found a question titled, *Who is called Sword of God?*

According to Wikipedia, Khalid ibn al-Walid ibn al-Mughira al-Makhzumi was an Arab Muslim commander who served the prophet Muhammad. He even led Muhammad's military in early Muslim conquests. Muhammad then appointed Khalid as a commander of the Muslim army and gave him the name of Sayf Allah—Sword of God.

Could this have to do with their sword?

"Check this out." She swiveled her computer for Drew to

see the article. "Maybe the antiquities are related to this. The timeframe doesn't work for the item Oliver mentioned, but it could fit with the other antiquities they're importing."

Drew studied the screen, then looked up. "Let's keep this in mind and see if Nick discovers anything related to it."

She turned her computer back. "Did you locate anything?"

He shook his head. "I'll keep searching."

Which he did. So did she. For hours.

"Nothing more here." She sat back. "Maybe when we learn how the others were murdered it'll help clarify things."

Drew looked at his watch. "I need to head out for my meeting with the Contis and Rossi."

"I'll keep searching." She looked at him, suddenly seeing him in a warehouse with the person who killed all of these men, and Drew in trouble. "Do you have any backup for this meeting?"

"Can't risk it," he said.

Her heart sank. "Please be careful. Very careful. And let me know the minute you're safe."

He stood, but didn't seem inclined to move. "I'll call you."

She stood with him. Needing to touch him before he put his life on the line, she took his hands. "I know you're not looking for a relationship, but you have to admit we've already formed a deep connection."

"Yes," he said, his tone low and husky. He lifted his hand to tuck her hair behind her ear.

A shiver cascaded over her body. "I'm really terrified for you. The stakes have skyrocketed since your last encounter with them. They've killed or had four people killed."

"I know." He swallowed hard.

"Then with these huge stakes, I think it only fitting that I give you a reason to be even more careful." She let go of his hand and wound her arms around his neck. "Kiss me, Drew. Like it's our last time together, and we'll want to remember it."

He didn't let a second pass, but lowered his mouth, crushing his lips to hers and jerking her body against his. The sense of urgency caught her off guard. He deepened the kiss even more, and she let herself get carried away, tightening her hold on his solid neck.

Pure joy flooded her, and she didn't want the kiss to end. Sure, it had been a long time since she kissed a guy, but never had she felt such a deep emotion. A feeling of oneness. Of the other person being made for her.

He suddenly pulled back, his breathing deep and ragged. He rested his forehead against hers. "We shouldn't have done that, but I'm glad we did. I don't know where this might lead, but maybe we need to pursue it when this op is over."

"Maybe." She closed her eyes tight to try to regain her emotional footing. "But for now, remember there are people who care for you and to be careful."

"I'll do my best." He squeezed her hand and headed for the door. He slid it open on the track, the sound groaning like her heart as he walked away from her, all alone and heading into danger.

17

Drew turned into the parking lot for the single story warehouse in the commercial area of northeast Portland. He scanned the area with his binoculars, noting a lack of signs save the address numbers on the building. Two SUV's were parked by a loading dock, one he recognized as belonging to Sal Conti. The other had to be Rossi's vehicle.

Nothing out of the ordinary.

It was show time.

He rolled slowly across the lot and backed his vehicle in for easy departure should he need to flee. After checking the magazine on his sidearm, he got out. The chilly night air under overcast clouds smacked him in the face.

Good. It would help to erase the lingering heat from his crazy kiss with Teagan. He'd never expected that to happen. The few detached brain cells he'd managed to retain kept screaming at him to let her go and stop kissing her, but she'd felt too good. Smelled too good. Thankfully, reality did finally seep in. He couldn't act on his feelings. No matter his desire. But man, with the way he responded, it was clear he wanted the kiss—wanted her. And he wanted the kiss to go on and on.

And a lot more with her.

In the ugly world he'd inhabited for the last year, she was pure and good and had given him hope.

"Don't botch this then, so you can get back to her," he said under his breath as he charged up the steps and pushed open the small metal door next to the big loading doors.

Inside stood Sal Conti, Rossi, and the same thug who'd been with Rossi when Drew and Teagan had first spied on the man here.

Sal pointed Drew's way. "That's Dylan."

The thug spun and marched across the room. "I'll take your gun."

Drew didn't want to relinquish his sidearm, but if he wanted to make progress with Rossi, he had no choice. He planted it in the thug's palm with undue force, noting the man wore latex gloves. The guy shoved it into his waistband and used his big paws to search Drew. Felt like a giant bear without the extended claws patting him down.

Drew had to bite his tongue not to say something that might get him in trouble.

"He's clean," the thug yelled. "No weapons and no wire."

"Join us," Rossi said. "Any friend of the Contis' is a friend of mine."

Drew wanted to hurl at the creep's congenial yet cocky behavior. "As Sal said, I'm Dylan Crane. And you are?"

"Chauncey Rossi."

Drew got straight to the point. "Well, Mr. Rossi, let's get this party started. Sal says you'll share your product in trade for our cash. But I gotta see the product first."

Rossi's eyes narrowed. "What? No time to get to know each other first?"

Drew firmed his stance but felt naked without his sidearm. "I've gotten to know the Contis this past year, and they can vouch for me. No reason to dance around the point of this meeting."

"He's right," Sal said, but his tone was indecisive. "We vouch for him."

Rossi eyed Drew. "As much as I respect Sal and his brothers, my supplier would expect me to be more careful before handing over our product."

"Supplier?" Drew didn't have to fake his surprise at this development. "I thought you were the big cheese."

"Oh, I am as far as you're concerned. The only time you'll meet my supplier is if you've made the unforgivable mistake of trying to double-cross us."

"That's not going to happen." Drew had to work hard to keep his mind from pouring over the fact that Rossi wasn't the top dog. Drew wouldn't cut off the legs of this operation simply by taking Rossi off the streets. "Let me tell you a few things about me so we can move forward."

Drew gave a concise description of his bogus past, making sure not to embellish too much, which was the sign of a liar. When people told the truth they stuck with the facts. Those who lied often added unnecessary details.

Rossi nodded and looked at the thug. "Let's get the man a sample."

The thug crossed to a crate that had already been opened. He pulled out items wrapped in bubble wrap and carefully set them on the floor. Next he took out a brick wrapped in cellophane and brown tape. The thug handed the brick to Drew.

He took a good look at the compressed white powder instead of the darker tan powder he was expecting, and his anger rose. He took a beat to swallow it down and eyed Rossi. "You trying to mess with me?"

"What do you mean?" Rossi blinked, acting all innocent.

"You think I'm stupid or something." Drew held out the

brick, likely a kilo or about two pounds of drugs. "This is coke not heroin like Sal said you'd be giving me to hold. Half the value and I'd have to hold a lot more product."

Rossi laughed off the comment. "Join me at the table and bring the brick."

Drew followed Rossi to an old wooden table covered in brown paper.

Rossi held out his hand. "The brick?"

Drew gave it to him.

Rossi slit open the cellophane and set it on the table. He tapped it with a small hammer. The exterior of the brick fell apart and inside was another brick, this one tan like heroin.

"We hide the heroin inside the coke to deceive our mid-level transporters," Rossi said.

Drew met Rossi's gaze. "Why on earth would you do that?"

"Our shippers charge higher rates for heroin versus cocaine shipments. Gotta keep the costs down whenever we can. And it helps us diversify with two products to move."

Made sense to Drew. "I'll need to have my guy test the quality."

"Of course." Rossi lifted his chin. "You'll find it to be topnotch."

Drew kept his gaze fixed on Rossi. "Once we confirm it's the good stuff, how much are you prepared to front?"

"Equal street value to the cash you're depositing for us to wash. If all goes well, you can hold that in inventory, and we'll keep funneling the money. Once we know you can handle the cash, we can talk about you moving that product for us too."

Drew smiled. "Exactly what I was hoping for."

Rossi looked at his thug. "Wrap this up and let this guy get out of here."

The thug took the brown paper and wrapped it with practiced ease before handing the package to Drew.

He casually tucked it under his arm as if he carried big dollars in cocaine and heroin all the time. The coke was likely worth thirty-thousand dollars or more and the heroin two times that amount. "I'll get back to Sal as soon as I can."

"See that you do." Rossi eyed Drew, the man's gaze dark and threatening.

Drew looked at the thug. "My weapon."

The thug looked to Rossi for approval, and he nodded.

Drew holstered his weapon as a sign of his trust and strode toward the door. The evil emanating from this man burned into Drew's back as he headed for the exit. Each step he feared a bullet to the back. He arrived at the door unscathed. He opened it and wanted to bolt but paused when he heard Rossi speak.

"Something about that guy I don't like," Rossi said.

"Maybe it's because he's as cocky as you are," Sal said. "You gotta be number one."

"I *am* number one, and I aim to stay that way. I want you to continue to keep an eye on him."

Drew had figured there would be additional measures taken once he was holding Rossi's drugs, but the Contis trusted him and he didn't think they would follow through. Still, Drew had to be more alert and more cognizant that he could be putting Teagan in greater danger if he spent time with her. Dating would need to stop, and he would also encourage her to back away from the investigation.

Yeah, right. Like she would go for that. Still, he had to try.

If the Contis did follow through, they wouldn't change their surveillance immediately, giving Drew plenty of time for Teagan to join him in taking the drugs to the Veritas Center.

He got into his vehicle and peeled out of the lot, making

sure he wasn't followed. When he was a safe distance away, he pulled over to call Teagan and hoped she would answer.

"Is everything okay?" Her tone was throaty and breathless as if he'd woken her or she'd run for the phone.

"Fine." He told her about the meeting. "I have the drugs and am heading to the Veritas Center."

"Give me a minute to get dressed again, and I'll be on my way."

Maybe he had woken her. Visions of her sleepy face and hair in a mess had him wishing some day in the future that he might wake up next to her. Whoa. She'd gone from being a distraction to being so much more. If only he were in another place. Another time and he could figure out what to do.

But now he had a job to do.

"I'm still in northeast Portland," he said. "I'll meet you there. Be careful and watch for any surveillance."

"You're scaring me."

"Just being overly cautious, and I want you to be too." He looked into the dark night, his thoughts running wild. "I don't want anything bad to happen to you."

Drew parked next to Teagan's car in the Veritas Center lot and checked his watch. Thirty minutes until Oliver arrived at the port. Drew should soon be hearing from the agent surveilling the guy. He tucked the package of drugs under his arm again and climbed out. How odd to carry a kilo of drugs into such a posh place. To carry a kilo of drugs anywhere might be odd for some people, but not for his job.

Pete met Drew at the door and Drew caught sight of Teagan sitting on a sofa under the floating stairs. She wore jeans again, and this time had put on a frilly top that heightened Drew's awareness of her feminine side. Her hair was down, damp, and flowing over her shoulders. She hadn't been sleeping but showering.

Pete opened the door, and she shot to her feet.

The security guard marched straight to the desk with firm but short strides, confirming for Drew that once a law enforcement officer, always a law enforcement officer in manner and actions. Teagan joined them, but Drew kept his attention on Pete, who was giving Drew the stink eye.

Pete clamped a hand on his sidearm, a power play if Drew ever saw one. "Got your ID this time?"

Drew shook his head, but didn't elaborate.

Pete shifted his feet and didn't look away. "I should read you the riot act. Coming here again like this, but I'll let it go since I already confirmed you once tonight. Don't much like it, but I'm thinking you must be undercover, which is a pretty dang good reason not to have your ID."

Drew ignored the comment and filled in the form.

"Let me give Dr. Lane a call." Pete produced a badge and handed the pass to Drew.

He slipped the lanyard over his head and turned his full attention to Teagan. Up close, he could smell her coconut shampoo and see her damp hair curled slightly as it lay on her shoulders. The jeans clung to her long legs, and the pink top, though frilly, revealed her curves. A causal outfit that was probably nothing special to her, but their kiss had changed everything about how he was seeing her now.

She took his arm and led him away from Pete. "So your meeting really went okay?"

Drew took a breath to erase the shot to his heart from her touch. "I think so, but I heard Rossi tell Sal to increase his surveillance on me. Which means we should probably stop dating, and you should take a step back from the investigation."

"No." She crossed her arms. "I'm in this for the long haul and won't be put off."

He took her hand and looked her in the eyes. "I figured you'd say that, but really it's for the best."

"For who?"

"You."

"I'm a trained and experienced detective, Drew. I can handle myself just fine."

He didn't want to get into an argument in front of Pete. "Then at least agree to hold off on the dating. That might keep Rossi from even finding out about you."

She gave a low, long sigh. "That I can do. And we can be more careful about meeting."

He squeezed her hand and released it. He honestly didn't like how easily she agreed to stop dating him, but he'd asked for it, and she was honoring his wishes. At least in one area. He would help facilitate the other area by limiting their meetings in the future.

The door at the top of the stairs opened. Drew shot a look to the landing. A woman with shoulder-length blond hair, dressed in jeans and sneakers and wearing a rumpled white lab coat stepped out, but held the door open with her back.

She waved at them. "Come on up."

Maya, he assumed. Teagan smiled and started to climb the stairs. He followed, and Maya held out her hand to Drew. They exchanged introductions.

He released her hand. "Thanks for meeting with us so late."

"No worries." She spun, her athletic shoes squeaking on the polished floor. "Follow me to the lab."

She turned and led them to the Toxicology and Controlled Substance Unit, which was located right inside the door.

She used the electronic reader to get them into a space that looked very much like Sierra's lab, with stainless steel tables in the middle and equipment along the edges. Different kinds of equipment, but new, state-of-the-art-looking things.

She went to a very large glass-fronted case that had gloves mounted in the glass that extended inside the case. She started dressing in orange, heavy-duty overalls. "I'll need to use the bio-safety containment cabinet to check the drugs. All our work with drugs must be done within the cabinet these days."

"Why's that?" Drew asked, though he thought he already knew the answer.

Maya tugged the suit up. "Possibility of fentanyl contamination. All it takes is seven hundred micrograms of fentanyl to kill. That's a mere half dozen grains or so. Plus, fentanyl sold on the street is made in clandestine labs and isn't as pure as the pharmaceutical version. Means the effect on the body could be more unpredictable." She added a face shield and heavy gloves.

Drew nodded his understanding. Criminals cut drugs with all kinds of substances. Some harmless like baking soda. Some harmful like benzocaine. Some dangerous like fentanyl. It was often used to help a product stretch further because it was cheaper than the drug they were selling. But sometimes it was used to enhance the drug and the high for their customers.

Drew stepped closer with the drugs and noted a Class 4 label on the cabinet. "How many classes are there?"

Maya held out gloved hands for the package. "Only four. And even a class three is probably overkill for this test. We normally don't deal with class four toxins, but we always like to outfit our labs with the very best. Costs more, but you can't put a price on safety."

Maya nodded at Drew. "If we find fentanyl in the drugs, you'll want to get rid of that jacket in our biohazard bin and scrub your hands clean before you leave."

He hadn't thought of that. "Aw, man, it's one of my favorites."

"Can't put a price on safety."

"The supplier didn't seem to hesitate to handle it so maybe that's a good sign."

"Or the supplier isn't too bright, which is often the case." She inserted the package into a glass container on the side and closed the door. She slid her arms into the sealed holes for the long, heavy gloves that were attached to the inside of the cabinet.

She pulled the sliding table holding the package into the main cabinet and began work using chemicals already in the cabinet. "You might want to take a seat. This will take some time."

Drew didn't mind watching but it was going on three a.m. He figured Teagan was tired, so he sat, hoping she would too.

"You do any more searches after I left?" he asked.

She nodded. "Didn't find anything but I texted Nick before I took my shower. He hasn't located anything either."

"Seems like the circle and sword aren't common."

"Or there's something missing in the spaces where the graves were dug that could give us the answer."

He nodded. "I really don't see Rossi or one of the Contis going to all this trouble to bury someone who bucked the status quo or made a mistake."

"Agreed. I think we're looking for a flunky they assigned to kill these men and who's got some sort of sick obsession."

"Could be Rossi's current thug," Drew said. "They didn't mention him by name tonight, but he's in the pictures you took of Rossi so Nick could come across his ID."

"I don't really expect him to find the guy." Teagan sighed. "I get that a lot of criminals post on social media, but I doubt someone who would do something like this would be on social media advertising his conquests, and I can't see other reasons his image might be online."

"Yeah." Drew leaned on the table and looked at Maya, who stood to put two frighteningly large-looking needles into the transfer port. She would confirm the drugs. That was a given. But could she also find something to give them a lead as to where they'd come from?

"Okay now we run this through the mass spec." She pulled out the needles and moved to a machine about the size of a microwave. She stabbed the first needle into a port on top of the machine. "I'm running these samples through mass spectrometry. The information is then sent to the computer, where it will compare the samples to a database of known chemicals and drugs. If a match is found in the database for both the drug and any chemical it was cut with, it'll be identified."

Drew had to admit he was impressed once again with the skill of the Veritas partners and the machinery of their lab.

Drew's phone rang. "It's Harris. Maybe she's calling about Oliver."

He answered and stood to pace as he talked.

"Oliver Rossi did indeed pick up a package at the port and has taken it to the family warehouse. You probably just missed them."

"Was his dad and Sal Conti still there?"

"No. The place was empty. Oliver went inside for a brief time and then went home." She paused for a long moment. "Of course our probable cause for a warrant is just hearsay, and if Steele is going to see the antiquity tomorrow anyway, that's a better route than trying to get into the warehouse."

"I'll let you know once she has a time and location for her meeting Oliver." Drew ended the call and returned to Teagan to update her.

She got out her phone. "No text from him, but then I would expect him to wait until morning."

"Makes sense." Drew studied her face and found a hint of unease. "I want you to convince Oliver to meet you in a public place like a park so I can observe the meeting."

"I don't think he'll go for that."

"Then you'll have to make him go for it," he snapped, and at the pain in her eyes, he regretted it. "I'm sorry, but your safety comes first."

"I get it."

"This could be big if you get a look at this antiquity, maybe take a picture of it, we can try to authenticate it and arrest him before he sells it to someone else."

"I'll find a way to get him to do it." Determination rang through her voice.

"Maybe when he contacts you, you should communicate via a video chat instead of by text. I know I would do just about anything when you smile at me." He couldn't believe he was admitting that to her, but it was for the good of the investigation, right? "Seems like he feels the same way."

"Hmm. Now that I know your Kryptonite, I'll be sure to smile much more often." She gave him a flirtatious smile.

His heart melted, proving his comment.

"The white powder isn't pure," Maya called out. "It's eighty-five percent cocaine hydrochloride adulterated with caffeine powder. The tan powder indicates a mixture of eighty-three percent heroin hydrochloride mixed with cocaine hydrochloride."

"No fentanyl?" Drew clarified.

"No. You can keep your jacket." Maya chuckled.

"And the drugs are about as pure as you find these days," Drew said, remembering statistics he'd read.

"Exactly. But that's not all."

"You found something else?"

She nodded. "Your heroin sample matched heroin known to come from Iran."

Drew had hoped for something like this, but he gaped at Maya for a moment. "You can actually tell us where it came from?"

She nodded. "The profiles in the database include samples proven to come from various countries around the globe and this is definitely from Iran."

"That's most helpful," Drew said, then gave Teagan a pointed look.

"Let me pack them back up for you." Maya went back to the cabinet and took the package out to rewrap it.

Drew stood and took it from her. "Again, thank you so much for the help."

"Glad to help if I can." She removed her face shield and dropped her gloves in the biohazard bin. "Can't say my hubby is glad when I work so late, but he's used to it. Besides he's an FBI agent, and he works horrific hours too."

"We totally understand that," Drew said.

"Let me show you to the stairs." She kept her suit on and led them to the stairway. "If you need any other help, let me know."

He shook Maya's hand. "Glad to meet you and hope to see you again sometime when I'm not asking a favor."

"That would be great. Now I need to get out of this suit and clean up so I can get at least a few minutes sleep tonight." She chuckled and turned to go back inside.

On the stairway and after Drew made sure the door had closed, he turned to Teagan. "We got more than we came for."

She moved closer, likely to keep Pete from overhearing. "Iraq borders Iran so the connection could be big. This could mean the drugs are actually connected to the antiquities."

"We need to pursue that for sure."

She nodded and led the way down the stairs. They dropped off their passes with Pete. He escorted them to the door. "Have a good night."

Teagan smiled at the older man. "Thanks, Pete, for taking good care of us."

He waved a hand. "Hey, glad to have someone come by this late at night. Keeps things interesting in a good way instead of a problem."

Drew stepped outside first, holding out his hand to keep Teagan behind him. He searched the area, confirming they were alone. Once certain, he walked her to her car, dropping the brick of drugs in his vehicle on the way. He wanted his hands free so he could go for his sidearm if needed.

He didn't like the thought of limiting his interactions with her in the future, and what he wanted to do was pull her into his arms and kiss her again, but that could be dangerous. The sooner he got Teagan in her car and on her way home the better.

She unlocked her silver Toyota Prius, a practical car, which fit her. "Call as soon as you're safely behind locked doors in your house."

"Will do." She hesitated for a minute as if she thought about kissing him, but then slid in and put on her seatbelt.

Maybe he was just hoping she was thinking of kissing him. He stood watching until she got on the road, and her car disappeared from his sight. His gut cramped. He didn't like the increased risk he was putting her in. Especially going to meet with Oliver tomorrow.

Drew couldn't do a thing to stop the meeting. She would

203

go with or without his approval. And if Oliver turned violent, Drew might not be able to stop him from hurting her before he could intervene.

He hated to face facts here, but the fact was, only God could keep her safe now.

18

Teagan raced down the hallway toward the autopsy suite, silencing her phone on the way. She'd gotten caught in traffic as she crossed town to the medical examiner's office located in the Portland suburb of Clackamas. It was housed in a large building with one of the state's regional forensic labs. She'd been to this building many times in her career but much preferred going to the lab side over the morgue.

She donned the last protective suit, mask, and face shield left in the outer area by the staff. Meant Drew must already have arrived and was waiting inside with the badly decomposed bodies.

Her stomach gnawed on her breakfast of eggs and toast. Why had she eaten? She'd been to a total of nine autopsies and had always gotten nauseous during the procedure. Thankfully, she'd never embarrassed herself by upchucking as some of her associates had done. Still, none of the autopsies were easy. Too bad she'd forgotten that a full stomach didn't help.

She sat to put on the paper booties. She'd believed she was done with these horrific events. How had she found herself here again?

Unbelievable.

She shook her head. The cuts today truly had to be the last ones she would attend. Surely, she would never be called back into action again.

She put on the mask and face shield and pushed through the swinging doors. The protective gear did nothing to stop the horrific smell of decomposition, and she had to force each foot in front of the other to head toward Dr. Albertson. The doctor was dressed much like Teagan and stood at the closest table with what Teagan hoped was the most decomposed body of the pair as she couldn't imagine seeing anything worse. Her assistant, Arthur, a thin guy Teagan had met before, strode to the table behind the doctor. A sheet still covered the body in front of him.

Teagan swallowed hard and shifted her focus to Drew, who stood stoically between both tables.

"Sorry I'm late," she said, swallowing again but couldn't seem to find any moisture in her mouth. "Traffic. Did I miss anything?"

"Arthur and I just finished the preliminary screen." Dr. Albertson looked up. "We're starting on the cut on this male you all have been calling victim three."

Teagan concentrated on Dr. Albertson to keep her gaze off the man. "Do we have a time of death for him?"

"Not exact," Dr. Albertson said. "But I know how you law enforcement types want an estimate. State of decomp puts him around April of this year. I'll need to research local temperatures to give you a more precise answer."

Teagan nodded. "What about an ID?"

"That one is simple." Dr. Albertson's eyes brightened. "His name is Kris Forte. We found his wallet with his driver's license in the back pocket. Same deal for the male on the other table. Carlo Romo. Before you ask, I snapped pictures of the IDs for you."

"Interesting." Drew tilted his head. "A destroyed ID on Smiley. No ID on the second guy, but if he was carrying something that could identity him, looks like the killer would've left it as he didn't care to hide their IDs."

Interesting. Indeed. Teagan was sure she'd never heard this man's name before, but now that they knew the names of these two men, she and Drew could research them to find their connection to Rossi. "What about cause of death?"

"You know I try to be helpful." Dr. Albertson went back to work, plunging her hands into the victim's chest cavity. "But you people always want the big three before we even get started. ID, time and cause of death often take time."

"I know," Teagan said, actually feeling bad for pushing the good doctor, but it wouldn't stop her. "I'm sorry, but do you know his cause of death?"

"Not yet." She lifted her head. "This level of decomposition will take some time to get through. But to save time so you can get out of here and find whoever did this, Arthur will start the preliminary pictures on Romo."

As if on cue, Arthur lowered the sheet to Carlo Romo's waist. "Oh wow. Take a look at this, Doctor."

Dr. Albertson continued to move something around in Forte's chest cavity then holding her hands in the air, spun and stepped to the other table. Teagan and Drew followed her.

Long stripes of torn angry red flesh covered the victim's torso as if attacked by a wild animal, shredding long angry paths down his skin.

"What in the world?" Dr. Albertson ripped off her gloves and bent closer.

Teagan forced herself to study the angry marks. "Animal attack? Maybe a bear. I know we have brown bears in Oregon."

Dr. Albertson grabbed fresh gloves and bent to examine

the stripes. "Not a bear. No animal that I know of. These patterns have only three claw marks. Bears have five. And these are fine. Sharp. Like made from metal points not the thickened claw of an animal. Maybe from a very sharp handheld garden implement."

"Metal?" Drew looked at Teagan. "Does that make any sense?"

Teagan quickly ran through the facts they possessed so far. "No. Not with what we know."

Drew shifted his attention to Dr. Albertson. "Doesn't look like the cause of death though, right?"

"No. These wounds are all superficial." Dr. Albertson bent even closer and pressed a gloved finger against a hole in the man's chest near his heart. "I would say this is your cause of death."

Teagan studied the triangular wound. "That's not round like a gunshot. Or straight like a knife."

Dr. Albertson raised her head. "I suspect the injury was sustained by an arrow. A three-bladed tip. Death from an arrow is very rare. In fact, I've only ever seen this once before. Turn the victim, Arthur."

Her assistant grunted as he shifted the body to expose his back to Dr. Albertson.

"The arrow fully passed through him." She pressed on a hole in the back of the man's chest. "Likely means he was motionless at the time."

"Arrow?" Teagan mused. "This is so odd. We have claw-like marks on the body and an arrow killing the man?"

"My preliminary guess for his cause of death, yes," Dr. Albertson said. "But I won't know for sure until I do the cut."

"Which came first?" Drew asked. "Claws or arrow."

"You can lay him down, Arthur." Dr. Albertson pointed at the largest gouge from a claw. "See how the edges of the marks are swollen and gape? This tells me it was definitely done antemortem. And I would guess that with the way the wounds fade as they go down toward the feet, that this victim was standing as was the attacker and the killer is taller than the victim."

"So this guy was first attacked by a person with a garden tool or something like that, and then he was shot with an arrow?" Teagan clarified.

"That's my best estimation of what occurred."

"Don't you find that odd?" Teagan asked.

Dr. Albertson shrugged. "In my line of work, I see many things that most people would find odd, but it's par for the course."

"And can you give us an estimate on this man's time of death?" Drew asked.

She gave Drew an exasperated look. "A guesstimate says he's been in the ground for three weeks so mid-November or so. But again, I have to consult temps and weather to be more precise."

"And what about Forte?" Drew asked. "Any indication that he died the same way as Romo?"

"No sign of claw marks on the remaining flesh. Can't say there weren't any before decomp set in. And right before Arthur called me over, I located a bullet near the heart. Large caliber from a rifle. I assume it will be his cause of death." She ripped off her gloves and returned to the first guy. "Let me get it out of there."

She gloved up and dug in his chest. She removed a mangled bullet, turning it then dropping it in a metal tray. "I'll get this over to the firearms unit at the state lab for analysis."

Teagan stepped closer. "We'd like to take it to Grady Houston, the Veritas Center's ballistics expert."

Dr. Albertson gave a firm nod. "Great. He'll work fast and give you the best results."

"I'm sure he'll make it a priority for us." Teagan looked at Drew and waited for his nod of agreement. She should have consulted him first, but why wouldn't he want an answer sooner?

"This is so odd," she said to him. "We have death by a sword, bullet, and arrow, and marring with claws, and we have one more victim to go. Our killer obviously doesn't have a favorite method. Will make him much harder to find."

"Or worse. " Drew's eyes tightened. "We could be looking for more than one killer."

More than one killer. Drew stripped out of his protective gear, hating the look on Teagan's face when he'd let those words slip out. Her whole body tightened, and her face paled to the same level as when she'd first laid eyes on victim three's body. All that said, they had to consider the possibility of multiple killers, but that really didn't fit. Still, most serial killers chose one method to end their victim's life and repeated that method for every victim. They felt comfortable with their choice, and by killing more than one person, they got better at committing the crime.

But this? Three different means of death? Maybe four? That was unusual for sure.

He tugged off his gloves, the latex clinging to his fingers like glue. "I need to go somewhere to list out the details we've learned, so I can analyze them and make a plan."

"*We* can use the whiteboard at my house." Teagan stuffed her suit into the biohazard bag. "I know you're wanting to limit our time together, but we need to discuss this together."

He wanted to argue, but she had a valid point.

Discussing the information with someone very familiar with the investigation could lead to a breakthrough.

He looked at his watch. "We have enough time to do some research before you meet Oliver, so let's head over to your place now."

Teagan reached for the bullet evidence bag sitting on the bench. "I'll text the photos of the victims' driver's licenses to Nick when I get to my car and drop the bullet at Veritas on the way home. Hopefully, he can run a quick background on the men, and we can find a connection between them and the Contis or Rossi."

"Nick won't have access to law enforcement databases, so can you email the pictures to Harris, too? She can work on pulling reports while we drive."

"Sure."

He shared Harris's email address and stood. "You think Nick can have something to us by the time we get across town?"

"If he's not too busy with something else, I would think we'll get a preliminary report."

"I could never bring this investigation to a close on time without their help."

Teagan nodded and started down the hallway at a fast clip. Drew had to hurry to keep pace with her. At the front door, he checked the area for any threats. Confident no one lay in wait for them, he turned to her. "Be sure to be extra careful on the drive. Watch your six."

She held his gaze. "You too."

He opened her car door and waited for her to send her text and email, then get on the road. Her stop at Veritas would make her trip longer than his, giving him a bit of time to update Harris on the murders. He leaned against his car and dialed her burner phone dedicated to his calls.

"This isn't good, Collier," she said. "You think we're looking for more than one killer?"

A question Drew expected. "I think it's possible."

"Or we have a very creative killer." She let out a long breath. "I've never encountered anything like it. I'll have someone search ViCAP for similar crimes."

The FBI's Violent Criminal Apprehension Program database was filled with solved and unsolved crimes from law enforcement across the country. The bureau created it so law enforcement officers could enter specifics of their investigations and search for similar ones.

"What else do you need from me?" she asked.

"The Veritas information specialist is already running background on these victims, but he doesn't have access to law enforcement records. Could you have someone run down any missing person investigations on these men? Teagan Steele emailed the IDs to you a few minutes ago."

"I'll check for it as soon as we're done talking and send the information to her email. What's happening with Steele's meetup with Oliver?"

"She convinced him to meet her in a nearby park." Drew shook his head even if Harris couldn't see him. "I can't believe the guy's going to bring out a stolen antiquity in public."

Harris snorted. "How many times have we seen a guy do something stupid for love?"

"Plenty." He'd never really understood it and hadn't counted himself as one of them in the past. But what would he do for Teagan if he wanted to pursue a relationship with her?

He would stop at almost nothing.

"Let me know if she gets something solid to move on, and if you need anything else." The line went silent, and he looked to see if the call had ended, but they remained connected. "Watch your back, Collier. This has seriously taken a turn for the bizarre and dangerous."

Harris's warning lingered in Drew's brain as he wound in and out of heavy traffic to the west side of town. She'd warned him only on rare occasions and that put him on edge. He took an even more circuitous route than normal, but so far no sign of being followed. He arrived at Teagan's house and parked behind her car. Her vehicle was empty so he jogged to the wide porch and rang the bell.

She opened the door, marker in hand. "Got the preliminary reports from Nick, and I'm putting the names and stats on the board. I started them printing too so we can make notes."

"Have you heard back from Harris yet?" He entered the foyer.

"Nothing yet. I have my phone set to alert for emails so we won't miss it."

He followed Teagan to the dining room, where she'd written three of the four victims' names on the board in cherry red marker.

She tapped the empty slot for the second victim. "I called Kelsey on the way over. She's just now getting the bones for victim two on the table to examine them and will call as soon as she has anything to share." She dropped the marker in the tray. "The reports from Nick should be finished printing. Let me grab them."

She marched out of the room, and her footfalls sounded on the hallway floor gradually disappearing.

He went to the board and studied the information they'd uncovered.

Grave 1 - Smiley/Lenny Spence killed by sword and died 2016.

Grave 2 - Unknown

Grave 3 - Kris Forte killed with rifle and died April of 2022.

Grave 4 - Carlo Romo killed with arrow and died November of 2022.

Drew ran his finger over each name written in precise strokes. "Who are you guys, and what do you have in common?"

"Hopefully these reports can help with that." Teagan handed a stack of papers to Drew and went to the board with her own set. "I also got an email from Harris. She's working on getting the files for the missing person investigations, but she wanted us to know that none of the victims has a record. Not even a speeding ticket."

He let that bit of news sink in as she wrote Forte's profession next to his name. *Hotel executive.* Next to Romo she wrote *alternative energy executive.*

"Might as well write enforcer next to Smiley's name," he said.

She jotted it on the board. "No obvious connection between the three of them. He might've been an enforcer, but he died before the others did and couldn't have killed them."

"Maybe the connection is career related. What could a hotel executive have to do with alternative energy?"

"A hotel chain could be using renewable energy at their hotels."

"Could be, I suppose. Or maybe they have something in their private lives that connect them." Drew grabbed the reports from Nick and sat to read through the basic facts. "Both Romo and Forte were both married. Forte had two kids. Lived in Portland suburbs. Forte in Clackamas and Romo in Sherwood."

Teagan turned the page on her report and ran her finger down the paper. "This is an article on Romo going missing. Disappeared while hiking near Mount Hood. Presumed dead."

Drew scanned the next report. "Next one is about Forte. He was last seen leaving his gym late at night. Didn't arrive home. Car was never found. Obviously neither was he."

Teagan sat next to Drew and met his gaze. "Death notification calls will have to be done. Can you do them with your UC status?"

"The op is winding down, and the information I could glean in participating will outweigh any risk of these women connecting me to my undercover personality."

"Yeah, odds are good they don't know anything about this."

Drew nodded. "Smiley has no family that we know of. If we find the unknown victim's ID, it shouldn't be as much of a shock for his family. He's been gone for some time, and they likely believe him to be dead. But Forte's and Romo's families will take it hard." Drew looked Teagan in the eyes. "I can do it alone if you want me to."

She shook her head. "It's part of the job."

"That you're only doing because I forced the issue."

"Whatever the reason, a Steele doesn't shirk their responsibility." She sat back, looking defeated.

A look he recognized as one that many law enforcement officers exhibited every day when faced with people in crisis. But they picked themselves up and found their resolve to go on and incarcerate the bad guys who hurt others. The stress took its toll, but the officers were willing to give of themselves, just like Teagan.

She took a long breath. "I wish we could have DNA confirmation before meeting the family, but that will have to wait. If the missing person investigation has DNA profiles it'll go faster, but otherwise we can collect samples when we meet with the family." Her phone rang, and she sat forward. "It's Kelsey."

She tapped the screen. "Putting you on speaker so Drew can hear."

Teagan set her phone on the table between them.

"I'm pretty sure I've identified the victim from grave two." Kelsey's voice rang strong and sure through the room.

Drew shot Teagan an excited look. "How?"

"I went through his personal effects again," Kelsey said. "As you know there wasn't any official ID, but the intern found a wedding ring and didn't think to mention it."

"And you could ID him from that?" Teagan asked.

"It was engraved, and I entered the inscription into ViCAP. It returned a missing person investigation for a Benton Hoyle. He was last seen on June 15, 2018, which certainly fits the time of death."

"And cause of death?" Drew held his breath as he hoped for an answer that would somehow tie these murders together.

"A sharp blade to his back that pierced his heart."

"Like a knife?" Teagan asked.

"No." Kelsey drew the word out. "Not that deep and much wider. More like a hatchet. My assistant is at Grady's lab looking for a weapon that could've left the marks on these bones, but I thought you would want the ID now. ViCAP didn't have DNA information, and now we can get the official process started to confirm his DNA."

Teagan looked at Drew. "Any other questions for Kelsey?"

He shook his head.

"Thanks, Kelsey," Teagan said. "Call when you're certain on the weapon."

Teagan tapped End on her phone and looked at Drew. "A hatchet. This is getting weirder and weirder."

"Agreed." He sat back to think. "This is really looking more and more like we're looking for multiple killers, but they have to be connected if all the victims were buried on the same site."

"Could be a secret group or society who kill and bury the dead on Smiley's land."

"That might fit with the antiquities aspect somehow too."

Drew picked up his phone. "I'll call Harris to add Hoyle to her list and get all of those files to us pronto. Time is ticking down on my approved investigation time, and it's time to ask for additional help too. No way I'll let these guys get away with multiple crimes, especially not murder."

19

Under gray skies threatening to spit rain, Teagan crossed the park toward Oliver, who was relaxing on the bench under cherry trees stripped of their leaves and sleeping until spring when they would put on a cotton candy show of color. The Columbia River surged along the length of the very popular waterfront park.

Oliver's arm was stretched over the back of the bench, his legs crossed, and a box sitting next to him.

The box whose contents she'd come to see.

"He's here," she said into her phone to Drew. "And he looks like he's here for a picnic not showing a stolen antiquity to a woman he barely knows,"

"Take advantage of that," Drew said. "Try to get as much information about the item and get him to pose for a picture if you can."

"I'll do my best." She ended her call.

Thankful she was wired again and Drew could hear the upcoming conversation, she marched across the lush green grass, one of the benefits of frequent winter rain in the area. Many places across the county had green grass in the summer due to abundant rain, but not Portland. Summer dried up, the foliage along with it.

She took a breath to put on her Meg Jacobs persona and stepped around the bench. Oliver shot to his feet. He wore jeans, expensive leather loafers, and what she thought was a cashmere sweater in a subtle green color that brought out his dark coloring.

"You came!" His eyes were alight with happiness. "I wondered if you would."

"Why?"

"Because you asked to meet out here, and I wondered if you didn't trust me for some reason."

"Not you in particular." She took a seat and tried to calm her jittery nerves. "I just like to be careful when meeting men I don't know. My dad taught me that."

"Sounds like a smart guy, but you can trust me."

"Good to hear." She tapped the box and didn't have to feign excitement. "Is this the antiquity?"

He nodded. "Would you like to see it right away?"

"I would," she said, making sure to sound breathless. She rested a hand on his arm to distract him from thinking about one of the few park visitors seeing the object.

A wide smile transformed his face into an extremely handsome man. Why on earth was he still single? Other than he seemed to be a chauvinist. There were women who didn't mind that behavior in a relationship. She just wasn't one of them.

He opened the box flaps and peeled back brown padded wrapping. She took in the limestone relief of a Persian guard that was only about eight inches square. She'd expected something much larger and had to admit surprise. Still, it looked old. Very old.

"This was part of a row of soldiers depicted on a

balustrade," Oliver said. "Experts who authenticated it for my seller say it was made sometime around 510 BC." Oliver lifted his shoulders. "It's the final missing piece of the relief. That's why it's so valuable."

Making it even more despicable to keep it from the Iraqis.

She faked an admiring glance. "Do you already have a buyer?"

"I do. A guy my dad has dealt with for years. He'll probably turn around and sell it for even more." He laughed. "Tomorrow night you'll be looking at a guy who made his first million. Or should I say multi-millions. Not bad for someone my age."

"I'm so impressed," she said, making sure she gushed.

"I thought you would be."

"You might think I'm crazy, but I'd like to take a selfie with us holding the relief." She still had her hand on his arm, so she squeezed it. "I find this so exciting, and the excitement is spilling over to you."

"I don't know." He frowned. "A picture could incriminate me."

"I would never show it to anyone. I promise." She leaned closer and batted her lashes. She either would come across as sultry or a woman who didn't know what she was doing as she had never flirted shamelessly like this before.

"You're tempting me." He grinned. "I just can't think when you look at me like that, and I need you to stop."

"The only thing that will stop me right now is a picture." She cast him a pleading look. "Just one. Then we can move on to talking about going on a date."

"No. Sorry." He shook his head hard. "I can't be seen in the photo with the relief."

She couldn't fail to get the picture that an expert could

review. Sure, they couldn't confirm the item as authentic until they saw it in person, but they could tell them that they were moving in the right direction. "Can I take one with just me in it then?"

He beamed her a smile. "That you can do."

She lifted the box, taking her time to be sure the relief displayed clearly as did the box label with the Northwest Geo Instruments on it and snapped a photo. She'd planned ahead and had the camera set on burst mode so it took multiple high-speed photos.

"Okay." He closed the box and placed it on his lap. "One's enough and it's for your own private viewing."

"Don't worry. I won't share."

"I'm not actually worried. If you did share it publicly, the photo could link you to a stolen antiquity, and you could be sent to prison."

"Ooh, I didn't think of that," she said, when she had indeed thought of that and many other ways to implicate Oliver. "Now that the box is closed, can I take a picture of you, though? You know, for late at night when I'm thinking about you."

Her last comment made her stomach turn, but she smiled.

"Of course." He sat back, preening.

She took shots of him holding the box. Sure, it didn't implicate him like a picture of the object, but it did connect a link from the box to the item that a jury might find questionable. The pictures were taken immediately following the one of her with the object, in the same location, and the odds that the box was empty as he held it weren't very high.

"Now," he said. "Let's talk about how soon we can start dating."

Drew's stomach continued to turn as he drove toward the Conti's warehouse. He'd hated watching Teagan flirt with Oliver, but he was thankful she'd seen the antiquity and gotten a picture of it. Harris could try to have the item authenticated, and they could sweep in and arrest Oliver before he made the sale. They might be poised to arrest this guy and were making some progress on the murders, but Drew still had to keep the op going by telling Sal that he'd confirmed the drug quality and would move forward with the cash. One thing he couldn't do was come out and tell them he knew the heroin was from Iraq.

He also wanted to see if he could learn the identity of Rossi's thug to see if the creep might be behind the murders.

Drew slung his backpack holding the package of drugs over his shoulder as he got out of the car. The overcast skies made it seem to be nighttime, and the Christmas lights twinkling on the outside of the building felt foreign to his UC life. Last Christmas he'd spent alone in his dinky apartment while the Contis were home celebrating with their families.

He could honestly see how UC officers could turn and embrace the criminal life—which did happen at times. The offenders lived a high life, and the officer was stuck in poverty and witnessing all that life could offer if they gave in and took a bribe. He'd be lying if he said the money and posh life didn't entice him at times. Like that Christmas Day. But then he thought of his mother. Of his faith. Of his oath to serve and protect. And he made it through another day to point his attention at bringing in the bad guys.

He climbed the steps and entered the lobby. He was greeted by the sweet smell of freshly brewed hazelnut coffee, so popular in the Northwest where hazelnuts were grown. He greeted Betty with a smile.

"Oh, sugar." She held a cup of coffee. "You're looking tired."

He ran a hand through his hair but didn't comment.

"You spending late nights with Teagan Steele?" She blew on the coffee.

"Not real late, but my social life has cut into my sleep for sure." He chuckled to make light of it.

"You really like her." Betty raised a penciled-in eyebrow. "I can tell."

"You're still my best girl." He smiled.

"Oh, you." She waved her free hand. "Only Sal and Aldo are in today."

"Vito's on the loose, huh? I thought those guys were inseparable."

She set down her mug and cast a conspiratorial look around the area. "Between you and me, they had a big blowout. Vito said he's tired of how they treat him, and he's never coming back."

Oh, wow. Interesting development. "You believe him?"

"Could be. He's so much younger than the other two and always wanted to be like them, but they really do pick on the guy. I could see him going postal on them if they're not careful."

Drew didn't realize the animosity went that deep. "Seriously? You think he might hurt them?"

She shrugged. "You never know these days with constant bullying and all. Maybe you could talk to Sal and Aldo. Tell them to take it easy on him."

"Yeah. Sure. I'll try." He tapped the counter a few times and then headed past the security guard, the same petite woman as yesterday. She had a tough-looking stance but gave him a nod as he passed her.

Drew entered the warehouse. He had no intention of

talking to Sal and Aldo about their brother. If their leads on the murders didn't pan out, he would press Vito for additional information on Smiley.

Drew took a long breath, further inhaling his Dylan identity and stepped into the door. "What's up, Contis?"

Sal glared at him. "Little Vito had a snit and rushed out. We're trying to make decisions without him."

Drew rolled his eyes. "Younger brothers."

"Yeah, well, if he doesn't come back today, I might actually write him off." Sal leaned back and clamped his hands behind his head. "What're you doing here?"

"Came to give you a thumbs up on the package from last night." He displayed the drugs from his pack and then quickly hid them again in case someone might come in. "My guy says it's the real deal, and we're good to go."

Sal dropped his arms to the chair. "Finally, one thing going right today."

"Other problems?" Drew settled in a chair and made sure his expression was filled with concern.

Sal studied Drew. "Nothing for you to worry about."

Drew had raised the man's suspicions—so time to move on. "Speaking of worry, I thought the meeting with Rossi went well. Guy seemed to be okay with me and my business."

"Yeah, he's fine."

Drew casually crossed his leg. "His sidekick was something else."

"Tony?" Sal chuckled. "What can I say? The guy likes old mafia movies."

Aldo looked up from his computer. "Wouldn't you if your last name was Gambino?"

Perfect. Now Drew had a name to research. "Ever think he might really be mafia?"

"Nah." Aldo waved a hand. "The guy's bark is far worse than his bite. Sure he'd protect Rossi, but he'd no more take someone out than he'd take out his mother if he could help it."

"Guess you don't have to be an enforcer if you look like one." Drew laughed. "He been working for Rossi long?"

"Took over, what?" Sal looked at Aldo. "Five, maybe six, years ago?"

"Yeah, around then. Rossi doesn't go anywhere without the guy." Sal grinned. "We joke that Tony even sleeps with Rossi and his wife."

Drew faked a laugh and considered the implications of this news. He would never get close to Rossi without Gambino present. Not that Drew thought he needed to get Rossi alone. The next time he saw Rossi, Drew planned to be arresting him.

Drew planted his foot on the floor and tapped his backpack. "Let's talk about the glitter supply. My guy wants a one-for-one dollar match on product up to the first half mil we deposit. Then we'll hold it until we can be sure you can turn our cash as fast as needed."

"That's a lot of glitter to put on hold." Sal ran his hand over his jaw. "I'll have to talk to Rossi, but I doubt he'll be able to make that decision. Will have to get back to you."

Drew clutched the backpack. "I'll take this for the deposit I already made."

"Gonna turn that back to you today minus our cut," Aldo said. "So keep an eye out."

"Will do." Drew stood and looked at Sal. "I'd like to get this going today or tomorrow or my guy will want to move on. Let me know when you're ready to rock."

Sal frowned. "It'll take as long as it takes."

Drew ignored the comment and strode out, waving to

Betty as he passed but not stopping as she would ask him if he talked to the brothers about Vito. She never had her own children and acted like their mother. She wanted them all to be happy and wouldn't like the plans Drew had for the brothers for sure.

He got his car pointed toward the city and called Harris. "I need you to run particulars on a Tony Gambino. He's Rossi's muscle. Maybe the killer we're looking for."

"Hold on." Keys clicked in the background. "Loading now. No priors."

"Doesn't mean anything."

"Likely because he hasn't been caught." She let out a noisy breath.

"Where do we stand on the missing person reports?"

"I received the last file and have a flash drive ready for you. I'm free right now if you can get to our rendezvous spot."

"Give me thirty minutes."

"I'll be there."

The call ended, and Drew resisted pressing his foot down on the gas pedal. His UC ride was already sketchy looking, and he didn't need to be stopped for speeding with a brick of drugs in his backpack.

As it turned out, even with precautionary measures taken to make sure he wasn't tailed, he beat Harris to their usual meeting place. She strolled down the alley, in her hand, a travel tumbler that she used to transport drives to him. It had a false bottom, which was where he would find the flash drive. In UC work, an agent never carried anything on their person that could be used to blow their cover unless it was somehow concealed. They especially never carried records like the ones Harris was providing, and if found, would out him as a law enforcement officer.

She handed him the mug. "How are you progressing?"

"Not as fast as I would like." He told her about his meeting with Sal and Aldo.

"Got word from upstairs." Her flat tone didn't let on as to what she was feeling about that call. "They want this operation concluded by the deadline. No exception. You've got less than twenty-four hours."

He ignored the panic threatening to make him snap and focused on his priorities. "Can't see the murder investigation concluding that quickly. There's no obvious connection to Rossi or the Contis. I'd need additional resources to delve into each victim to meet that deadline."

"No can do." She pushed back her leather jacket and rested her hands on her waist. "If you can't resolve the murders, then turn your focus back to the drugs and antiquities so we can close out the UC op on a win."

She didn't seem to care that four men had been murdered. She was worried about her case closure rate. As were the agents upstairs. It was all about the statistics at times, a frustrating reality Drew had faced too often.

"You can't let them get away with the murders." He eyed her.

She didn't bat a lash. "No one's getting away with anything. County can take over. If they prove one of our guys is connected to the murders, then the suspects will be sitting in jail waiting for additional charges to be brought against them. A win/win."

Not the answer he wanted. Not at all. He fisted his hands. "I don't agree with this, you know."

"I know, but you don't have a choice." Her tone had gone low and gruff. "Get the Contis and Rossi on the other charges and do it within the next twenty-four hours."

"And if I don't," he challenged.

"At the very least, I'll write you up for insubordination." She held his gaze. "Push it too far, and you'll lose your job."

She turned and marched off.

He watched his career evaporate with each of her steps because there was no way he would back off the murder charges. No way. He would find the killer no matter the personal consequences.

20

Teagan had never seen Drew mad, but he marched in angry steps around her dining table, mumbling to himself, his eyes tight and hands in fists. To her surprise, after he'd said they shouldn't meet here, he'd arrived to start printing the missing person investigation files. He'd gotten them on a flash drive from his supervisor, who had issued an edict. One he didn't like. Not at all. And he didn't know what to do, so he stormed around to clear his head and think.

"Printing should be done by now," Teagan said to interrupt his pacing and get them moving ahead.

"I'll get it." He charged out of the room.

She'd also never seen him this indecisive. It wasn't unusual in law enforcement to run into budget constraints and have to close a case and move on. But in this instance, they'd barely begun the murder investigation, and she knew how much he wanted to bring the killer—or killers—to justice. Being UC for so long had made this personal to him. He not only didn't want to let Rossi or the Contis, or even a higher up, get away with murder. He wanted to be the guy to slap the cuffs on their wrists and haul them in.

She understood. Completely. So what should she do?

She couldn't encourage him to ignore his supervisor's directive. She could assure him she would work the murders until the killer was found while he closed down his undercover operation. Better than nothing, she supposed. But she doubted that would be enough to appease him.

She turned to study the board that she'd updated with Hoyle's information

Grave 1 - Smiley/Lenny Spence killed by sword and died 2016. Enforcer. Went missing while ?

Grave 2 - Benton Hoyle killed by a hatchet and died June of 2018. Went missing while ?

Grave 3 - Kris Forte killed with rifle and died April of 2022. Hotel executive. Went missing from his gym.

Grave 4 - Carlo Romo killed with arrow and died November of 2022. Alternative energy executive. Went missing while hiking.

Drew rushed back into the room and dropped a tall stack of papers on the table. Reports that would take hours and hours to go through with a fine-toothed comb. Not one time. Likely many times to find that hidden lead that would move them forward.

He planted his feet and faced her. "Forget what Harris said. We go forward on the murder investigation as planned. I can't have Harris shut us down. Means we'll need to use your resources only, but we can do this."

She'd worked enough homicides to know it wasn't that simple. And those were individual murders. But four of them? That took manpower. "Can I make a suggestion?"

"Sure."

"You mentioned asking for extra help, and I'm assuming Harris turned you down."

"She did."

"What if we asked my family to help? Londyn and Ryleigh are still sworn officers and the others have recently left law enforcement. They all have the skills to review these files and look for connections."

"I don't know." He frowned, the indecision back in his expression. "The risk of something leaking might be too great."

"First of all, none of them will leak info. Second, we need help and Harris won't provide it. My department likely doesn't have the staffing to do so. If you want to catch this killer or killers, my family is your best option."

"Fine." He planted his hands on the table. "But let's not call all of them in right away. Mackenzie seems to know something's off, so we start with only her."

"I'll call her." Teagan quickly dug her phone from her pocket and made the call before Drew changed his mind.

When it connected, she said, "I need you to come home. I need help with something I'm working on."

Mackenzie blew a frustrated breath through the phone. "I'm kind of in the middle of something myself."

"My something involves murder," Teagan said to pique her sister's curiosity.

"Be right there." She ended the call.

"Nothing like murder to get a sister's attention." Teagan smiled to try to lighten the mood, though there was nothing light about murder.

Drew grabbed the paperwork. "Let's get these reports organized."

"It would help to put them in murder book format in binders. I know that will take time, but then we can flip through them easily and not waste even more time searching for what we need."

"Agreed."

"We have all the supplies in the office. I'll grab stuff while you separate that stack by investigation." She took off to the office shared by all the siblings and cousins.

She loved this room. The dark paint set the mood. The long wall of original bookshelves overflowing with law enforcement reference books dating all the way back to their grandad's days as a detective added to the moodiness. Instead of a desk, they'd placed a small dining table in the middle of the room with four chairs so more than one person could comfortably work in the space at the same time.

A closet in the corner held the supplies she would need. She took empty binders, dividers, markers, highlighters, post-it notes, and a hole punch to the dining room.

Drew had separated the reports into three stacks and stood over the first one. He looked up. "Which investigation do you want to take?"

"We don't know much about Hoyle, so I'd like to start with him. See if he's the link to the others."

Drew slid a stack of papers across the table to her.

She scanned the detective's report sitting on top. "He was a supervisor for an airplane manufacturing plant, and he went missing while out biking. They found his bike on the side of the road. Never found him."

"Explains the cycling clothes found in his grave." Drew went to the whiteboard and added Hoyle's details to his name, then tapped each employment type. "Enforcer. Alternative energy. Hotels. Airplanes. What do they all have in common?"

"Hotels and airplanes go together, but the energy company and enforcer are the odd ones out. Hopefully, the answer is in all of this paperwork." She started sorting Hoyle's files into mini piles that she would divide with tabs for easy access.

Drew tugged the pile with Romo's records across the table. "Their personal lives could give us the lead we need.

Though if the way they disappeared tells us anything, it looks like they were into different activities too."

She looked up at him. "Could the connection be related to the dates they disappeared or were murdered?"

"Good question." He went to the board and tapped the first two dates with his finger. "We have a two-year gap between Smiley and Hoyle, then four years between Hoyle and Forte. Only eight months between him and Romo."

"So what might that mean?"

"I don't know." He ran his fingers through his hair and clutched the back of his neck. "If we're looking at some sort of anniversary, it would likely be annual. Or something that occurred every fixed period of time and none of these fit that pattern."

"And then we really don't have enough information about Smiley to consider his relationship to the others."

The front door opened and Drew spun, his hand going to his sidearm.

"Relax. It's got to be Mackenzie." Teagan heard her sister's shoes drop to the floor, confirming Teagan's thoughts.

Mackenzie soon padded into the room in slippers. She wore a navy blue and white tie-dyed maxi skirt with a navy blue lacy blouse. As Chief Information Officer for the company, she was in charge of keeping details and facts, but at heart, she was a freethinking philosophizer, and her clothing reflected that more than her business side. Teagan often thought as the middle child, Mackenzie purposefully marched to the beat of a different drummer as a way of standing out.

Her gaze went straight to Drew. "Dylan."

"About that." Drew gave her a sheepish look. "My real name is Drew Collier, and I'm an ICE agent."

"I knew it! Law enforcement." She looked at Teagan. "Mom and Dad won't be happy you lied to them."

"Couldn't be helped. Drew is undercover. I had no plans to introduce him to Mom and Dad, but he showed up and Mom insisted he stay for dinner. You know how that goes. She asks and you comply."

"I can see that, but will she be okay with it?" Mackenzie's attention drifted to the whiteboard, and her eyes widened. "You said murder, but didn't mention four victims."

Trying hard to remain calm, Teagan brought her sister up to date, making sure to share every detail that they'd learned so far.

"Wow!" Mackenzie shook her head as she dropped into a chair next to Teagan. "You really stepped into it, didn't you?"

Teagan nodded. "And now we need additional help but our agencies can't provide it. So we figured you'd like to offer your assistance."

"Of course I'm in." She leaned forward as if eager to work. "Where do I start?"

Drew slid Forte's file to her. "Create a murder book with Kris Forte's missing person's report. We're organizing so we can quickly share the info and reference it as we go along."

"You got it." She dug right in, her focus pinned to her work.

Teagan got out her phone and opened her photo app to show Mackenzie photos taken at the grave site. "We found this circle and sword in the middle of the four graves. Ever seen anything like it?"

Mackenzie took the phone and swiped through the pictures. "Doesn't ring a bell, but seems medieval."

"Could be except they didn't use rifles in medieval times," Drew said. "Might be a secret society. That could explain the varied causes of death."

Mackenzie set the phone down and looked at the board. "Maybe it references a movie or book. Or even a video game."

"Could be. Nick is running a search for us on the weapons, but he didn't locate anything when searching for the sword and circle that fit our situation. Neither did we."

"Have you talked to the victims' families?" Mackenzie asked.

"Not before we get up to speed on the investigations so we know the right questions to ask." Drew shared a pointed look with Teagan. "After we get these records organized and review them, then we'll do death notification calls and question the next-of-kin."

The Romo's house smelled like garlic and oregano, and Drew could imagine Carlo Romo coming home from a hard day at work. Kicking off his shoes at the door. The children he might have in the future running to greet him. A traditional Italian meal at the table waiting for him and his family. But the man wouldn't be coming home again. The children wouldn't have a father to throw their arms around.

If only Drew could bring comfort to the sobbing widow sitting across the coffee table from him and Teagan. But he couldn't. He knew that from when his dad died, and today's death notification calls to deliver bad news.

As expected, Mrs. Hoyle hadn't had such an intense reaction. Her husband had been missing for years, and she'd presumed he was dead, but she was upset. Mrs. Forte and Daniela Romo still retained full hope that their husbands would return.

"We're very sorry for your loss," Teagan said, her tone gentle and comforting.

Catapulted back to the loss of his father, the emotions hung heavy on Drew like an icy quilt.

God, where were You then? Where are You now?

"How did he die?" Daniela asked, bringing Drew back.

The last thing this woman needed right now was to find out some creep mauled her husband's body and shot him with an arrow. The details could come later.

"We're still working out the details," he said. "But it was under suspicious circumstances."

"You think he was murdered?" Daniela clutched her chest.

"We do."

"But who?" She gaped at them. "Who would want to kill him?"

"We hoped you might be able to answer that question," Teagan said.

"No one, that's who." She planted her hands on her knees. "He's the kind of guy everyone likes. Always in a good mood. Friendly. I'm the antisocial one, but not him. He made friends everywhere we went." She released her knees and twisted her hands together in her lap. "Why? Just —why?"

Teagan leaned closer. "I recently lost my cousin in a violent death, so I know how tough news like this can be. But are you up to answering a few questions?"

"I don't know. I...I just don't..." She searched the room of her small apartment as if answers hung in the air and she could pluck them down. Tears ran from her already puffy red-rimmed eyes.

Teagan handed the grieving wife a small packet of tissues. "Your answers might help us find whoever did this, but if you're not up to it we understand."

"I can do it." A sob wrenched from her throat, and she shook her head. "For him. For my Carlo."

"Could you tell us a little about him? Like what he did for a living and what he liked to do when he wasn't working."

Daniela dabbed her tears. "He sold alternative energy products. I'm not sure of the details. But he traveled most every week. His territory was the Middle East."

Middle East. Antiquities or heroin connection? Could be.

"He loved every minute of it," she continued. "Not me. I hate to fly. I never went with him. I should have. Especially since we were still newlyweds and my job would've let me off to go. Why didn't I?" Daniela looked at Teagan for answers.

Teagan gave a comforting smile. "You're going to find yourself asking all kinds of questions like that, and it's okay, but don't beat yourself up. It doesn't help."

Daniela crossed her arms around her stomach. "Does the pain get better?"

"Different." Teagan's anguish darkened her tone.

Drew should have realized these calls would remind her of her recent loss and come alone for these calls. He wished more than anything at this moment that he could draw her into his arms and hold her until the pain passed. But it never would. Never did when you lost someone you loved, and it was doubly hard to get over when the death was sudden. Even more so with a violent death where the loss made no sense.

"What things did you two like to do together?" Teagan asked.

"We watched movies." A wavering smile crossed Daniela's face. "All kinds. I love romcoms, and he would watch them with me and never complain. He is—was—so sweet that way. But otherwise, we did things alone. He was a big sports fan. We have a cable sports package, and he watched anything and everything sports related."

"Did he play any sports?" Drew asked.

"In high school and college. Soccer and hockey." She tipped her head. "I guess those were his favorites. I honestly think he liked the fights."

"But he didn't currently play in any league?" Teagan asked.

"No."

"What about hiking?" Drew asked trying to work them around to Carlo's disappearance. "Was he a big hiker?"

She nodded. "But I didn't like the steep trails he needed to get the workout he wanted so we didn't do it together very often. I should've gone with him the day he disappeared instead of dropping him off on my way to see my sister."

"Did he usually go alone?" Drew asked.

"No. He went with a couple of guys from work, but they weren't available that day. I tried to convince him to stay home, but he'd been traveling for three weeks straight and wanted to work off stress."

"Anything else he liked to do in his free time?" Teagan asked.

"Not really."

"I saw in the records that detectives in my department took his laptop, but since returned it," Teagan said. "If so, could we take it with us?"

"I wish I could give it to you but it belonged to his company, and I turned it over to them. He used it for personal use too. Due to all the travel, the company let their employees do that. They gave me a drive of all the personal information it contained."

"Did you look at it?" Teagan asked.

Daniela nodded. "I scrolled through the files. It was just pictures from his travels. Really just meaningful to him, so I haven't done anything with it."

"Could we take it?" Drew tried to hide his enthusiasm, so

she didn't notice it and waste her time searching the pictures for information that might only make sense in connection with the other murdered men.

"Let me grab it from the spare room." She jumped up and fled as if being chased.

Teagan faced Drew. "I assume you caught the Middle Eastern connection to potential antiquity theft and heroin."

"I did." He let his enthusiasm into his tone. "Let's hope this drive contains information that finally makes some sense of these murders."

21

Teagan trailed Drew into her dining room where Mackenzie was still hard at work. Mackenzie had tacked large sheets of paper on the wall, one for each victim, and had listed additional details for each of them. Perfect. Not only did she provide great information, but Teagan's worry lessened just by having her sister at her side in this investigation. After years of living together, they had an unspoken code between them that no one else could match. That would help find these killers. Teagan was sure of it.

"Nice work." Drew approached the papers. "Did you find anything to connect them all?"

Mackenzie sat up in her chair. "They all formerly played sports and loved it, but none of them were currently active in any leagues. And I couldn't find anything in the sports themselves that connected them."

Teagan thought back to their previous research. "Rossi is a soccer coach for kids second through eighth grade. Maybe our victims played in his league when they were little."

"Sounds possible. Grab a book and let's see if we have that info." Mackenzie pushed one of the murder books to Teagan and another one to Drew.

He pulled out a chair for Teagan, and she smiled at him, letting her gaze linger a moment longer than necessary.

"Um-hmm," Mackenzie said. "Just like I thought."

"You have a lead?" Teagan pulled her chair in.

"No. Just observing the two of you."

Teagan wouldn't get into a personal discussion now so she shook her head at her sister and flipped open Benton Hoyle's binder. "Good job in finishing the books, by the way."

"Glad to help." Mackenzie smiled, but it was more of a smirk holding a residual knowing look. "I have to admit that I kind of miss this. Not enough to go back, but I miss it."

"Me too," Teagan said, glad at the change in subject. "But after working this investigation, I'll be happy to return to running a business."

Drew had been ignoring them. Or if he was paying attention, he didn't comment. He just kept running his finger down pages in his book and flipping them with a frenzy. "Here it is. Forte grew up in Salem. Makes it unlikely that he was in Rossi's soccer league."

Mackenzie tapped a page in her book. "Romo lived in Tillamook. That's an hour away like Salem, so Rossi probably didn't coach him either. Not impossible for either one, though."

Teagan continued reading until she found the needed information. "Hoyle was raised in Gresham. I remember reading that Rossi's league was neighborhood specific for the most part, but they did take kids from other areas. Gresham might be on the other side of the city, but we can't rule Hoyle out." Teagan grabbed her phone. "I'll text Nick to see if he can locate old team rosters."

Drew looked at Mackenzie. "I didn't see any sign of sports betting in Forte's file. Did you come across it in the other files?"

"Maybe," she said. "Forte and Romo both went to Vegas recently, but not at the same time. The detectives on each investigation looked into their finances. Nothing odd there. If these guys *were* gambling, they were finding a way to do it under the radar."

Drew draped an arm over the chair next to him. "Which means they couldn't be losing money as they couldn't very well hide withdrawals from their accounts."

"And if they were winning," Mackenzie said. "They were hiding their earnings as they weren't buying extravagant items."

Teagan gave it some thought. "They could still be losing, just not their own money. If they borrowed it, they could've been into someone for the money they lost."

"Failure to pay could be a reason to kill them, I suppose," Drew said. "Though they would be better off alive to their bookie."

Teagan looked at Drew. "Are the Contis involved in organized gambling?"

"I've never heard anything to that effect, but I don't know what all Rossi has his hands in."

Teagan faced her sister. "Can you tell if the wives went on these Vegas trips?"

Mackenzie's eyes narrowed. "In each case, two airfares were charged to their credit cards. I assume that it was the wife as any guy having an affair shouldn't be dumb enough to charge it to their joint credit cards."

"Never know what someone might do." Drew looked at Teagan. "We'll have to follow up on this with the families."

"I'll start a list of follow-up questions." Teagan got out her phone and made a note in the app.

Drew closed his book, his gaze pensive. "None of the wives had any idea why someone would want to kill their husbands. We'll need to interview friends and coworkers next. See if they tell a different story. And in Forte's case, we need to check with other gym members."

Teagan added that to her notes. "We can do that first thing in the morning."

"We should also interview the detectives in charge of the missing person investigations," Mackenzie said. "You know how as an investigator you have gut feelings in an investigation that don't make it into the reports."

"Can you take care of that?" Drew asked.

"Glad to." Mackenzie's whole body lifted to attention.

Teagan loved seeing her sister so alive. She'd been kind of down this last little while. Teagan thought she needed a vacation and would suggest that when this investigation was over. Teagan should take one too, but they both couldn't be gone at the same time, and Teagan wanted her sister to have first dibs on time off. After all, it was Teagan's job to make sure everyone flourished in the company.

"What about Romo's travel?" Drew asked. "Might he have run into these guys while on the road?"

Mackenzie grabbed Forte's book, flipped to the back, and slid the binder across the table. She tapped the page. "This is a list of hotels owned by the company he works for. We could cross reference the list to Romo's travel schedule if we could get his schedule."

Teagan ran down the list. "None of these hotels are in the Middle East, which was Romo's territory."

Drew frowned. "Then it's not likely the hotel connects Romo to Forte, but Hoyle had quite a few airline tickets booked on his credit card statements. Could they have connected at some time?"

"Anything to the Middle East?" Teagan asked.

"Not that I saw," Drew said. "But he died a while ago, so it would have to have been before the summer of 2018. We don't have records for Forte and Romo back that far and will have to request the financials and talk to the family."

"I'll add it to my list." Teagan tapped the information into her phone.

"For now," Drew said. "Let's look at Forte and Romo starting with the last three months. Social media is listed in the reports but not as related to travels. We should check that too."

"I already did," Mackenzie said. "Didn't take long. They each had Facebook accounts and never really posted anything."

"So we start with financial records then." Teagan pulled Forte's book closer to her.

Mackenzie grabbed her laptop. "I'll create a spreadsheet where we can log the travel dates for comparison."

A logical move for Steele Guardians' Chief Information Officer. Mackenzie, despite her free spirit, loved to organize data and information and present it in a logical way so they could all make decisions. Having someone devoted to just that was a true blessing to Teagan.

"Thanks." Teagan flipped to Forte's financial section and found the credit card statements.

"Romo was in Qatar from November first to the eighteenth," Drew said.

Mackenzie's fingers flew over the keyboard, her eyes narrowed with concentration.

Teagan ran her finger down Forte's credit card statement for April. "Forte had airline tickets for BGW at the beginning of April. Not sure where that is."

"I'll look it up," Mackenzie said, her fingers already typing. "Baghdad International Airport."

Teagan's pulse kicked into gear. "So they both traveled to the Middle East before they died but not at the same time. Could it have to do with the stolen antiquities?"

Drew nodded. "Or could even have to do with drugs."

Teagan held Drew's gaze. "We need to call Hoyle's wife first thing in the morning to see if he went to the Middle East too." Teagan added the information to her list.

Mackenzie yawned.

"You should head to bed," Teagan said. "We'll start again in the morning."

"You don't have to tell me twice." Mackenzie chuckled and stood. "I hope starting in the morning includes you making breakfast for us."

Teagan smiled. "I can."

"Then good night." She swept out of the room in a flourish, her skirt swishing as she walked.

Drew sat back. "I like your sister."

"Me too, but don't tell her that." Teagan laughed.

"I always wanted siblings, but my parents were never able to have another child. And then my dad died, so..."

"I can't tell you how many times growing up I wished I was an only child, but that was pure foolishness. Losing Thomas really put in perspective how much family means to all of us."

"Family who won't appreciate me lying to them."

"They'll get it. Maybe not at first, but they're all in law enforcement so they'll understand."

"Listen to us. Talking like I'll be seeing your family after all of this is done."

She wasn't sure how to respond, so she would just lay everything on the line and go from there. "I would like it if that happened."

"I'm kind of leaning that way too."

"You are?"

"Ever since I kissed you." He took her hand, his warm and rough. "But I don't want to mislead you. I still haven't worked through my issue. I'm trying, though. You're so worth it."

"Shouldn't you let me decide if I want to risk potential pain?"

"Yeah, I should, but I just..." He shook his head. "Whenever I think of my mom after my dad died, it cuts me in two. She was in such pain. Had a complete mental collapse. I just..."

"Then let's agree to not decide anything until after this investigation is over. Give both of us time to think about what we want and what we're willing to risk."

"I don't deserve you."

"What? Why?"

"Because you're so understanding when I know this is something I should just be able to let go."

"You experienced a deep trauma. First with losing your dad and then with your mother suffering so much. It's not just blink and it will go away. It will always be with you in varying degrees." *And hopefully, you can come to grips with it*, she didn't add as she didn't want to put any pressure on him right now.

"I appreciate you saying that." He lifted her hand and kissed it.

Her heart flooded with warmth and longing, and everything good—so different from when Oliver had done the same thing.

He released her hand, and a cool mask went down over his face. "You up for reviewing Romo's flash drive before we call it quits for the night?"

She nodded, though she had to admit to disappointment that he'd moved them back to the professional world so quickly. Even if she *had* agreed to wait on anything personal.

Her laptop still sat on the table so she grabbed it,

plugged the drive into the side, and opened the file. "Hundreds of pictures."

"Open the ones from his most recent trip."

She clicked on the first December picture. "He's attending a soccer match."

Drew leaned closer and pointed at the screen. "Not just any soccer match. See the banners on the stands? It's a World Cup playoff game."

She clicked through the action pictures of the game and paused on a closeup holding Romo and a guy with inky black hair, a neatly trimmed beard and broad nose, wearing a green soccer jersey.

"That's the Iraq flag on the guy's chest," Drew said. "And Romo is beaming at the man like he's something special."

"Let me do an internet image search." She uploaded the photo to a search engine, and it came back with many listings for the name Nasim Jabal, a former Iraq National soccer player and a man revered in his country.

She read down the entries. "Looks like he's a legend in Iraqi soccer."

"Makes sense," Drew said. "Romo seems excited to meet him."

She looked at Drew. "You think this means anything?"

"Could I suppose, or it's just something that happened on this trip."

"Should we get Nick looking into it?"

"Sure, but only after he finishes searching for the youth rosters."

Teagan sent Nick a text, praying this could be what they were looking for even though she seriously doubted the murders had anything to do with a famous soccer champion.

22

The next morning, Teagan ended the call with Benton Hoyle's wife and looked across the dining table at Mackenzie and Drew, who were still eating the rosemary quiche, fruit, and toast Teagan had gotten up early to make for them. Drew hadn't been followed by anyone last night or this morning. Thankfully, that meant he felt more comfortable coming to breakfast.

He swallowed the last bite of his second large piece of quiche. "What did she say?"

"Boyle *did* travel before he disappeared but not to the Middle East. He went to Moscow for work. His company has a training facility there where he trained their workers."

"Not at all related to the other two then." Mackenzie stabbed a bite of cantaloupe.

Teagan shook her head. "I asked her if he took any pictures while there, and she said she'd look and forward anything she finds to me."

Drew drained his orange juice glass. "I need to move some money to the Contis first thing this morning and pay them a visit. After that we can visit our victims' workplaces and gym."

Teagan's phone chimed. "Text from Nick. He's emailing the soccer rosters he found and a background report on Nasim Jabal along with pictures he says we should look at pronto."

She pushed her plate away and grabbed her laptop so they could view the photos in larger format. Drew and Mackenzie both came to stand behind her.

When her computer dinged, she quickly clicked on the message and opened the first of three photos. "Nasim Jabal and Benton Hoyle. At a World Cup match, too but in 2018."

"That's a strong connection to Romo," Mackenzie said.

"Anything for Forte?" Drew asked.

She selected the next picture and gaped at it. "It's Forte with Jabal."

Teagan glanced over her shoulder at Drew. "Who do you think this Jabal guy is?"

"Obviously that's what we need to find out." Drew held her gaze. "Open the last picture."

She clicked on the photo showing Jabal and Rossi at one of his youth soccer matches, where Jabal was holding a clinic for the kids.

"The final connection." Mackenzie returned to her seat.

"It's soccer and this Nasim Jabal guy." Drew shook his head as he circled the end of the table to sit. "But what does it mean?"

"Surely, Jabal didn't kill these guys over some soccer match," Teagan said.

"Not likely." Drew stabbed a final piece of cantaloupe.

"Could Jabal be Rossi's antiquities or drug connection?" Teagan asked.

Drew swallowed his bite. "What does the background report say?"

Teagan looked at the screen. "He was a professional soccer player until 2015. The highest scoring player in all of

Iraqi soccer. Extremely revered and a legend. Now he's a spokesman for Iraq's soccer league and travels extensively around the world promoting the national team."

"Which would give him a chance to smuggle drugs or antiquities on his travels," Drew said. "Or make contacts to move products."

"So could our victims be part of his network?" Teagan asked.

"We need to finish charting each guy's travel dates," Mackenzie said. "And also figure out if Jabal was in Oregon when these men were killed."

Teagan looked at Drew. "Harris would be our best bet to get a warrant for Jabal's travel and other information we need, but she told you to stand down on the murders."

"I don't care." Drew jumped up. "I'll try to tie it to the antiquities to get her to agree to that."

Teagan appreciated his willingness to go out on a limb. "While you make the call, Mac and I can check the schedules we have in the books and call the wives for more details."

"We should also find out where Jabal is right now." Drew dug his phone from the cargo pocket of his pants. "I'll get Harris on that too, but maybe Nick can find him faster."

Teagan nodded. "I'll give him a call."

Drew gave a sharp nod and stepped out of the room.

Mackenzie grabbed the nearest book. "I'll get started on the dates."

Teagan called Nick.

"Yo," he answered. "You get the information I sent?"

"Yes, thank you."

"Seemed important. I'm still working on a deep dive on the guy. He's pretty private, so it'll likely take some time."

"Thank you for keeping after it." She took a breath. "I

hate to ask another favor, but any way you can locate Jabal for us?"

"Figured you'd want to know so I already have his location."

If he were sitting in front of her, she would be gaping at him. "How did you do that? Especially since he doesn't have much info out there."

"You don't want to know."

"Okay," she said as she assumed it involved hacking that might be on the fringe of legality. "So where is he?"

"Flew into PDX last night."

So he'd flown into Portland, but what had he come to do?

Drew stowed his phone near the dining room table, hardly able to believe what Teagan was telling him as she looked up at him with wide eyes. Nasim Jabal was not only in the country, but he was in Portland. Somewhere. Doing what, Drew had no idea. Maybe planning to kill another guy. But why? Who?

Drew had to find out and do it quickly. "Did Nick say where Jabal was staying?"

"All he could tell me was where he wasn't," Teagan answered. "No hotel booked or house rental. No car booked either. So either he took a rideshare or someone picked him up and is chauffeuring him around."

"Do you have his flight info?" Drew asked, his mind racing with details and plans.

She nodded. "Nick just texted it to me."

"Forward it to me. I'll have Harris get the airport security footage. Maybe we can find out if he was picked up and by who."

"I can do that," Teagan said. "Or we can wait on Nick. He said he had a contact who could give him the info right away."

"Then we wait."

"What about Harris getting us a warrant for the records we need?" Mackenzie tapped the open binder. "There's not much in these files about travel except for Romo."

"She agreed and will jump on it."

"Once Nick tells us who picked Jabal up," Teagan said. "We need to get surveillance on him twenty-four/seven."

"I doubt Harris will spring for that," Drew said.

Teagan frowned. "I can try County, but honestly, if we want it done fast and done well, we can either tap my family again or hire Nighthawk Security."

Drew searched his memory for any info she'd shared about the team that had offices in the Veritas building. "The team for the guy who went to Harris on your behalf?"

She nodded. "They'd likely reduce their rate for us, but my family is free."

Mackenzie looked up. "This is none of my business, but I have to weigh in. If you want top-notch protection, go to those guys—but we can do the surveillance without a problem, and we can get it going like yesterday."

"Let's assume Nick will come through and go ahead and schedule your family," Drew said. "But I want the first shift as I want to lay eyes on this guy for myself."

"I'm joining you." Teagan looked at Mackenzie. "You're great at scheduling. Figure out how many people we need and get others on the phone to see who can fill the slots."

Drew glanced between the sisters. "When you read them in, it has to be with very limited information."

Teagan arched an eyebrow. "We won't skimp on what they need to know to be safe. They have to know they'll be trailing a man who could've killed four other men."

"I have no problem with that. Let's get it going." Drew's gut tangled, but at the same time adrenaline flowed through his body, and he was eager to act, not sit here and plan. But he knew the success of any op was in the planning. He didn't just get up one day and decide to be Dylan Crane. It took months of planning to create his cover and identity. To lay out his approach and make sure he would succeed.

They didn't have months to prepare for tailing Jabal, but they could at least do their best in the limited time they had. If he really was a serial killer, their lives could depend on it.

Teagan parked across the road from Rossi's large home in Happy Valley and turned off the key on their rented BMW, Drew in the passenger seat. She slid her seat back for extra room and took a long look at the seven-thousand square foot house. She'd located the address online and found pictures of the place with every amenity and a view of Mount Hood. Which she couldn't see because the sun had already set, leaving a clear sky with sparkling stars.

Drew shifted, his long legs making him look uncomfortable. "Can't say as I ever surveilled anyone in such a well-appointed car."

"We fit right into the neighborhood, and no one will ever mistake this for an undercover police car."

"I wish we could've gotten the larger model."

She did too. Not because of her leg room but because she wouldn't be sitting so close to Drew. With all the commotion and information learned this morning, she'd managed to put her developing feelings for him on the back burner, but sitting this close? Seeing his strong profile? Catching the scent of his sandalwood soap?

She wanted to forget Rossi and her job and just be with

Drew. Enjoy the time. But she couldn't. In fact, she had to work extra hard not to think of him as a man but as a fellow officer on a stakeout. Problem was, on every stakeout she'd participated in, the talk had always turned personal. It couldn't with him. She wouldn't let it with him.

He grabbed his binoculars and watched the house. "Only two cars in the drive, but he has a four-car garage. Who knows how many vehicles are actually here."

"I'd love to get a closer look, but we don't want to tip our hand this early in the game."

"Wait," he said. "Garage door going up. Black SUV backing out. Tinted windows. Can't tell who's inside but there are two people in the front."

"Could be Rossi and Jabal headed out to kill someone." She looked at Drew. "Should we tail them?"

"Yes."

She started the car and waited for the SUV to get a good lead before pulling from the curb. She tapped the car's phone interface and told it to call dispatch to run the plates.

"Registered to a Chauncey Rossi." The dispatcher read off the address which matched this residence.

Teagan ended the call and fixed her attention on the road. "I hope we're not making a mistake in following them."

"Could be, but it's the best option." Drew pointed ahead. "He's getting on the freeway that leads to Rossi's warehouse."

"Maybe this is about the antiquities or drugs."

Drew leaned forward. "We really need to get that detailed report on Jabal from Nick soon."

"He'll provide it as soon as he can." She focused on the road so she didn't accidentally creep too close and put Rossi on alert.

They stayed on the freeway until they neared the

airport and turned off to the industrial area holding Rossi's warehouse. He pulled into his company drive, and she killed the headlights, then coasted to a stop in the same spot where Drew had paused on their last surveillance.

He lifted his binoculars. "Gambino got out. He's doing a perimeter check. Get ready to back away if he comes close."

At the threat of being discovered, her heart kicked into gear. She shifted into reverse, ready to gun it if needed. She kept her eyes on the driveway and wished she had a better view of the men.

"He's headed back to the car. Opening the passenger door. Guy getting out. Not Rossi. Jabal." Drew leaned forward. "Opening the back door now. Rossi getting out."

She strained her eyes but could barely make out the movement.

"Okay, they're hustling inside. They seem super on edge. I say we leave the car here tonight. Not risk driving into the lot. I'll hoof it across the space. You stay here." He looked at her. "Someone needs to take backup in case I get into trouble in there."

She wanted to argue, but he had a valid point. "If you're not back in fifteen minutes, and I haven't heard from you, I'm coming in."

"Roger that." He reached for his door handle.

She grabbed his forearm and waited for him to meet her gaze. "Be careful, Drew. I don't want to lose you."

The warehouse was dark and the air stagnant. The big air ducts at the ceiling were still, the HVAC likely turned down for the night to save money. Drew had scanned for body heat signatures and found the three men in the front of the building exactly where Rossi had met with Sal Conti the other night.

Drew slid along the exterior wall until he was in hearing distance of the men. He lifted the binoculars that hung around his neck to get a good look at Jabal. He looked exactly like the guy in the pictures with the victims, but different too.

Gone was the fan smile. Gone was the cheerful and relaxed countenance. Here stood an intense, deadly-looking foe. His dark eyes were narrowed below thick eyebrows. His jaw set. His focus locked on Rossi. The thin guy shifted on his feet, acting uncomfortable and nervous, telling Drew that Jabal called the shots. He was Mr. Big.

The guy Drew had been seeking.

Drew got out his phone to record the conversation. He didn't have a warrant and couldn't use the recording in the investigation, but it might come in useful in other ways. At the very least, Teagan would want to hear it.

"I don't like it." Jabal took a step toward Rossi.

Gambino moved closer.

Jabal spun on the man and stabbed a finger in his thick chest. "You make another move toward me and it will be your last."

"It's okay, Tony," Rossi said. "Nasim is a friend. He would never hurt me."

"Don't be too sure." Jabal eyed Rossi. "Now tell me why we want to let our product sit with this local we don't even know."

"To grow your business. We wash his money for now, but he has strong connections to move product. The more connections we make, the more product we move. The more product we move, the happier you are."

"He into the antiquities too?" Jabal asked.

Rossi shook his head, his silvery hair whispering over

his forehead, and he shoved it back in place. "Strictly the powder."

"Twenty-percent cut on the laundering isn't enough if I have to let my product get stale with him. I want you to renegotiate. Get me another ten and we will move forward."

Rossi frowned. "He'll never agree to that."

"Then it's his loss. We aren't in the cleaning business. If I'm carrying that risk, I'm going to get a just reward."

"Okay." The uncertainty in Rossi's tone hung in the air.

Jabal glared at him. "You think the Conti bozos are up to handling this?"

"Sal and Aldo for sure. Vito is a weak link."

"I want him gone. I have never even been suspected of anything illegal in all these years, and that's because I don't abide weak links."

"We can take care of it." Rossi didn't even blink an eye.

"No." Jabal rested his hands on a nearby crate. "I'll take care of it. You just get me my thirty percent. Now let's get this stash put into safe keeping, and I'll let you know when the job is done."

"You heard the man," Rossi said to Tony. "Put it in the upper deck, bay six."

Tony strode across the room and hopped onto a forklift. He started the engine and it rumbled to life, the sound echoing from the high ceilings.

Drew turned off the recording and bolted, letting the engine noise cover his steps as he hurried out the door. His mind raced as fast as his feet.

Was Jabal the killer? Had he killed Smiley and the other men? Sure seemed like it, but what about the varied ways the men were killed? Why do that? It just didn't make sense.

Drew hoofed it across the lot, trying to keep his footfalls from sounding on the asphalt. He powered through the ditch and into the rental car.

"They're leaving soon." He buckled his seatbelt. "Go!"

Teagan gave him a frantic look. "Go where?"

"Assume they'll go back home and get into position to follow them where they can't see us."

She floored the gas, and the car shot back in reverse. She backed onto a nearby street and maneuvered into a hidden spot. All was done with minimal, but precision effort. He had to admire her driving skills.

She shifted into park and turned to him. "What did they say or do?"

Drew quickly played the recording while keeping his eyes on the road and waiting for the SUV to appear. "Once we get across town, we'll have to split up. You stay on these guys, and I'll have Harris come for me."

"Why?" Her tone ratcheted up another notch.

His fault. He'd been hyper since he'd left the warehouse. He needed to bring things down a notch. "I need to locate Vito, bring him in. First, to make sure he stays alive. Second, to try to flip him."

She turned her face from the road and looked at Drew. "You'll have to blow your cover."

Yeah, he would. He swallowed away the unease of revealing his true ID. "The op is coming to an end anyway. If Vito rolls over, we'll have our case made. Harris can't say no to us bringing this killer to justice."

23

Teagan finished her surveillance shift at nine p.m. when Londyn and Peyton came to relieve her. She thankfully drove off from the boring task and headed for the Steele Guardians' office. She'd seen no additional action at Rossi's house and figured the men were in for the night. But not her.

No. She might be tired, but she was amped at the same time. She had to do something constructive. Nick's report had arrived in her Inbox right before she'd ended her watch. She would print it out and study every word in hopes of blowing this investigation open.

She pushed through the door, surprised to see Gretchen still sitting behind the reception desk. It was unusual to find her there after six. Not so unusual for Teagan. She often worked this late, usually the last one in the family to leave the building for the day. Mackenzie often worked late too.

No life outside of work for either of them—zero.

Okay, maybe they both went to Sunday worship and family dinners, but otherwise, Teagan likely could be found behind the four walls of Steele Guardians. And she didn't mind that. Not one bit. She'd had her share of relationships fail and didn't have the energy to even start one, only to have it end when the guy got upset over all the hours she put into her job or didn't like that she was a strong force to be reckoned with.

The exception to that seemed to be Drew.

She paused by the desk and smiled at Gretchen. "You're here late."

"Your dad asked me to stay. He and your uncle are expecting a potential new big shot client who could only come tonight, and they didn't want it to look like the business couldn't afford a receptionist to greet him."

"Sounds like Dad and Uncle Gene." Teagan shifted her laptop case on her shoulder and started for the stairs, but halfway there she stopped. If she worked at the conference table down here, she could spread out the papers as she organized herself.

Plus, she didn't want to be alone. Gave her more of a chance for her thoughts of Drew to intrude in her solitude. Which is why she hadn't gone home. Mackenzie would give her the third degree, and Teagan wasn't ready to admit to anyone—not even herself really—that she was all in on a relationship with Drew when the man was obviously on the fence.

She crossed the room and glanced at Gretchen. "I hope it won't bug you if I work at the table."

"Bug me? No way. It'll be great to have the company." Gretchen got up and stretched, then ran both hands through hair dyed a blondish gray color that month.

Teagan issued a warning look. "Just so you remember I'm working."

Gretchen wrinkled her nose. "Point taken. I'll keep quiet until you ask me something."

Teagan doubted that would happen, but if she didn't want to be alone with her thoughts, she needed a distraction. Thoughts like if Drew had found Vito? He hadn't texted so she figured he was still looking for the guy, but a quick update wouldn't have hurt. Still, she wouldn't bug him any more than she would bug another associate in a situation like this.

She opened her computer and sent Nick's report to the printer. It was only six pages but she was old school in that she liked to take notes on a hard copy. The older detectives she'd worked with had teased her about using their methods when she was so young.

"I'll bring your printing to you," Gretchen said. "It'll give me something to do so I don't poke my eyes out in boredom."

"Thanks." Teagan opened the photos from the crime scene, looking one more time at the sword in the circle in case there was an obscure reference to it in Jabal's information. Then she took another long look at the picture of the claw marks on Romo's chest. Not that she really thought Nick's report would address that. She just wanted to remind herself what a sick guy Jabal was if he was their killer, so she was even more motivated to keep working.

"Ew," Gretchen's voice came from behind Teagan. "Looks like that guy was attacked by Wolverine."

Teagan quickly closed the picture. "You mean the Marvel Comics character, Wolverine?"

She nodded. "One of the guys in my cosplay group bought metal claws online."

Teagan knew cosplay was short for costume play. Basically, adult dress-up.

Gretchen bent over Teagan. "And that looks like the logo for Blood and Sorcery."

"That really violent video game? I've heard about it but never played it."

"I did. Once and only once at a guy's house. Great graphics. Too realistic if you ask me. And the weapon choices are brutal."

Teagan's nerves started tingling. "Are there claws like the Wolverine's?"

"Yeah, why?"

"How about a hatchet? Or even a bow and arrow or rifle?"

"Yeah, I think so. Not a hundred percent, though. Want me to research it for you?"

"Go for it while I read my report." Teagan reached for her phone to tell Drew about the lead, but she snatched her hand back. She would read this report and let Gretchen confirm the weapons before contacting him. Once she had all the information in hand, she would call him. No point in interrupting him if this lead went nowhere.

Teagan drove through the dark night alone, heading for Smiley's property. She'd tried calling Drew, but her calls kept going to voicemail. She couldn't let that stop her. Let the killer get away with murder. If she could prove her theory, they would be one step closer to bringing him in. She also couldn't risk the evidence being destroyed. She'd have preferred Drew accompany her, but with Rossi and Jabal under surveillance, she was perfectly safe going alone.

She turned on to his road and slowed as she approached. A light flickered out of the window on Smiley's house. Like a computer or TV screen lighting up the room.

What in the world?

She slammed on her brakes and pulled over, cutting the headlights as she did. She sure didn't expect to find anyone here. Especially not at this time of night. And the electricity had been cut off in the house, so the light had to be coming from a battery-powered device or someone set up a generator.

She cut the engine and listened. No generator. She picked her way through the brush to the driveway, where a large black truck loomed. Keeping her focus on the house, she inched ahead for a closer look at the vehicle. Crickets chirped in the background and an owl hooted, but no sound came from the house.

She reached the truck. White lettering on the door declared Northwest Geo Instruments. Rossi's business truck.

Was Rossi inside? If so, how did he get out of his house without Londyn or Peyton seeing him?

Teagan pinned her attention to the house, but moved back to her car. It was hidden by thick brush. She felt free there to text her cousins without the light from her phone giving her away.

Rossi still there? she texted.

Londyn replied immediately. *Yes. Just saw him step out for a smoke.*

What about Gambino? He or Jabal leave?

No one's left the property since we arrived.

Odd. So who was in Smiley's house?

Only one way to find out.

She silenced her phone and stepped onto the property to evaluate. Any hint of danger, and she would call for backup from County.

Drew had exhausted every possible location in an effort to find Vito and had given up for the night. He'd tried to return Teagan's call, but she wasn't answering her phone. She'd said she was going to her office to work, so he parked in the Steele Guardians' parking lot and approached the door. The inside light clicked off, and their receptionist stepped out with key in hand.

"Remember me?" he asked.

She startled but quickly recovered. "You came to see Teagan. Dylan, right?"

He nodded and didn't correct her on the name.

"I'm Gretchen by the way." She held out her hand, her nails painted all black except her index finger was a baby blue. "Teagan's not here. She went out about an hour ago."

Out? At this time of night? "Did she say where she was going?"

Gretchen shook her head. "I know she was looking at pictures from an autopsy. I saw one. It was really odd."

"Oh, yeah." He played it down, but his interest was piqued for sure. Which autopsy picture had Teagan been viewing? The most unusual would be of Romo's wounds on his torso. "The guy have long scratches on his body?"

"Yeah, so you *have* seen it." She inserted the key into the lock. "I shouldn't have been looking over her shoulder, but I still told her what I thought."

"Which was?" He continued to play it cool when his heart rate was starting to kick up.

She kept her fingers resting on the key. "I think the scratches look like they could be from Wolverine."

"As in the movie character?"

She nodded. "I'm big into a cosplay group and one of the guys got metal claws online."

Costume play. "That's interesting. Thanks for sharing."

"Sure, is there anything else I can help with?" She twisted the key and the lock snicked into place.

On a hunch he took out his phone and displayed the photo from the circle and sword. "Any idea what this might be?"

"Wow, you and Teagan think alike. She had that open too." Gretchen waved a hand. "That was an easy one."

"Care to enlighten me?"

"It's the logo for Blood and Sorcery."

"Blood and Sorcery? Is that some kind of cosplay?"

She snorted. "Sorry. No. It's just. Well, I figured most everyone under forty had heard of this video game."

"Why's that?"

"It's the most violent game on the market and has been under a lot of controversy this past year."

The time he'd been under and not paying much attention to the real world. But it was odd that Nick didn't know about it. As a tech guy, he was most likely into video games. Even if he'd heard the stories, there were so many games on the market that it would be hard to recognize the logo for all of them.

"Tell me about it," he said.

"The graphics are very realistic, and you have choices of a ton of brutal weapons. I told Teagan the game has claws like Wolverine's, and she had me look online to see if there were other weapons. She especially wanted to know about a rifle, hatchet, and bow and arrow. Once I told her there were, she raced out of here."

Drew's heart kicked fully into gear. He appreciated the information. Figured it would be most helpful. But didn't like that Teagan had run out as if she was following a lead on her own.

He forced calm he didn't feel into his tone. "But she didn't say where she was going?"

"No. She has her cell. You should try calling her."

"I have been. She's not answering."

Gretchen frowned. "That's not like her at all. She's the most conscientious in that area of all the Steeles. She says she never knows when it might be the call that will help their business thrive." Gretchen studied him. "She probably knows it's you calling. Any reason she might not want to talk to you?"

"Not that I can think of." He tried to keep his tone neutral but failed big time. "Can you call her? See if she answers for you?"

"Sure." She rummaged around in her purse to get out her cell. She tapped her foot, worry taking her expression. "No answer. I could call her sisters to see if she's home."

"Do that," he urged while panic was fighting to gain purchase.

She looked at her phone and thumbed down the screen.

"Mackenzie, it's Gretchen. Teagan's not answering her phone. Is she home?" Gretchen's eyes narrowed, and she looked at Drew, then shook her head.

His gut cramped. Hard. A knot of steel.

Something was wrong. Very wrong.

Please don't let whoever is here have discovered the graves have been excavated, Teagan prayed as she inched toward the truck. If it's the killer, they might think they don't have anything to lose.

She felt the vehicle's hood. Warm. Whoever was in the house hadn't been there long. She would get a look at what was going on inside. She couldn't waste limited County resources by calling for backup without knowing someone was in danger. She'd get details first so she knew what kind of response to request.

Light shone from the front room of the small house, spilling out like a beacon to lead her deeper into the property. She made her way to a tree and paused behind it to assess. Her mind filled with visions of the gruesome discovery they'd found on this property. Her stomach churned, nausea mixing with fear of what she might soon discover.

You have to be strong. Ignore the fear. Move ahead.

"No! No!" A male's agitated words burst out of the broken windows like two gunshots, echoing through the quiet night.

Oh no. No. She knew who it was. She'd worked with him and his brothers for years.

Vito Conti.

And he was in trouble. She had to move faster.

She zigzagged to the house, ducking behind a rusty car. A tree. Then another.

She made a final mad dash to the nearest window. Broken. Good. She would be able to hear better. She spotted Jabal with a gun pointed at Vito, who was violently trembling. A laptop computer sat on a dusty table that had been turned upright, a video game on the screen.

The music played, and she recognized it from when Gretchen was researching Blood and Sorcery.

"I said play," Jabal demanded.

Vito held up his controller, his gaze pleading. "But I—"

Jabal jabbed Vito's shoulder with his gun. "Either play or I will kill you right here."

"You're going to kill me anyway," Vito said, a hint of rebellion in his voice. "Why make me play the stupid game?"

"I am giving you a chance to live. Win this level and I will let you go. Lose and you will die the same way your character dies."

Ah-ha! That explained the varied weapons used to kill the victims. He let the victim play for his life and used the weapon that killed his avatar to end the player's life. Meant he would have to come prepared for many scenarios.

She searched the room and saw a large duffle on the floor. Could it contain all the needed weapons? If so, it could pin all of these murders to Jabal. She couldn't risk Vito's life, but she also couldn't miss out on apprehending Jabal and seizing the weapons.

She had time. At least as long as Vito played along. Which she figured he would do to buy time.

She backed her way to the driveway and then the road. She didn't want to leave Vito alone with a killer, but she couldn't risk being overheard or having Jabal see the light from her phone.

She dialed Drew. Got voicemail. "It's Teagan. I'm at Smiley's place. Vito is here. So is Jabal. He's going to kill Vito if I don't intervene. Will call County for backup."

She ended the call and phoned dispatch to report her location and ask for backup.

"Nearest unit is en route now, but he's thirty minutes out," the dispatcher said.

"Tell him to book it." She hung up and double-checked her phone to be sure it was in silent mode before starting back for the house.

She reached the clearing. Not more than twenty feet to the house.

The front door flung open.

"Run!" Jabal's excited voice came from inside.

She bolted toward the house. Pressed her body against the side. Vito came charging down the steps.

No time to think. She raced for the landing. Got behind the door. Waited.

Jabal burst out, a full-sized ax in his hands. She stuck out her foot. Tripped him. His hands flailed out, but he lost his balance. Tumbled down the steps.

"Police, don't move!" She started for the stairs—her weapon outstretched.

She lifted a foot to step down.

The earth rolled beneath the deck. Shifting. Shaking. Hard.

She tried to regain her stance. Lost her balance. Fell from the platform. The ground continued to move. She blinked hard. What in the world?

Oh no. No. No. No.

Earthquake! Rare but not unheard of in Oregon.

Please don't let the ground open up and swallow me whole.

24

Drew raced toward Smiley's property. Thankfully, there was little traffic at this time of night, and he could floor the gas, moving at high speed. At the speed his heart was traveling. How could he have missed Teagan's call? His phone didn't ring but suddenly showed a voice mail. Had to be because of sparse cell towers in the rural area.

The ground shifted beneath the car. "What the—?"

The earth shook harder. A large pine tree came plunging down over the road. He slammed on his brakes and skidded toward the tree. He braced for the point of impact.

His bumper slammed into the solid wood.

Airbags deployed. Slapping his face.

His vehicle rocked to a stop, but the ground kept shifting.

He'd experienced earthquakes before but not this strong. Still, the tree had likely been damaged or sick if it was so easily uprooted.

The rolling stopped as fast as it started. The ground felt solid beneath him again.

He'd never experienced such a helpless feeling. The

whole world below him moving. No way to stop it. Threatening to swallow him.

Teagan. Was she okay? He had to get to her.

He dragged in a breath. Another. Mentally assessing any injuries.

His chest hurt. Face hurt. From the airbag. But he was good to go.

He punched down the fabric and released his seatbelt to stumble out and evaluate the damage to his car. Front end smashed. Bumper dangling.

So what? Did the condition of his car even matter?

No way he was getting around this tree. If Teagan was in danger, she would have to get out of it without him.

Teagan stumbled to her feet, the earth still moving.

Jabal was faster. He had his gun on her. "Don't move or I shoot."

The shaking stopped. She took a breath. Another one. Assessed.

Didn't see Vito. *Good.* At least he'd gotten free.

"Why are you here?" Jabal asked, his English perfect and barely a hint of an accent.

She wanted to unload on him but decided to take a calm approach. Maybe he wouldn't shoot her unless provoked. "To stop you from killing another person."

"I have not—"

"Save it," she said. "We found the bodies and your connection to them. All we don't know is why you are doing it and why this way."

"I don't have to explain my actions to you." He lifted his chin, a haughty expression on his face. "What's the point anyway? You aren't going to live beyond the night."

"Just humor me." She tried to remain calm, but her mouth had gone paper dry. "Did you kill Smiley or only the other three?"

"Smiley was my first." A sick smile slid over his face, and his eyes glazed in a dark stare.

She searched the area for a way to get free but there was no escaping a speeding bullet. She had to keep the man talking until backup arrived. "I understand you wanting to kill Smiley. He must've been threatening your business. But what about the others?"

"We lost."

"What?" She eyed him.

"My football team," he said, simply naming his soccer team as if that was a good answer. "We lost the night I met these men. Big losses. Important matches. They'd each won a promotion to dine with me and go to the games with me. I blame them for the losses. They had to see what it felt like to lose too."

Unbelievable. She blinked at him. "But it was just a soccer match. You made them play with their lives."

"Football *is* my life!" His pointed gaze burrowed into her. "It was taken from me by a stupid injury. I did not want to retire. There is no high like playing. Winning. Defeating others." A mean look narrowed his eyes. "Well, this is a very similar high. Maybe better."

A piece to help complete their puzzle, but it still didn't explain everything. "You were right there with these men. Why wait to come all the way to the United States to kill them?"

"I have such a nice place to dispose of their bodies and no one caught on."

"Until now."

"Yes, until now."

She looked around again, glad to see that Vito had not

come back. "And you thought you had Vito to kill tonight, but I let him get away."

"This does not matter." His voice was low and terrifying. "I have another person in his place. I have you."

Drew called County. Yelled at them to hurry. To cut down on the ten minutes they were out from getting to Teagan. But like him, they were on the wrong side of the tree. Unlike him, they could now detour from their location thanks to his call. But he would have to backtrack for thirty minutes. If he could even get the car to run. He could make it on foot faster than that. There was nothing for it but to run.

He grabbed a vest and rifle from his trunk and started off. He got into a rhythm, pounding the ground. One thing he'd insisted on while UC was continuing his workouts, and right now, he was thankful he had.

He kicked into high gear, passing trees. More trees. And more trees. Climbed a hill.

Headlights rose over the top, beaming their way toward him.

A car. He could commandeer it.

No way anyone would stop for a guy toting a rifle. He hid it behind his back. He waved his other arm and jumped up and down in the middle of the road.

He had no identification other than his bogus driver's license for Dylan Crane. Even his vest didn't say police on it as he couldn't risk having that in his trunk. So, fine. He'd have to tell this driver who he was, but if they didn't give him their car, he wasn't above pulling his rifle on them.

The sedan slowed and crept closer. Drew waited for the vehicle to stop, and he eased close to the driver's door.

Thankfully it was a guy. He should be less skittish than a woman stopping for a man in the night.

"Tree down from the quake. My car's on the other side. I have a law enforcement emergency and need to take your car."

The man ran his gaze over Drew. "You got some ID?"

"No, sorry. Had to leave home without it."

"Then I'm not giving you my car."

Drew swung the rifle around his side, careful not to actually point it at the man. "Leave the car running and get out. Keep your hands where I can see them."

The man's mouth fell open. "Don't hurt me. Please. I have a family. You can have the car. Just don't kill me."

"I really am a law enforcement officer. I won't hurt you."

The man fumbled to open the door, undid his seatbelt, and got out.

"Can you call someone to come get you?" Drew asked.

He nodded.

"My name's Drew Collier. I'm an ICE agent and work out of the Portland field office. My supervisor is Gala Harris. Call the office tomorrow, and we'll arrange to return your car."

The man glared at him. "This is wrong."

"I'm sorry, but a woman's life is at stake, and I have no choice." Drew stepped toward the man. "Go sit on the side of the road where I can see you."

The man bolted across the pavement.

Drew hopped into the car. Locked the door so the guy couldn't try to get back in. Drew stowed the rifle and made a three-point turn. He got the older model sedan up to speed as fast as possible. The car vibrated under him, but he pushed it harder. Harder.

Please, please, please, don't let this car conk out. And don't let me be too late.

Teagan took her time climbing the steps to the trailer, part of her wishing the ground would tremble again and Jabal would lose his footing. But she reached the door and stepped onto the stained carpet without any incident.

The light blinded her. She blinked to clear her vision.

The laptop screen had gone dark.

Jabal skirted around her and woke the computer. "I'll load the menu so you can choose your weapon."

Right. She needed to pick the method that if she lost this level, he would use to kill her.

She would likely do best in the game with a handgun or rifle, but that would mean immediate death if he told her to run like he'd done with Vito. Same with the bow and arrow, though she would lose the level much faster as she'd never shot one. He would have to catch her to use a sword, hatchet or the claws. He could throw the hatchet, though.

Listen to her. Evaluating the best way to die. Or not to die, which would be far more preferable. Hysterical laughter threatened to erupt. She swallowed it down.

Jabal waved the gun. "Pick one now, or I'll pick it for you."

"The sword."

"Select it with your controller." He gave her a quick lesson on how to move in the game. He was thorough and answered her questions almost as if he wanted her to survive the level for longer. It probably gave him more of a thrill.

"Could I have a practice session?" she asked.

"No. We go live now. Press the red button."

She took a breath and focused on the screen and hit play. Enemy foes came at her with swords. One. Another. And another. She had to concentrate to battle them off. She lost track of everything around her. Of time. Of space. And played her heart out.

Moving forward through the medieval world. Slicing her opponents. Gasping when blood gushed from them as if real.

"Yes. Yes." Jabal's satisfied voice seemed far off.

Gretchen was right. This was an intense and violent game.

Teagan's stomach revolted, and she swallowed away the bile.

"You're great at murdering people." Jabal sounded so impressed with her skill.

She lifted her shoulders. Seriously? She cared about what a serial killer thought of her?

She lost focus. Just for a split second.

A guy came out of nowhere. Sword in hand. Sliced into the air. Cut off her avatar's head. Her avatar dropped to the cobblestone. Bleeding profusely.

Laying lifeless.

Her heart sank. Her hand was slick with perspiration on the controller and cold panic seeped in.

Would she suffer the same fate in real life? Would she lose her head?

Drew raced around a corner. The shadowy figure of a man stood in the road. Drew slammed on his brakes. Skidded on the damp pavement. The man looked up. Drew yanked the wheel right. Narrowly missing the guy.

The car slid to a stop. Drew jerked open his door. "You all right?"

"Dylan? Is that you? Man, I'm glad to see you."

"Vito? I've gotta go. Teagan's in trouble."

"I know."

He what? Didn't matter at the moment. "Get in the car and tell me what's happening."

He lumbered to the passenger door and climbed inside.

"Buckle up and talk." Drew pressed his foot to the pedal as Vito told a story of Jabal taking him captive outside his favorite bar and bringing him to Smiley's house. Jabal made Vito play a video game that Jabal challenged him to before he tried to kill Vito. Blood and Sorcery. Teagan and the earthquake saved him.

Drew fired an angry look at Vito. "And you left her with a killer?"

Vito lifted his hands. "I freaked out, okay, and ran. Then the earthquake knocked them down, and I figured since she had a gun that she would come out on top."

"And you don't know if she did?"

"No."

Drew wanted to strangle the man, but he wasn't surprised that Vito ran. Many people would. Their first thoughts were to save their own lives. Just the opposite for law enforcement. They ran into danger.

"I'll be going into the house when we get there," Drew said. "You get down on the floor and stay hidden in the car. Resist the urge to look up no matter what you hear."

Vito grabbed for Drew's arm. "You can't take me back there."

Drew jerked his arm away before the guy could take hold. "You'll be fine in the car. There's a deputy on the way. If anything happens to me, he'll take care of you."

"I don't like it." Vito shuddered. "That man is terrifying. If I'd known he was Rossi's boss, I would never have agreed to get involved with Rossi."

Drew realized Vito still thought he was Dylan. In all the excitement Drew had forgotten. He must not have let anything slip to give his status away, and he had to be careful that he didn't until it benefited him to reveal his real identity.

"You really like Teagan, don't you?" Vito asked.

"I do."

"She's great. If I was younger, well..." He shook his head. "What am I saying? She's way out of my league. But still, a guy can fantasize of what might've been if he didn't stay in the shadow of his two bullying brothers."

"Why have you?" Drew asked.

"Because we're family."

"Well someone in that family sold you out if Jabal tried to kill you."

"Yeah, that's what he told me. Said that I was the weakest link, whatever that means. I haven't done anything wrong. I haven't done anything really. Maybe that's the point. But I told him my mouth was shut. I would never tell anyone about him."

"He didn't believe you. Couldn't risk you talking. Not after he'd kidnapped you and you could ID him."

"Yeah, figured as much." Vito sat back. "Gotta give him props for his creative way to end a life, though."

Drew wouldn't give the killer props for any of it. Especially not if he'd already taken Teagan's life too.

Jabal removed a shiny sword from his bag of tools. "You know the drill. Run!"

Teagan stared at the guy. She couldn't comprehend that she'd lost and would have to run for her life. Who knows. Maybe she was in shock.

He lifted the sword and expertly stripped the controller

from her hands. It hit the floor and bounced a few times before coming to a stop under the table.

Jabal ground his teeth. "I said run or I will end your life right here."

She looked into his eyes. Found a disconnect with reality. The evil. The excitement.

She took a breath and bolted. Charging across the room. Out the door. Over the porch. And toward her car.

If she could get inside her car before he caught up, she would survive. But he was a former soccer player. Forward. He'd once had great speed and endurance while moving a ball downfield. Now his feet were free to run without a ball. Maybe the sword would slow him down. Or his career-ending injury. Maybe not.

She charged over the damp grass. Thick. Heavy. Tangling in her shoes. Wanting to take her down. She raised her stride. Lifted. Powered ahead.

A car pulled into the drive. The lights dark.

Could it be Drew?

No. It wasn't his car.

Drew! She yelled in her brain, but knew it wasn't him. Maybe it was Rossi. Or Gambino. Come to help.

To stop her.

They would cut her off at her car. She had to veer into the woods. Find a hiding spot. Watch. See if Jabal stopped.

She plunged into the tree area. Grass thinned. But saplings were thick. The sharp branches snapped at her body. Biting into her face. Stinging.

Too bad. Keep moving. Must keep moving or you will die.

25

Drew shoved the car into park. He couldn't believe what he was seeing. Teagan raced across the property, Jabal close behind, a long shiny sword in his hand.

"Remember to stay down," Drew warned Vito as the car rocked to a stop, and Drew jumped out, gun in hand.

He bolted for the area where he'd seen the pair disappear into the woods. If Jabal had seen Drew's car, he didn't let on. He might be too intent on the hunt to notice.

Drew dove into the woods but had to slow. Too dark to see. Wouldn't do to slam into a tree and take himself out.

Teagan needed him.

He spotted the flash of Jabal's sword ahead and charged in that direction. He couldn't see Teagan.

Had she fallen? Knocked herself out on a tree? Let her feet get tangled by a sapling?

Jabal suddenly skidded to a stop.

Drew slowed to keep his footfalls from giving him away. He moved swiftly but stealthily through the dark, closing the distance to Jabal. Drew was still too far away to affect an arrest without having to shoot the man.

Drew moved a few yards. Stopped. Listened. Nothing.

Had he lost Teagan too?

A twig snapped ahead.

Jabal took off running.

Drew bolted after him.

Jabal slammed into something and catapulted backward. The sword went flying.

Teagan leapt out from behind a tree. Dropped onto Jabal. A scuffle ensued.

"Stop, police," Drew yelled.

Neither of them stopped.

Drew ran closer. "Stop, Jabal, or I'll shoot."

The man must've known Drew couldn't get a clean shot off or he was too crazed with hunting to stop himself. He kept scrapping with Teagan.

Drew caught up to them.

By the time he did, Teagan had the man on his stomach. His arms behind his back.

Drew knelt down. Put the gun to Jabal's head. "Stop moving."

He went still.

Drew didn't have handcuffs. No rope. No zip ties. Nothing to use to secure Jabal.

"Secure him with your belt," he told Teagan when all he wanted to do was sweep her into his arms and prove that she was okay.

She released Jabal's hands but remained with her knee in his back as she slid off her belt and tightened a loop on his right wrist then fashioned a knot on the other side. She jerked it tight.

Jabal moaned.

"It's the least you should suffer for what you've done." She stood and glared at the man.

"That should hold until the deputy arrives," Drew said, keeping his gun trained on Jabal, but glancing at Teagan.

"Are you hurt?"

"A few bumps and bruises, but that's all." She held his gaze for a long moment, her eyes carrying the heavy weight of what could've happened. "He had Vito, but he got away."

"I know. I picked him up on the road."

"Is he all right?" With trembling hands, she got out her phone and tapped the screen.

"Shaken up and afraid, but fine. Thanks to you."

She lifted the phone to her ear. "Deputy Steele here. What's the ETA on the unit I requested?"

She tilted her head, and in a sliver of light from the moon, he saw her hands shaking. "Tell him we're in the woods to the east of the house, and we need a prisoner escort."

She disconnected. "Nearly here. So I assume Vito told you what happened and about this madman's stupid game. He played it to find the adrenaline rush he lost when an injury forced him to retire."

"I'm not a madman," Jabal protested loudly. "Just a sportsman who needed the adrenaline high again."

"You could've gotten your rush in so many legal ways," Drew said between teeth. "And hunting another person? Sadistic and depraved."

Jabal muttered something under his breath.

"What'd you say?"

"They needed to die," he snapped. "To avenge my team's losses."

"Sicker than I thought." Drew shook his head and couldn't wait to see the cuffs slapped on this man and him being hauled away in the back of a patrol car.

Then Drew would take Vito in too and threaten all kinds of charges to get him to roll over on his brothers. All Drew thought he'd have to do was play his recording with Rossi threatening to end Vito's life and the guy would be singing.

~

Teagan cleaned up in the Clackamas County jail's bathroom down the hall from the interview room where she and Drew would interrogate Vito. Thankfully, the earthquake hadn't been severe enough to cause any major damage. She'd checked in with her family to ensure they were all okay while Drew drove them to the city on the alternate route. They'd arrived safely at the jail, only experiencing a minor aftershock.

She forced herself to look in the mirror. Red welts covered her cheeks and forehead, and shades of purple ringed her right eye from where Jabal's elbow had jabbed hard in their struggle.

She'd managed to subdue him. Just barely. She wouldn't have been able to hold him for arrest if Drew hadn't arrived.

Thank you. Thank you. Thank you.

Her body had flooded with relief when Drew raced to her and stood strong and tall nearby. She'd wanted to let Jabal go and throw herself in Drew's arms. She might be a deputy and trained for life-threatening situations, but that didn't mean such an encounter didn't send terror to her heart. Seeing Drew had released a flood of pent-up adrenaline, and her muscles had threatened to melt. Couple that with the realization that she'd nearly lost her life, and she wanted the man she'd come to care for to hold her tight.

But she settled for professionalism. Not for herself. Not even for Drew. But for the creep Jabal. She didn't want him to see how much his attack had hurt her. Didn't want him to know he had scared her. Had troubled her one iota.

So she'd settled for being stoic and took the time as they waited for the deputy to get Vito to think about what she might say to Drew. When she thought she might die, her life's choices had flashed before her eyes. Mainly the bad choices. And the real reason she avoided relationships became clear. She'd been rejected too many times by men who couldn't deal with a strong woman, and she didn't want to feel the pain again.

Talk about cathartic and tear-inducing. But she'd held it together until the deputy drove off with Jabal in the back of his unit. She still wanted to collapse into Drew's arms, her infamous strength gone. But then, there was Vito Conti, watching from the vehicle Drew commandeered. She wouldn't let him see she wasn't the consummate professional either.

That left falling apart until now. In the stark, sterile bathroom that held so many unpleasant odors she didn't want to remain in the room any longer than she had to.

"Get it together. You can wait to fall apart when you get home." She clenched her hands, gave herself a mental pat on the back, and exited the room.

Drew had a shoulder propped against the wall, and he came to his feet. He lifted a hand as if he planned to touch her face but let it fall. "I didn't know you'd bruised your eye."

"Jabal's elbow."

"I'm so sorry this happened to you." His face contorted in pain. "I should've kept my phone on for your calls and been there with you."

"You were undercover, and your safety had to be your top priority."

"But I..." He shook his head. "I never want to see the people I care about suffer. It tears me up inside."

"I imagine it reminds you of you losing your father," she said though she didn't want to add to his pain.

He nodded.

"So you've avoided letting others in." She studied his tight expression. Should she share her newfound revelation? She had to at some point but in the jail hallway?

Of course. Time or place didn't matter. As long as she let him know how she felt. "I've been closed off too. Not for the same reason. I thought it was because I didn't have time for work and a relationship too."

"And now you don't think that?"

"When you're about to die, things become real clear, and you see things in a different light."

"What did you see?"

"My true motivation to remain alone, I guess. I'm a straight-forward woman with an intense drive to succeed. Not something most men like. At least not the men I encountered. I never found a guy who really appreciates me for who I am. So I spent years trying to be what I thought they wanted me to be."

His gaze softened. "That must've been hard."

She nodded. "And I couldn't sustain it, so the relationship always ended. But subconsciously, I accepted that I don't have a lovable personality, and I was better off embracing my work. But guess what? Thanks to meeting you, I figured out I need to keep putting myself out there because caring about someone makes life a whole lot richer."

She expected a positive response from him, but he frowned. "Except then you can open yourself up to a world of pain too."

"Pain that makes me know I'm alive. Which I have felt when I'm with you. I would like to get to know you better after we close this investigation." She took a deep breath, hating the stale-smelling hallway, but she needed to say this before she lost her courage and retreated back into herself. "In fact, I think I've fallen for you. As in, I'm falling in love with you."

"I..." He shook his head again. "I feel the same way."

Okay. Again. Not the response she expected. "There's a big but coming, isn't there?"

"Sort of. I mean, I need you to know I still have reservations about getting involved. After seeing you physically hurt, I know even more how much I care for you and how much I don't want to see you suffer. What if something happened to me? What if I have an aneurism too and keel over?"

"Then I'll deal with it. I..." Footsteps coming down the hall took her attention, and she turned to see the deputy leading Vito toward them.

The deputy opened a door and nodded at Teagan and Drew to follow.

"To be continued," she said and went down the hall to the room, taking long breaths to clear her brain of Drew and make room for the questions they needed to ask.

Vito had settled in the chair with his back to them. She circled the table and sat on a cold metal chair.

"I'll be right outside if you need me." The deputy went to the door and closed it behind him.

Drew sat next to her, facing Vito. "Can we get you some water or coffee?"

Vito crossed his arms and glared at Drew. "We trusted you, and the whole time you were playing us."

"I was." Drew's unapologetic answer hung in the air.

"And what?" Vito lifted his palms. "Now you'll trump up some bogus charge and put us in prison?"

"Your future is up to you." Drew took out his phone. "But before we talk about that, I wanted you to hear a conversation Rossi had with Tony and Nasim Jabal."

Vito's eyebrow raised. "Where did this conversation take place?"

"At Rossi's warehouse over a crate of heroin and cocaine." Drew set his phone on the table. "Listen to this."

The audio started, and Rossi's deep voice rumbled over the speaker. Vito sat back, the cocky look remaining on his face.

Rossi mentioned Vito's name and Jabal said he must die.

Vito's face lost color. He sat up straight, planting his hands on the table. "Why mention me? I'm no snitch. No more than either of my brothers are."

"Apparently they don't have any faith in you," Teagan said.

Vito crossed his arms. "They're wrong."

"Are they?" Drew asked. "I know you would never want to turn against your family, but think about how Sal and Aldo treat you. About how they let you walk off and didn't come looking for you. Sal told me if you didn't go back to the office after your fight that he was going to write you off."

"He really said that?"

"He did."

"You're lying to me."

"I'm not." Drew's eyes narrowed and gone was the nice guy. "Think about it, Vito. If I wanted to lie to you, I'd make things sound even worse so you would really think badly of Sal. But I'm telling you the truth so you can tell us the truth. I can let the DA know that you cooperated. He can go easier on you."

"I can't."

"They will, you know?" Drew asked.

"Will what?"

"Blame you for the drugs and antiquities exactly like they blame you when anything else goes wrong. And then there are the murder charges."

"Murder?" Vito's jaw dropped. "We didn't kill anyone."

"Then explain why we found Smiley and three other men buried on his property," Teagan said. "A property that Rossi continued to pay the taxes on, likely so no one found the graves."

Panic settled into Vito's eyes, and his gaze flitted around the room. "The only thing I know about Smiley is that he died and that the Jamal guy took me to Smiley's house to kill me with some stupid game."

"You wouldn't have been his first victim, but number five."

"No. No." Vito shot his gaze from Teagan to Drew and back again. "You have to believe me. Please. We had nothing to do with that."

"Are you sure your brothers didn't know about it?" Teagan pressed. "Think for a moment, and you'll know we're right. It's in your best interest to tell us everything you know."

"I don't... I just..."

He was starting to cave, and Teagan would take full advantage of it. "I get how you feel. I have two sisters. We fought as you can imagine three girls would do. And it could result in two sisters ganging up on the third." She didn't go into any details as it honestly didn't happen often. "They'll leave you hanging out there to take the blame while they go free."

He bit his lip and then sighed. "Sure, they'd bullied me. All the time actually. I don't like that, but they won't let me take the fall."

"Okay." Drew stood. "We just brought both of them in too, so we'll see what Sal has to say. After he rolls over on you, remember that I offered you the first chance to reduce your sentence and keep you from going away for an accessory to murder."

"Wait." Vito lifted his hands. "Sit. I don't know anything about the murders, but I'll tell you what I know."

Drew took his time taking his seat and shifted a few times on the chair. "Then start talking, beginning with the first time you sold stolen antiquities and illegal drugs."

~

Drew parked in front of Teagan's big Victorian home. Vito had confirmed the many suspicions Drew had of the family's activities. Sal and Aldo remained tight-lipped. For now. And Oliver? They'd brought him in too, along with the antiquity for evaluation. He wouldn't turn on anyone. Just clammed up and asked for a lawyer.

A night stewing in a cell might help them change their minds. At least Drew hoped so.

He'd left the vehicle he'd commandeered at the Clackamas County Sheriff's Office for the owner to retrieve, and Teagan had taken Drew to retrieve his own car that thankfully ran despite the front end damage. He followed her to make sure she arrived home okay.

She didn't much like the idea of him seeing her home when he told her his plans. Was it because he'd been so indecisive on a future for them or because she didn't need to be escorted home and could fend for herself? She'd proven that with Jabal. She had him down for the count. But seeing her at the mercy of that ruthless serial killer left Drew so unsettled his gut ached. If he didn't see her walk into her house safe and sound tonight, it would ache all night.

He got out and opened her car door for her. She slid those jeans-encased long legs out, the knees grass-stained from her adventure. The color around her eye had deepened to a dark purple, raising his anger.

She didn't speak but locked her car and started up the walkway.

Drew followed and tried to let go of the earlier conversations with not only the Conti brothers, but Rossi, and Jabal too. He was the most closed-mouth of them all. The entire time Drew and Teagan interrogated him, he sat with a cocky face. Acting superior. The supreme ruler and everyone was his subject.

Sure, Drew wanted to slam a fist into the arrogant guy's face for the murders. But mostly for what he'd done to Teagan. Drew had to keep his hands in his pockets or he might've unloaded on the creep and given the guy a lawsuit to bring against them.

The only point of interest in any of the conversations was that it was clear Rossi and the Contis didn't know about multiple graves on Smiley's property. They all reacted with genuine surprise to the graves. Other than Smiley's.

So Jabal had done what most serial killers do. Acted alone.

At the door, Teagan turned to Drew. He shoved the night's turmoil into the back of his mind and concentrated on the amazing woman standing before him. He didn't know what he should say to her, so he kept quiet and waited for her to speak.

"I was thinking on the way over. Christmas is next week," she said. "Would you like to spend it with my family? Your mom would be welcome to join us too."

Not at all what he'd expected her to say, and he didn't know how to answer. He didn't want to lead her on, but he had to be with her. That had become clear. How could he do both?

For now, he could be noncommittal. "I can ask my mom."

Teagan's shoulders drooped. "Does that mean you want to be with me for the holidays?"

Just as much as he hated seeing her physical injuries, he hated seeing this very strong woman so uncertain. He had to tell the truth no matter the consequences. He took her hands. "Yes."

She smiled, soft, luminous, and his pulse sped up.

Her eyes brightened under the twinkling Christmas lights lining the porch. "I have to warn you that Christmas starts on Christmas Eve day at one. My sisters, cousins, and I go stay with our parents on the farms where we grew up. My grandparents have a place between my parents' property and my uncle's property. We split into teams and go out to our sixty acres and cut down a tree. It's a fierce competition to see who can bring home the best tree."

"Sounds like fun."

"It is." Her face glowed with a happiness he hadn't seen before. "We get three trees. One for each house and we all decorate them while consuming our weight in Christmas cookies baked by my gran. Then we go out to the hayloft in the barn to prepare for Christmas dinner. My grandad invites law enforcement officers and military friends who don't have anywhere to go on Christmas, and we make sure they have a great day. After we get it all ready, we have a family meal at my grandparents' house and go to church at midnight."

A real family Christmas celebration he'd always wanted since his father died. "Again, sounds great."

"We sleep over in our old rooms on Christmas Eve, and the next morning it's time for our immediate families. After we've had breakfast and opened presents, we go to my grandad's dinner and later more presents with them."

"Sounds great. I think my mom would like that too."

"Perfect." She squeezed his hands. "So if you would ask her and get back to me as soon as you can, I can tell the family to expect two more people. That would be great."

"I will." He pulled her closer. "Will you tell your family about my real name or do you want me to do that?"

She tilted her head. "I can do it. Better to get it done before Christmas."

"Or we could arrange to meet with them before that," he said. "I would like to look them in the eye and apologize."

"We'll have to get together this week to work on our statements and the final task force report. You could come over for our midweek dinner."

"Sure. We could...that...yeah, that works." What he really wanted to say was, can't we do something to be alone? But he chickened out. He was normally a decisive guy. How could he let simple emotions hold him hostage like this?

"I guess that's settled. All we have to do is say goodnight."

"Maybe." He looked up. "You do have mistletoe above the door. Maybe we should kiss on it."

She frowned. "Do you think that's a good idea?"

"I don't know, but honestly, it's all I want to do. I'm going to kiss you if you don't stop me."

"Why would I want to stop you?" She gave him an enticing grin.

He circled his arms around her waist and pulled her slender body tight against his. He locked lips with her, hers cold in the December night, but they quickly warmed to his touch.

A foreign emotion overcame him. A powerful emotion. He never wanted the kiss to end. He vaguely heard a car pull to the curb and stop, but he could no more stop kissing her than he could stop breathing.

His mind was reeling as she curled her arms around his neck and dug her fingers into his hair, drawing his head down tighter.

"Ah-hem," a female voice wound its way into his brain. "Your PDA will get all the neighbors talking."

PDA. Public Display of Affection. Right. He'd lost control. Was making out on a quiet residential street with potentially nosey neighbors.

He tried to lift his head, but Teagan held firm for another few seconds before releasing her hold.

He looked into her eyes and found the love she spoke of burning there. He probably was looking at her with the same longing.

Mackenzie stepped closer. "I knew this was simmering beneath the surface."

"Thought we hid it better than that," Teagan said, not looking away from Drew.

"Maybe from the average person but not a former detective." Mackenzie laughed. "I've finished talking to the officers in charge of the investigations. Nothing new, but you'll have my report by morning."

"Thanks. We wrapped things up tonight." Teagan updated Mackenzie.

"Congratulations." She looked at Drew. "It looks like we'll still be seeing more of you."

"Likely," Teagan answered. "I've invited him and his mother to Christmas."

"Then be warned to get a lot of sleep the night before," Mackenzie said. "Our tree hunting experience is pretty cutthroat. The team who wins gets the golden tree and bragging rights for the entire year."

"Golden tree?" he asked.

"Our take on an Oscar." Teagan smiled at Drew. "You'll see when our team wins."

"Hold on, now." Mackenzie's tone was steady and lower pitched. "There's no way we'll let the two of you be on the same team."

"You can't stop it," Teagan said, her gaze pinned to Drew. "It's the luck of the draw, and since I met Drew, I feel lucky. Very, very lucky."

26

Christmas Eve, and the unusual cold snap had Drew drawing his jacket closed and zipping it up. He opened the car door for his mother and took a long look at the Steele's farm. A big two-story white house with black shutters and wrap around porch sat ahead of him. A traditional farm-house. Or at least from what he'd seen on TV and in movies. Down a slight hill in the distance stood a red barn that looked old but well-kept. A green tractor sat out front of the barn's big open doors and someone moved in the shadows inside.

His mom shielded her eyes from the early afternoon sun and looked around the area. "I never figured you to fall for a farm girl."

Drew either. "Teagan's lived in the city all her adult life. If she hadn't told me she was raised on a farm, I wouldn't have had a clue."

The shadow morphed into a person who exited the barn. A woman wearing overalls over a flannel shirt, paired with heavy boots and a baseball cap hefted a bale of hay into the tractor's bucket and then slid the barn door closed. It groaned along the metal tracks. She climbed onto the

295

tractor, the engine rumbled to a start, and she backed out. At the bottom of the drive, she paused to look at them and grinned.

Teagan. It was Teagan. His pulse kicked up.

He hadn't seen her since the family dinner three days ago, which had gone quite well. As she predicted, her parents fully understood his UC role and forgave him for misleading them. Her dad had given Drew a solid stare, and said, "That doesn't mean we condone lying. If you ever do it again for any reason other than job confidentiality, we'll have a special talk. Just you and me out by the woodshed."

Teagan had groaned, but Drew didn't mind the warning. It showed how much Hugh loved his daughter, and Drew would never lie to them again unless his job required it. Which he doubted as his UC days were behind him. They'd gotten Vito to turn on everyone on the drug and antiquities charges, and surprisingly, Oliver caved too, in hopes of a reduced sentence. And they all denied anything to do with the murders. DNA confirmed Jabal on those charges, and they didn't uncover any evidence to charge the others.

Now they all awaited trial where some high-priced lawyer would try to get them off. Drew and Teagan would be there to do their best to stop that from happening.

The tractor puttered up the drive and stopped before them. Teagan hopped down and hurried the rest of the way. She ripped off a glove and held her hand out to his mom. "You must be Drew's mom. I'm Teagan."

His mom grabbed Teagan's hand and gave it a firm shake. "Ellen Collier. Pleased to meet you."

"And you too, Mrs. Collier," Teagan said. "Sorry I wasn't at the house to greet you. I got a late start on my chores and thought I could get them done before you arrived."

"Please call me Ellen." His mom gave Teagan a welcoming smile before letting go of her hand. "And we should be the ones apologizing for being early. We thought traffic would be heavy due to the holidays, but it wasn't."

Teagan nodded and turned her full attention to Drew. It felt like the sun had come out brighter and shined warmly on him.

"Hi," she said almost shyly.

"Hi," he said back to her, sounding like a teenager with a crush.

"Oh, my," his mother said. "You are smitten, aren't you, son?"

He felt his face color. "I'll get your bags, Mom."

"I'll help." Teagan offered.

He went to the trunk, and she came around the back. Once he'd raised the trunk and reached for his mother's overnight bag, Teagan bent in and kissed him on the cheek.

He turned and planted a fast but hard kiss on her lips, then waggled his eyebrows at her. "I like seeing my farm girl at work."

She giggled. "Then maybe you can help me finish my chores before we go out tree hunting."

"Sure thing."

He lifted out his mom's and his bag. "Nothing for you to carry but you can close the trunk."

"This way." She closed the trunk and hurried toward the house as if she couldn't wait to get alone with him.

Or at least he hoped that was her plan. They'd seen each other every day until the dinner, and the past few days he'd missed her drastically.

They went in through the front entrance, the screen door snapping behind them. Teagan's mom came to meet them, and she introduced herself to Drew's mother.

"Let me take you to your room so you can settle in before the big tree hunt." Ruby took his mom's bag from Drew. "Do you have some boots to wear?"

"In my bag." His mom looked a little flustered. "After seeing what Teagan's wearing though, I'm afraid you'll laugh at them. Not very practical for the woods, I guess. But it's all I had."

Ruby waved her hand. "Not to worry. We have about every size of boot you could want here if you want to trek all over the woods, but I was hoping you would stay back with the rest of us old folks to judge."

His mom let out a thankful breath. "That sounds good."

"I'm going to take Drew out to help me finish my chores," Teagan called after her mother.

"Breaking him in right." Ruby crinkled her nose, and Drew could see Teagan in her mom's face.

Ruby had aged very gracefully, and he suddenly wanted to know Teagan when she was the same age.

She grabbed his hand, and he dropped his bag to let her lead him out the door.

"What's the rush?" he asked.

The moment it snapped closed, she slid her arms around his neck and pulled his head down. "This."

She kissed him long and hard, and he forgot about time and place again. Forgot to wonder where her dad might be. Or her siblings. Until he heard a car rumble down the drive. He lifted his head and looked over her shoulder. An early fifties classic Chevy pickup lovingly restored to all its former glory rolled down the drive and stopped in front of the house.

"Oh, man. She's beautiful." He left Teagan behind and jogged down the steps as her dad climbed out of the driver's side.

"Did you do the restoration work?" Drew ran his hand over a curved fender.

"Yeah, me and the girls."

Drew spun to look at Teagan. "You like to restore cars?

You didn't say when I told you it was my hobby."

"The subject got changed, and then it never came up again. I like to work on the engines, but I'm not keen on bodywork or interiors. Mackenzie loves doing the interiors, and Ryleigh helps with bodywork."

Drew looked at Hugh. "You have other vehicles?"

"A few. Got a big garage out back."

Drew turned back to Teagan. "I don't have room to work on vehicles at my place, so I keep them at my mom's. I'm refurbing a '65 Mustang right now. Or at least I was before I went undercover."

Her eyes lit up. "I haven't worked on a car in years, but I wouldn't mind doing it again."

Hugh held out the keys. "Want to take it for a spin?"

"Are you kidding? Absolutely." Drew whipped the keys out of Hugh's hands before he changed his mind. He glanced at Teagan. "You coming with me?"

She frowned. "Can't. I have to finish my chores."

"I can do them for you," Hugh offered.

"Seriously?" Teagan gaped at her dad. "I think I've only heard you say that once in my entire life and that's when I had the flu."

"I know you're running late from helping your gran and grandad this morning. I'm proud of how you pitch in all the time. How you run the company. Of you."

Teagan threw her arms around her dad, and the man blushed as red as his pickup.

"And you've only ever brought home a guy for Christmas once in your life." Hugh extracted himself from the hug. "You should spend it with him."

"Still, I feel very honored that you would do my chores."

"Now don't go making a big deal of it. Don't tell your sisters, or I'll be doing chores all day." He looked at his watch. "Tree cutting time in forty minutes. Don't be late."

"Are you kidding?" she asked. "And let my sisters and cousins rig the drawing? No way."

She circled her arm in Drew's. "Let's get going before my dad changes his mind."

Drew liked this day already, and it had just begun. He knew there would be other surprises, but would there be any as life-changing as the way he felt about this woman at his side?

~

The forested area smelled like pine and fresh air, something Drew didn't get much of in the city. His year undercover in a dirty business left this country air somehow feeling fresher and more tantalizing. He could easily see Teagan and her family as she was raised out here with grandparents Drew could only have fantasized about.

He'd lost both grandfathers before he was walking and his grandmothers in his elementary school years. Then his dad. His mom's mental breakdown. Was it any wonder he felt the way he did about loss? Didn't give him a good reason to hide behind the feelings, but gave him a good reason to be reluctant to form any future attachments.

He hopped out of the utility vehicle driven by Teagan's Uncle Gene, their other teammates, Peyton and Mackenzie, piled out of the back seat. The family, along with fiancés and boyfriends, had split up into three teams of four, leaving his mom, Teagan's grandparents, mother, and aunt back at the house where they would select a winner.

The teams had one hour to find a tree, cut it down, and have it mounted in the tree stand at the assigned house or they were disqualified.

Two utility vehicles holding Teagan, Bristol, Nate, and Brent raced past them, yelling slurs on Drew's team as they passed. Drew had barely had time to meet the other men, but looked forward to getting to know the fellow law enforcement or prior law enforcement guys.

"Are you going to just stand there staring?" Gene shouted. "C'mon. We have a tree to find and only fifty-five minutes to do it in."

"I'll grab the tools." Peyton ran to the back of the vehicle.

"Follow me and try to keep up." Mackenzie grinned at Drew.

She took off at top speed, likely born from years of playing in these woods and from prior tree hunting. Gene came behind them, and Peyton, carrying an ax and hatchet, caught up.

Drew had a flash of the image of Hoyle killed with a hatchet but let it go. It was too nice of a day with the kind of family he only read about in books or saw in movies to let the actions of a killer ruin the afternoon.

Mackenzie wound in and out of trees, but Drew didn't let her get too far ahead.

She came to an abrupt stop near a clearing with smaller trees and reached out to a nearby bluish-green tree with long needles. "How about the Noble fir?"

Gene circled the tree as did Peyton, the sunlight catching her red hair as she moved. She looked a lot like their grandmother, but not the siblings.

"Well?" She planted a hand on her hip.

"We should never take the first tree," Gene said.

"How many times have we seen one right away, gone looking only to almost miss the deadline, and go back to the first tree?" Mackenzie asked.

"Yeah, but other times we don't," Peyton said.

"Then let's split up," Mackenzie said. "Set a timer for fifteen minutes and yell if we find a better tree in that time. Otherwise, we meet back here to cut this one down."

"Sounds like a plan." Gene set an alarm on his phone. "Drop the tools, Red, and come with me."

Mackenzie tapped her phone screen and looked at Drew. "Guess that means you and me."

She set off at that quick clip, her head swiveling as she took in the trees.

Drew followed, his feet crunching over dried pine needles and cones. "I don't really know what I'm looking for."

"A tree with perfect symmetry and just the right amount of space between branches to hang ornaments. Must be over ten feet tall but not above eleven to perfectly fit the room."

"Basically, like the one you just picked?" He chuckled.

She laughed. "Exactly. But Uncle Gene sometimes likes to complicate things. Still, we can look as long as we make it back on time. Couldn't ask for better weather."

"This is a lot of fun."

She glanced over her shoulder at him. "What kind of Christmas traditions do you have?"

"Not many. Most of them died with my dad. Since it's only my mom and me, we don't make a big deal of the holidays."

"Oh, man, are you in trouble."

"Why's that?"

"Teagan's birthday is the beginning of December so she claims the whole month as hers and that includes Christmas. It's the only time of the year that she really has a lot of fun. Whoever marries her will have to make room for boxes and boxes of decorations in his life."

"I get that she likes Christmas, but she didn't mention all the décor. And the fact that she's a workaholic isn't a secret. Doesn't bode well for any guy in her life."

Mackenzie stopped to finger a tree and look it over. "That's going to change. I had a talk with her last night and told her I planned to step up and take on more of the duties so she can work less."

"That's good of you."

She shrugged. "It's not like I have a guy in my life right now either, and I doubt there'll be one in the near future."

"Why's that, if you don't mind me asking?"

"Don't mind at all." She resumed walking. "I'm just not ready to be tied down. I'm pretty much an adventure girl. Or at least I was before I went into law enforcement. Before then I used to seek out as many new experiences as I could find."

"And that changed?"

"Yeah. I saw so many bad things on the job that my joy dried up." She stopped to frown at another tree. "When I left the force, I started a podcast on faith and life. Not sure why I did, but it's deepened my faith and brought back some of my joy."

Interesting. "And you don't want to be tied down when you finally have that adventuring spirit back."

"Exactly." She glanced over her shoulder. "I can see why Teagan has fallen for you."

"I don't know if—"

"Don't be shy." She shook her head. "You know she has, and now the ball's in your court."

Yeah, the ball was in his court, all right. Too bad he still didn't know if he would summon up the courage to get off the bench and into the game.

Teagan wished she'd been allowed to be on Drew's team. She wanted to introduce him to her kind of Christmas—a family gathered with love to celebrate Jesus's birth and enjoy His many blessings—not be in competition with

Drew. But she still wouldn't let her teammates down and stood proudly in front of the tree they'd cut for her grandparents' house. The judges had already evaluated the other two trees and took in this last one with the whole family looking on.

"Oh my." Her gran clutched her chest. "The first two were simply amazing and this one is too. This year is going to be the hardest one yet."

"Must be due to all the new male blood in the group," her grandad said, earning him an eye roll from Teagan's gran.

"You have to admit it's good to see so many of our young ladies paired up." He looked at Mackenzie and Ryleigh.

"Oh no, you don't, Grandad." Mackenzie looped her arm in his. "You're here to judge the trees not comment on our love lives."

"Someone needs to nudge you in the right direction," he said. "Like luring in a fish. Let's get some bait dangled in front of you."

The group laughed, and Teagan's love for her grandad and the others confirmed the capacity she had to love so many people and still do everything else in her life. She could love a man too, and he would fit in like her other family members. That guy was Drew.

Her gran looked at the judges. "Follow me to the kitchen to get the trophy so everyone can get on with decorating."

Teagan glanced at Drew, who hung with his teammates on the far side of the room. She wished the judges would hurry up with their deliberations and pronounce a winner so she could join him. She couldn't believe how happy she was to see him here with her family. And the earlier ride in her dad's truck?

Amazing.

They'd talked vintage vehicles and engines, proving they

had far more in common than they'd known. Not that they needed more than the feelings they'd developed for each other.

The kitchen door opened, and the judges paraded out.

Her grandad cleared his throat. "And now awarding this year's trophy is our special guest, Ellen. We are so pleased to welcome her and hope this means she will be coming to Christmas for years to come." He winked at Teagan and gave Drew a pointed look.

Drew blushed a deep red matching the Christmas stockings hung on the fireplace behind him.

"Grandad," Teagan warned.

He shrugged and grinned. She could never be upset with him. He was the finest grandfather a girl could hope for.

"I know this might seem like nepotism," his mother said. "But the vote was unanimous. This year's trophy goes to my son's team."

Drew's team erupted in cheers, and Mackenzie shoved him ahead to go get the trophy. He took the shiny gold tree from her grandad and held it up, a victorious smile on his face. "I can't take much credit for the tree, but I'm glad to accept on behalf of my experienced teammates."

"Don't worry, son." Her grandad clapped Drew on the back. "Years from now you'll have the experience too."

Drew cast Teagan a sheepish look. She smiled to reassure him that he didn't have to commit to a long-term relationship with her, but secretly she hoped he would before the day was out.

～

Drew had followed the whole family out to the hayloft in the barn to prepare for the big Christmas dinner that would be held the next day. Someone had already set up ten long tables and covered them with green and red tablecloths. Big outdoor heaters warmed the space, and an electric fireplace was mounted on one wall with stockings hung along the mantle. The tallest live tree Drew had ever seen stood in one corner and many of the family members, including Teagan, were busy stringing lights and hanging brightly colored ornaments.

Drew and his mother were on table duty. He was setting out white stoneware and polished silverware while she was arranging pine boughs, cones, candles, and bows in the center of the tables.

He was still a bit embarrassed that his team sent him to accept the tree trophy. Seemed like it gave him too much credit when all he did was chop a few times and carry the tree to the vehicle after the others did all the hard work. That was really all he'd done. Still, it felt like a monumental achievement in his life when Teagan put the star on the top of that tree and stood back, a beaming smile as she gazed on it like a child she might have given birth to.

Yeah, she loved Christmas, all right. She'd expertly strung lights, and they all loaded down the tree with family ornaments.

All the time, he felt at home. Not awkward at all. Was partly due to Ruby. She floated around filling hot cocoa and handing out cookies until he could burst.

His mother leaned closer. "You're in love with her."

"What?"

"Teagan. I see how you look at her. You're in love with her."

He thought to deny it, but his mother was too perceptive for him to lie. "Yeah."

"And she returns the feelings if I'm not mistaken."

"Yeah."

"What are you going to do about it?"

He shrugged.

She grabbed his arm. "You're not still hiding behind that old thing of not wanting someone to get hurt by you potentially dying young like your father, are you?"

He shrugged again, but yeah, that was exactly what he was clinging to.

"You know I'm whole again, right? Have been for many years. Your father was the only man for me, but I'm still living a full life."

"I know, but..."

"But I had a season of grief. Pain. Almost unbearable pain. You saw it and had to help me through it. But it's gone, and if I had to do it all over again, I would choose love even if it ended the same way."

He heard her words. Knew she believed them, but he couldn't internalize it. Not with the terrible anguish he'd seen her suffer.

"Look at this family. They had a huge tragedy in losing their Thomas, but they are coping Are they sad? Yes, I've only been here a short time and have seen it. But I've also seen the kind of love I wish for you, son."

"But I'm in law enforcement and what if—"

"Stop the what ifs. Teagan is a strong woman. Much stronger than I was. From what I can see she's made of steel." She smiled. "Yes, pun intended."

The vision of Teagan fending off a serial killer came to mind. Yeah, she was one tough cookie. "She is, isn't she?"

"Yes, so don't close yourself off. Open up your heart. Embrace the Steele family. Join them." She squeezed his arm. "Besides, I want them to adopt me too."

He laughed, gave his mom a hug, and turned, Teagan in his sights. It was about time he let her know how much he'd already come to love her and start talking about that relationship he'd been fighting against for what seemed like his entire life.

~

Teagan finished the tenth string of lights she'd put on the tree and still had bare areas to fill at the bottom. Her grandad had gone in search of additional sets, and he approached with another long string, his eyes solemn behind his glasses. This meal was one of his big service projects for the year, and he took it very seriously. The whole family was blessed to serve the men and women who, without this meal, would be alone on Christmas, helping to repay them for years of service.

"Everything okay?" she asked him. "And if not, can I help fix it?"

"Things are going great."

"Then why such a serious look."

"Just thinking about your guy, Drew. I'm glad to see you finally brought a guy home." He handed her the string of lights. "I like him."

She didn't want to be having this conversation out here where others could overhear, and she'd rather be talking to Drew. It looked like he was trying to get across the room to her, but kept being stopped by others. She loved her family, but they'd been in the way all afternoon of her getting some alone time with him.

"Like him as what?" She plugged in the lights to be sure they worked. "A law enforcement officer?"

"Sure, yeah. From what you said of the investigation, seems as if he's a good one. But that's not what I was thinking."

"A team player on the Christmas tree hunt, then?" The lights glowed bright white in her hands.

"You can stop that right now, young lady. I might be getting old, but I know what you're doing. I mean as your future husband."

"Grandad!" She had to act offended, but she'd known this was coming. "We've only known each other for a little more than a week."

"So what? When you know—you know." He started to uncoil the lights. "I'm not saying marry the guy this week, but give him a chance. You've let the business take over your life. Trying to make up for losing Thomas and make things better for everyone. You've done a bang-up job, and now that you have a sister and two cousins in the business, it's time to give them more responsibility and focus on yourself."

"I know."

"Then what's stopping you?"

"Drew." She explained his issues as she worked with her grandad to untangle the wires.

He stilled and locked gazes. "I'm sorry he was hurt so badly. His mom too. Want me to talk to him?"

"No!"

"Then say you'll do your best to change his mind, or I might have to."

"I'll do my best." She pointed at Drew. "He's on his way over here. Please let me handle this alone."

Her grandad dropped the light string and swept her into a hug. "I only want the best for you, sweetheart, and my gut tells me he's the best."

"Mine too." She gave him a tight hug, let go, and ran her fingers through her hair.

"I'll get these lights put up." Her grandad stepped toward the tree, giving Drew a pointed look as he passed but not speaking.

She let out a sigh of relief.

Drew stopped in front of her. "Looked like things were kind of tense between you. Hope I'm not interrupting."

"Not at all. Can we go outside for a minute? I'd like to talk to you without so many ears listening in." She gave her grandad a pointed look.

"I was hoping to get you alone too." He gave her a playful smile.

Her heart tripped into action. They hurried to the coat racks to grab jackets, then slid the massive barn door open and stepped into the chilly afternoon. Clouds hung in the sky, covering the sun and threatening rain.

The temperatures had plunged to near freezing.

"They were saying we might get snow," he said.

"It's a good possibility. We're at a higher elevation here than the city and get snow more often."

"You didn't want to come out here to talk about the weather, though, right?"

"Right." She didn't know if she should continue, so she stopped.

"Mind if I go first?"

"Go ahead." She steeled her reserves as she feared he might tell her that it was great to meet her family, but he still didn't want to make a commitment.

He looked her straight in the eye. "I was talking to my mom about us. She helped me see how strong you are."

Teagan let her nerves get to her and mocked making a silly weightlifter's pose.

He laughed. "Strong that way, too, but I mean inside. You seem to take what's thrown at you and still thrive. I mean, fighting off a serial killer is not only a physical thing but mental. You needed courage to even approach him."

"I had no choice," she said honestly. "Vito's life was at stake."

"You had a choice. You could've fled. Many people would

310

have had an easy choice. To stay safe and call in reinforcements. But you have the strength of conviction to protect others. Just like I do. And I worry that will keep putting me in danger and something could happen."

"But if it—"

He pressed a cold finger against her lips. "If it does, you can handle it. Mom helped me see that."

She took his finger and laced her hand in his. "So does that mean you're game for dating?"

"Not only game but willing and ready."

Big white flakes of snow landed on his face, and she brushed them away. "I'm so happy and snow falling is like the glitter on top of it."

He smiled. "A white Christmas with you would be the best one ever. And on a positive note, maybe we'll get snowed in." His smile morphed into a playful grin.

"Oh, yeah." She smiled back at him. "Being snowed in together would give you a chance to not only steal my heart but the hearts of my whole family. A girl couldn't ask for anything more." She paused, wondering if she should go on, but if this relationship was to work, she had to be honest at all times. "I could ask how your faith is surviving."

He frowned. "Still struggling with the why's, but twenty-four/seven influence of the bad things is gone. And with the chance to go to church again along with the goodness in you and your family, plus my mom, I'm confident it will be restored."

Her heart lifted. "I promise to do everything I can to help. Starting with being with you every minute I can to let some of this goodness rub off on you." She grinned.

He pulled her close. "How about a kiss to aid the process of letting it seep in?"

"I'm game for that anytime." She circled her arms around his neck. "Anytime at all."

STEELE GUARDIAN SERIES
Intrigue. Suspense. Family.

A kidnapped baby. A jewelry heist. Amnesia. An abducted socialite. Smuggled antiquities. And in every book, God's amazing power and love.

Book 1 – Tough as Steele

Book 2 – Nerves of Steele

Book 3 – Forged in Steele

Book 4 – Made of Steele – November 1, 2022

Book 5 – Solid as Steele – February 1, 2023

Book 6 – Edge of Steele – May 1, 2023

For More Details Visit -

www.susansleeman.com/books/steele-guardians

NIGHTHAWK SECURITY SERIES
Protecting others from unspeakable danger

A stalker. A mother and child being hunted. And more. All in danger. Needing protection from the men of Nighthawk Security.

Book 1 - Night Fall
Book 2 – Night Vision
Book 3 - Night Hawk
Book 4 –Night Moves
Book 5 – Night Watch
Book 6 – Night Prey

For More Details Visit -
www.susansleeman.com/books/nighthawk-security/

THE TRUTH SEEKERS
People are rarely who they seem

A twin who didn't know she had a sister. A mother whose child isn't her own. A woman whose parents lied to her. All needing help from The Truth Seekers forensic team.

Book 1 - Dead Ringer
Book 2 - Dead Silence
Book 3 - Dead End
Book 4 - Dead Heat
Book 5 - Dead Center
Book 6 - Dead Even

For More Details Visit -
www.susansleeman.com/books/truth-seekers/

The COLD HARBOR SERIES

Meet Blackwell Tactical- former military and law enforcement heroes who will give everything to protect innocents... even their own lives.

Book 1 - Cold Terror
Book 2 - Cold Truth
Book 3 - Cold Fury
Book 4 - Cold Case
Book 5 - Cold Fear
Book 6 - Cold Pursuit
Book 7 - Cold Dawn

For More Details Visit -
www.susansleeman.com/books/cold-harbor/

ABOUT SUSAN

SUSAN SLEEMAN is a bestselling and award-winning author of more than 45 inspirational/Christian and clean read romantic suspense books. In addition to writing, Susan also hosts the website, TheSuspenseZone.com.

Susan currently lives in Oregon, but has had the pleasure of living in nine states. Her husband is a retired church music director and they have two beautiful daughters, two very special sons-in-law, and two amazing grandsons.

For more information visit: www.susansleeman.com

CPSIA information can be obtained
at www.ICGtesting.com
Printed in the USA
LVHW102137021122
732257LV00022B/378